P9-DWH-177

BREATHE

BREATHE

sarah crossan

GREENWILLOW BOOKS
An Imprint of HarperCollins*Publishers*

 Printed in the United States of America. For information address HarperCollins Children's Books, a division of HarperCollins Publishers, 10 East 53rd Street, New York, NY 10022.

www.epicreads.com

The text of this book is set in 12-point Fournier

Book design by Paul Zakris

Library of Congress Cataloging-in-Publication Data

Crossan, Sarah.

Breathe / Sarah Crossan. — 1st ed.

p. cm.

"Greenwillow Books."

Summary: "In a barren land, a shimmering glass dome houses the survivors of the Switch, the period when oxygen levels plunged and the green world withered. A state lottery meant a lucky few won safety, while the rest suffocated in the thin air. And now Alina, Quinn, and Bea—an unlikely trio, each with their own agendas, their own longings and fears—walk straight into the heart of danger. With two days' worth of oxygen in their tanks, they leave the dome. What will happen on the third day?" — Provided by publisher.

ISBN 978-0-06-211869-1 (hardback)

[1. Science fiction. 2. Survival—Fiction. 3. Adventure and adventurers—Fiction. 4. Insurgency—Fiction. 5. Environmental degradation—Fiction.] I. Title.

PZ7.C88277Bre 2012

[Fic]—dc23 2012017496

12 13 14 15 16 LP/RRDH 10 9 8 7 6 5 4 3 2 1

First Edition

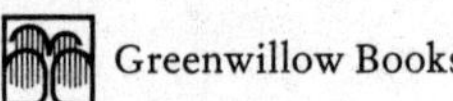

Greenwillow Books

To Andreas

Oxygen is essential for most living things.

For 2.5 billion years, it was the most abundant chemical element on Earth.

Until the Switch.

PART I

THE POD

1
ALINA

Breathing is a right, not a privilege, so I'm stealing it back. I'm nervous, but I'm not scared. This is the mission I've been training for. I'm ready to lead.

I squeeze Abel's hand and he looks at me. "Now?" he asks. He puts his other hand into his pocket.

"No, no. Not yet," I whisper. Several cameras are trained right at us and there's a steward only yards away. I pull Abel close and nuzzle his neck. We aren't a couple, but posing as one makes us less conspicuous.

"Tell me when," Abel says.

We get to a cluster of silver birches and join the group gazing up at them. The tour guide is giving a detailed explanation of what is required to keep the trees alive in here and the tourists, mostly Premiums, are eating it up. "It took twelve years for this particular species to grow. Nowhere else on Earth will you find such a specimen." I resist rolling my eyes and even pull out my pad to take a picture so I seem like a real tourist.

An announcement comes over the loudspeaker, the voice firm: *"The conservation area will close in five minutes. Please leave the biosphere. The conservation area will close in five minutes. Please leave the biosphere."*

"We're too late," Abel says, letting go of my hand and heading for the exit. I throw my arms around his neck. In training he was so cocky; I could never have imagined fear setting in like this.

"We can't backpedal," I say. "We've been saving for months to pay the entrance fee. And we need those cuttings. We aren't leaving without them." I glance around. Everyone is coming our way. Including the stewards. I kiss the tip of his nose. He pulls back.

"Why can't your aunt or uncle do this?"

"I already explained it once," I snap. "They're in agriculture and they don't get permits for this part of the biosphere." The tour group shuffles by and heads for the gift shop. I grin at an older couple watching us and they return the smile, linking arms with each other as they move on.

"If I get caught . . ."

"We won't get caught," I say, though I can't know this for

sure. All I know is that I've never been caught before, and Abel's hesitation is only putting us at greater risk.

I lead him back to our planned spot, where only camera four can see us. "It's to your right," I say. "Do *not* miss." He nods, rummages in his pocket, and pulls out a fist, so I know he has the rock in his hand. I want to kiss him for real now, but there isn't time, and anyway, he might not want a real kiss from me.

As the camera scans in the opposite direction, I elbow Abel, and he launches the rock into the air. I hold my breath. And I want to shut my eyes because I can see that the rock is going to miss. We're going to get caught. And it won't be jail time for us. We'll simply go missing.

"Shit," Abel says.

Instead of hitting the camera, the rock bounces against a tree then down onto the head of a tourist. I gasp. Stewards come running as he starts to howl.

"I've been hit!" the tourist shouts. "I've been shot."

"I have to get out of here," Abel says. "Now. You don't understand."

"Do you have another one?" I ask, grabbing his elbow so he won't run. He nods and pulls another, larger rock from his pocket. He tries to hand it to me. "*You* have to throw it," I say. "Your aim is better than mine." The camera continues to pan the area. "Quickly!"

"If I miss, this could kill someone."

I look down at the rock in his hand. He's right. It's huge and jagged, and Abel is strong.

"Then don't miss," I say. The stewards are calling for a stretcher. If anyone turns our way and spots us off to the side like this, we'll be flagged for sure. Abel has to throw it now, or we have to get out. "Do it!"

The rock spins through the air. It hits the camera, smashing the lens to pieces. Glass and plastic shower the pathway and more stewards appear. Abel glances at me, then runs forward to where the crowd is growing.

"That could've killed someone!" he shouts. "This place is a death trap!"

I take a deep breath and slip under the ropes. I sprint through the trees, crouching low, hopping over roots. Most auxiliaries can't run like this; their hearts wouldn't cope with the strain. But that's why we spend our nights in alleyways chasing one another up and down, forcing our hearts to pound and breathing in unlicensed quantities of oxygen.

I pull out a hand-drawn map of the biosphere with an *X* marking the spot where the elm is growing. But even without the map, it wouldn't be hard to find: its branches, like splendid wings, are spread so wide it looks like it is ready to take flight.

My breath catches at its grandeur, but I have no time to stand and admire it. I open my backpack, take out a rope, and hurl it over the lowest, thickest branch. I grab a pair of clippers from the backpack, too, stick them into my pocket, and climb. When I reach the lowest branch I let go of the rope and begin to scramble up the tree using the branches and knots as handles and footholds. I don't think about failure. I think only of the cuttings and getting them to The Grove. I scuttle along a branch and snip, throwing the cuttings to the ground as I go.

I would like to stay here, have Abel join me, and spend the afternoon breathing real air, nestled in the arms of this elm. Or his arms. Not that it's allowed; *No romance between members of the Resistance*, Petra insists. It complicates things and compromises our decision-making. And she's right. When I chose Abel for the mission, I didn't care that he wasn't really ready. I just wanted an excuse to train with him.

But I don't have time to worry about that now. Soon the stewards will have swept up the camera pieces and injured tourist and everyone will be filing toward the exit. I hasten to the ground, gather up my equipment and the clippings, and race back, my heart hammering.

When I near the space in the trees where the yellow pathway reappears, I get down onto my knees and inch forward. No one notices me as I stand and saunter over to Abel. He turns his head, smiles, and steps away from the fringes of the crowd.

We follow the last of the tourists through a revolving door into a dark tunnel separating the biosphere from the rest of the pod and the air changes; it no longer tastes real and green but plastic. And once we reach the end of the tunnel, we calmly walk away, careful not to go above three miles per hour in case a speed camera flashes us or a steward notices.

We are in Zone One, with its clean boulevards and mirrored buildings. Every person we pass is pristinely dressed, with facemasks strapped to their self-satisfied faces and connected to airtanks tied to their hips. They are all Premiums, of course, and when they see us, their gazes shift away. Ever so slightly.

We move steadily forward, and while there are no walls or electric fences, no barricades separating the different zones in the pod, when we enter Zone Two there can be no doubt we've left behind the elite. Here, closer to the center of the dome, houses have turned into squat apartment buildings. Open boulevards are now narrow streets and the place is swarming, not with suits, but with stewards, because this is where they live. We keep our heads down.

Before long we reach Zone Three. The apartment buildings, built to house one thousand people each, reach up toward the glass dome of the pod, and the roads are so dark it could be night: all the natural light is swallowed up by the concrete. We slip into a gloomy alleyway between two buildings. They are poor substitutes for the grandeur of the elms and alders.

Abel rubs his hands together and dances on the spot with excitement. "We did it! Did you get everything you needed? Can I see? I'll take care of everything if you like. Hand it over." He is back to his old self.

"I got a heap of clippings. Silas won't believe it. Petra will probably promote me!"

"You were amazing!" he says, and grabs my hips to draw me in toward him. He is smiling and so close the tips of our noses are practically touching. I push him away playfully, not ready to begin whatever it is a kiss would start.

"Me? The way you threw that rock and distracted everyone. I'm glad Petra found you, Abel. You're going to be very useful to us." I don't know why I continue to make our relationship all about the Resistance. I don't know why I can't tell him I'm glad he's around whether we're working together or not.

"So are we going to deliver them to The Grove?" he asks.

"Yes. Will you come with us?"

Abel beams. "Of course I'm coming!" We slink back into the street and Abel throws his arm around my shoulder. My insides tumble.

"Do you trust me?" he asks. He tickles my neck with his fingers.

"Cut it out, Abel!" I say. "We're comrades, not a couple." I want him to contest this and tell me he can't live without me. He doesn't. He just laughs. And I do not push his arm away.

But unlike him, I'm not laughing.

2
BEA

Ten candidates sit around the glass table. Many of them are fidgeting. One girl is chewing her nails and spitting them onto the table. A boy is eating the insides of his mouth. I try to appear calm. When I look at Quinn sitting across from me, he grins to show he isn't worried for either of us; he is as relaxed as he always is and leans back into his chair, his hands behind his head.

We are waiting for the professor. We are waiting for the debate. We've all spent over a year studying and it's time to prove how well we can outwit one another. Everyone else in the room is a highly groomed, prepped Premium, and apart from Quinn, who isn't in the least bit snobby and who you'd never know is a Premium unless you were close enough to see the circle tattooed onto his earlobe, I feel small next to them. Like Quinn, most of them probably had tutors preparing them for the debate, so they're ready to pull me apart.

When the professor sweeps into the room, he doesn't look at any of us. He turns his back as though he hasn't even noticed we're here. We freeze and peer at him as he powers up the screen at the front. When he speaks, his voice is metallic.

"The following exam requires rigorous brain functioning. Those of you who have taken the exam before and failed"—he spins around and eyes a boy with beads of sweat spotting his neck—"will remember that we are not looking for the *right* answer. We are looking for plausible arguments. Strength of reasoning. We are looking to build leaders who have the logic and fortitude to run the pod. You have been chosen because you performed exceptionally in your preliminary tests under simulated debate conditions. The only true test, however, is human-to-human contact in a real debate. This examination is being watched by several governmental officials and by directors from Breathe, the sponsors of this leadership program." Quinn glances at the mirrored walls. I guess he's wondering whether or not his father, a senior director at Breathe, is here. "The examination will be recorded, and you will be informed on your pad of your status as soon as you have been assessed. We will recruit no more than two of you. And we may recruit none of you."

It is not an ordinary debate, with one team on one side and another team on the other. We all sit around a conference table, much like we're in a board meeting, and take sides simply by listening to one another and deciding which candidates we agree with. At any point in the debate the professor can eliminate a student he deems aggressive, too quiet, or irrational. The key is to stay calm, stay in the game, and get others on your side. The professor settles himself into the high-backed chair at the front of the room and assigns us numbers by which to address each other. "If we have a situation wherein you all agree, points will be awarded for those among you who can act as a devil's advocate. I won't explain what this means—you all passed the preliminary tests." He turns to the screen, flicks a switch, and a statement appears:

Trees are no longer essential to our survival, nor our progress.

Obviously. What else does anyone ever talk about? A boy in a crisp white shirt jumps in first. "Trees were essential, historically, but now they're dead, we can do without them. One only need enter the pod to witness how happy and healthy every citizen is." Of course. A Premium *would* think of the pod as a paradise. But he's jumped in without thinking through his argument and there's no way he's going to be able to maintain that position for a whole hour.

"I disagree," I say. "Auxiliaries can't afford to buy extra oxygen to exercise. How can we be healthy?" And so it begins. We argue. Teeth are bared and voices raised. A few pushovers are easily eliminated. Then more. And at the end of the hour only two are left: me and Quinn.

"What type of progress are you talking about?" I ask. "Are we happier than our predecessors?" Quinn tilts his head and looks at me carefully. We are facing each other, a table between us. Quinn's fingers twitch. He glances at the professor.

"But progress and happiness aren't the same thing. We have more sophisticated technology than before The Switch because the loss of trees forced us to advance," he says. He looks apologetic because I know he doesn't want to battle with me. When we were given our test dates and saw we had been scheduled together, he threatened to quit until I convinced him otherwise.

"I didn't claim that progress and happiness are the same thing. I'm asking how we *define* progress." I pause, waiting for Quinn to respond, but he doesn't. He just shrugs, a little defeated. I'm sure he has an answer, and I don't want him to *let* me win. Before I can push him into responding, the gong sounds and Quinn lets out a sigh of relief. Then he smiles, not smugly or with any self-satisfaction but in a congratulatory way. I smile back.

"Thank you, candidates," the professor says, tidying his things. "A notice will be sent to your pads in due course."

• • •

Once outside the Scholastic Institute, Quinn turns to me, grabs my hands, and says, "You did it, Bea! You were better than all of us. And you were so tough. I can see that tattoo on your ear already!" He hugs me, and I smile, both because Quinn has me in his arms and also because I'm sure he's right: I argued perfectly.

"So *now* do you have time to hang out with me?" he asks. I'd been seeing Quinn less often as I prepared for the debate. Now that it's over with, we can get back to living in each other's pockets.

"I would *love* to," I admit.

"Cool. Because I have something massive planned: a camping trip out of the pod. Three days. What do you think? We have a school holiday coming up."

"Are you serious?"

"I've got to get a few things first, but I think we could go this Sunday, if your parents will let you. We can't go Saturday because I have a soccer match."

"Great, I'll ask. But . . . oh . . ."

"What?" He steps closer to me and pushes his hair from his eyes.

"There's the mock trial on Monday evening," I say. "I'm the lead lawyer for the defense."

"Oh, right." He bites the inside of one cheek.

"I'd love to go on a trip, but I've been working on the trial for ages."

Quinn shakes his head. "Don't be silly, it's important," he says. He puts his hands into his pockets and rocks back and forth on his heels, thinking. "You know what, I'll skip the match and we can go on Saturday morning instead. I'll tell coach it's a family trip." He looks up and nods.

"No way. You love those games," I say. And I love watching him play.

"Nah. I need to get out of the pod. And we need some time together to work out what you're gonna do once you become Premium." He takes my hands again and we sway together as though we're in some black-and-white movie. "You'll be dancing in the streets, Bea."

A woman pushing a stroller passes us and elaborately clears her throat. "Stop!" I laugh, pushing him away. "We're going to get arrested." We aren't moving energetically enough for what we're doing to be illegal, but I'm self-conscious dancing with him out in public.

"Do you wanna skip school today? We could go back to my house and watch a movie. I know . . . let's get drunk. Dad never locks up the booze," he says, laughing. I push him again. He's teasing because he knows I've never missed a day of school in my life and, unlike him, I can't drink more than a glass of anything alcoholic without falling over.

"I can't. The mock-trial team is having a meeting. Anyway, don't you have a history test?" I say.

"Thank God I have you to keep me on the straight and narrow, Bea," Quinn says, taking my bag and throwing it over his right shoulder, his own bag already over his left. Walking together in Zone One feels so natural, I forget for a moment I don't belong here. But walking along wide streets and enjoying the light, being with Quinn, of course, are things I could definitely get used to. I shouldn't, but I start to plan for a new life—a life as a Premium.

I spend the whole day dreaming and planning and recalling my victory in the debate, so the message that lights up my pad as I'm waiting in the school foyer for Quinn to finish soccer practice doesn't make any sense at all:

Dear Ms. Whitcraft,

We regret to inform you that your recent candidacy for the Breathe Leadership Program has been terminated. We encourage all failing candidates to maintain high scores in standardized tests to increase the chances of being recalled next season to stage-one enrollment.

Professor Felling

I stare at the message for a couple of seconds, stand up, and march out the double doors of the foyer. I walk as quickly as I dare down the street, slumping onto a bench several blocks away. I reread the message several times, and when I'm certain I haven't misunderstood, I turn off the screen and push the pad into the deepest pocket of my backpack. I sit looking down at my hands.

A small part of me wants to storm into the Scholastic Institute and demand justice. But I don't know how to be brave or pushy. Instead, I stand up and quietly walk home from school wiping my eyes and nose along my sleeve whenever the tears get the better of me. I think about calling Quinn, but if I didn't make the Leadership Program, he probably did, and hard as I might try, I'd find it difficult to be pleased for him.

I take the winch up to the fifteenth floor of my building, walk down a corridor ablaze with fluorescent tubes, and press my thumb against the fingerprint scanner. The outer door to our small apartment buzzes open and as I step inside, it closes with a gulp before the inner door automatically slides open. The apartments are airtight and fitted with oxygen meters so the Ministry can monitor our intake—if they have to pump in any more oxygen than our taxes cover, we pay extra.

Mom is already in the hall, where she clicks on the light so she can see me better. I must be red and puffy. "Bea?" Mom's face is deathly pale, her wrinkles so deep they could be scars. She has blue circles beneath her eyes. I just can't help it; I imagine how much longer she has to work and struggle without ever taking a break, and I start crying again.

"I don't want you to die," I whimper.

"Goodness, Bea, what's gotten into you? I'm not dying. I'm tired, that's all." She wraps me up in her bony arms for a moment, and when she lets go I notice my father sitting at the dining table. A steaming bowl sits in front of him, but he is so tired that he has fallen asleep in the chair, with his fork standing upright in his food.

"I failed the debate. I'll have to wait a year to reapply."

"Oh, Bea." Mom hugs me again, pressing my face deep into her shoulder. She doesn't tell me not to worry because she knows I will. And she worries, too, when she wonders how we'll live if I don't manage to reach Premium status soon. "Let's go for a walk," she says. Yes, a walk: we can afford that.

We stroll along the choked streets of Zone Three into Zone Two, where the buildings don't appear to be toppling into one another quite so much. The schools are here, the hospitals, the steward academies, and the housing for low-level Ministry workers. I could live here one day if I trained as a nurse or something. But I don't want to live here. I want to live in Zone One on the pod's edge with all the light. I want to live in a spacious house on a wide, linoleum lawn. Getting to Zone One is easy—you just walk in a straight line from any direction toward the light. Staying is quite another thing.

When we reach it, we peek through stocky gates at the few families who have their lamps on and blinds open for a glimpse into what we're missing: antique dining tables salvaged from The Outlands with a gaggle of plump children surrounding them; platters of real food; glinting chandeliers.

At the world-viewing post, only a block from Quinn's house, we sit on a metal bench looking out at the air-recycling stations connected to the pod with thick rubber tubing and listen to them whir. Beyond the stations lies an expanse of cleared land punctuated by faint patches of rubble, and in the far distance, the remnants of the old city. A steward passes by with his hands behind his back, glares at us, and when he is satisfied we are behaving ourselves, moves on.

"Haven't they anything better to do than watch us?" Mom grumbles.

"I should get a job. We need the money," I say.

"No, Bea. I want a better life for you than the one I've had. And that means school. Your job is to study." She squeezes my hand. Sitting with my mom, looking out at our starry-skied, oxygen-starved planet, I'm no longer sure I'll ever get my family out: I rely on my brain, but it doesn't look like that will be enough.

"Your grandfather hiked a trail over there. Every spring," she says, pointing. "But, gosh, I haven't been out of this pod since the honeymoon. We saved up for a year and were out there for three full days. It was spectacular. Scary though. When the sun goes down it's dark—no artificial lights anywhere." She turns and waves at the streetlamps gently illuminating Zone One. "We slept during the day and hiked at night just so we could enjoy the stars. We got as far as Marden. No, Maldon. Oh, I can't remember its name." She points to a spot we can't see because a low hill hides it from view. "They used to have boats you could take out on the water."

"I wish I could live in The Outlands."

"Don't fill your head with nonsense, Bea," she says with a sigh, though she's the one who's wistful. "And anyway, it's sad out there. Desolate. The land *and* the sea." She is meant to be cheering me up, but she isn't doing a very good job; if anything, I'm starting to feel worse, and I wish it had been Dad who'd discovered me so upset. He would've made jokes.

We stand up and stroll along a walkway looping the pod. A group of Premium runners rush by in facemasks, mini air-tanks attached to their waists with BREATHE printed in yellow on the side. They are panting and sweating and rather ugly-looking as they exercise, but even so, Mom smiles after them, her eyes as wide as dinner bowls.

"Where do people get the money?" she wonders aloud,

staring after the group. "They probably have twelve children apiece, too." I ignore her and try to enjoy the view.

"I was asked to go camping," I say.

"Camping?" She touches the curved, thick glass of the pod.

"Quinn invited me."

"But it's January, and we haven't got warm clothes. There's no climate control outside, love. And the airtanks. We just can't afford it," she says.

"The oxygen is a gift. And Quinn has plenty of stuff I can wear."

"I bet he does," she says. She looks away. She likes Quinn but hates his parents. She thinks they're stuck up, which they are, and she considers his father personally responsible for most of her problems, especially when she receives an oxygen bill.

"You should marry him," she says.

"What?" I think I've misheard her.

"If you marry Quinn, you'll get a perfect purple circle on your earlobe and everything would change. You'd be one of those wives who goes around with a purified airtank." Mom teases me about Quinn sometimes, and maybe she knows how I feel about him, but she's never before suggested anything like this. I want her to laugh and elbow me and turn what she's said into a big joke. She doesn't; she stops walking and turns to look at me. "I think you're brilliant, Bea, and I know you can be anything you want. But Quinn has it easy, and with him you would, too, and we wouldn't ever have to worry again." Her voice is earnest. "If you married Quinn Caffrey, do you think his father would allow the Breathe Leadership Program to refuse you a place?" I can't believe that my mother has even thought about this. Does she know what she's saying? I'm still at school and she's planning my wedding.

"Quinn took the exam, too. I was better. He won't have passed if I didn't," I say, simply to counter what she's suggesting. It wouldn't be fair, but there's every chance Quinn will have passed.

"We'll see," she says. "I just want you to have children if you want to, lots of them, without worrying about how you're going to pay their air tax, without having to tie them to their cribs when they're toddlers to stop them from moving around too much and sucking all the oxygen from the apartment. I know how you love to dance. I can never give you that. Quinn though, he *can*."

The question is, would he ever want to? The way Quinn and I are together and the way he treats me, I can't blame her for imagining he feels something he doesn't. The number of times he's given me a "spare" airtank or checked in on me when I've been sick would be enough to fool even the most cynical person. Only last week I left some supplies at school and wasn't able to do my technology homework without them; when I called Quinn to complain about it, he pretended he had to get off the pad, and then he went all the way back to school, got the stuff I needed, and turned up at my apartment door an hour later with them. Then he rushed off home so he wouldn't miss dinner.

"You wouldn't be saying this if I'd been born a boy," I say. She must be desperate to push like this. We're standing under a street lamp and I can see every furrow in her face, every vein in her eyes. How can I be annoyed when my mother looks so old and works so hard just so I can breathe?

"I would want my son to marry a rich girl. Then he could run and climb and kiss and do whatever he wanted without checking himself. I want you to have what I never had. Quinn's good-looking and clever and, well, rich. You can love someone rich or you can love someone poor. Why not love a Premium, huh?" I want to say, *But I do!* I do love a Premium. And I don't care how rich he is. If Quinn were a poor auxiliary, but loved me, that would be perfect.

Instead I say, "I'm still only sixteen, Mom."

"And in two years you'll be eighteen and I will be forty-nine and your Dad will be fifty. Just think about it." Think about it? I spend my life thinking about Quinn Caffrey, for all the good it does me, and it doesn't matter how much I want him; the fact is that he does not want me.

"He doesn't feel that way about me," I say. I have never admitted this out loud, so when I hear the words spoken in my own voice, clear and undisputed, I could cry. I look at my mom steadily.

"Is that so?" she says. At that moment my pad vibrates. It's a message from Quinn: *I thought we were going for shakes after school? U ok?* "Just think about it," Mom repeats.

3
QUINN

The vaccination line winds all the way from the nurse's office to the back of the damn gym. It's my lunch period and I'm starving, but this is the quietest time of the day, so I stand and wait for my jab. Not that I'm dying to be jabbed. I can't stand injections. The school announcer is reminding us every hour that we're required to go to the nurse to be inoculated, so it's better just to get it done, get it out of the way.

I've been waiting twenty minutes, passing the time reviewing formulas for a physics test, when Riley and Ferris saunter up to my place in the line.

"Thanks for holding our places, man," Riley says.

"Yep, really nice of you, dude," Ferris adds. I turn around to look at the students behind me. They scowl. As they should.

"Guys, everyone else has been waiting," I say, pointing at the grim line that's formed down the corridor. Ferris grunts and forces his way in next to the wall so he's firmly in front of me. Riley does the same. The students behind us are younger and apart from grumbling, there isn't much they can do.

"Wanna play soccer after school?" Riley asks, nudging me in the chest.

"Watch it!" I say and push him.

"We need a goalie," he says.

"And we thought about how much you like grabbing hold of balls. Right? Right?" Ferris sneers. I roll my eyes and pull out my pad, scrolling through to the school display where my tests and quizzes are logged.

"I can't play," I say. "The old man says my grades aren't good enough."

Ferris and Riley squint down at the screen. "Ugh," Riley says.

Ferris laughs. "I suppose you can't have it all, Quinn. Looks, money, smarts. You've gotta lose somewhere." I want to tell him that getting low As and high Bs isn't exactly losing and that if it weren't for my father, I'd be quite happy with my grades. Anyway, they're a lot better than what I know *he's* getting. But before I have a chance to finish the thought, both Riley and Ferris are engrossed in games on their pads—it doesn't take a lot to distract them.

I feel a tug on my arm, and when I look up, standing there is, quite possibly, the most outrageously beautiful girl I've ever met in my life. And that's not an exaggeration. She has large green eyes, the pupils dilated in rage, and her long hair is haphazardly heaped on top of her head. She looks like she is about to hit me. I smile at her.

"I've been here for ages, and out of the blue your little buddies come along and slip right into line," she says. "I don't think so." Riley and Ferris have headphones in so they can't hear a word she's saying, and even though I *can*, I've pretty much lost the power to speak, which is new. "Are you there?" she asks and waves her hand in front of my face. I continue staring but manage to close my mouth. "Go to the back," she says, pulling on Ferris's elbow when she figures she's getting nothing from me.

"What do you want?" he snarls, turning and yanking off his headphones.

"You have to go to the back."

"Who says I do? *You?*" He laughs. Riley turns and takes out his headphones, too.

"What's happening?"

"This bossy cow wants to take our place in line," Ferris says.

"Cool it," I say, stepping between Riley and Ferris and the girl. "You two pushed in first."

"Be careful who you take on, babe," Ferris continues, stepping forward and standing taller.

"You don't scare me. Pompous Premium. You think you can do whatever you like," she says, pushing me aside. I take a quick look at her earlobes; she isn't tattooed. She must have noticed ours right away and that would have riled her even more.

"I actually do get to do whatever I like," Ferris admits. He raises his eyebrows lasciviously. I want to tell her that she shouldn't really mess with these guys because they aren't afraid to hurt girls, but I have a feeling that nothing I say is going to stop her.

"You're pathetic," she says. She snorts and turns to me. "Nice friends you have there." As I begin to apologize for them, she stomps off.

"What was that about?" I say, shoving Ferris.

"I know, what a nut!" Ferris says. "She's a hottie though."

"I don't mean her, I mean you two. Why don't you grow up?"

"Us? You've gotta be joking," Riley says.

"He's gotta be joking," Ferris repeats.

I've had enough. Enough of standing in line and enough of trying to reason with two idiots. I pick up my bag and take off after the girl.

"Quinn!" Ferris calls after me. "Tell Bea I'll call her

tonight." I ignore him and keep going.

She doesn't rejoin the inoculation line as I expect her to. She walks straight past the end of it and into the canteen, where she joins the lunch line instead. I grab a tray and follow her to the counter. The menu for today is flashing above the food stations.

"They aren't usually that bad," I say. She didn't notice me coming after her and turns with a start.

"It's you," she says.

"Pleased to see me?" I ask, even though she doesn't look one bit pleased.

"Whatever," she says and leans in to speak to the server. I wait until I see that all she has on her plate is some dry toast, and I order exactly the same thing. The server smiles. The girl doesn't. She edges down the counter away from me.

She pays and sits alone at a round table by the window. When I take a seat next to her she says, "I'm waiting for someone," and looks up at the large wall clock.

I pretend not to have heard in case she goes on to tell me that she's waiting for her boyfriend. "I wanted to get my vaccine before lunch. I don't have time after school," I say. She doesn't look up. As she eats, her hair starts to come loose. She pushes the stray pieces behind her ears. "To be honest, I'm kind of sick of getting stabbed with a needle every other week. What can it be for this time?"

"They're immunizing for the green flu," she reminds me, biting into her toast. She points to a revolving billboard above our heads that has the words GREEN FLU INOCULATION DUE blazing in neon letters. I laugh, hoping she will, too. She doesn't. She gulps down some water and squints at me as though she isn't quite sure what she's seeing.

"Wasn't the green flu last month?" I say.

"That was the copper flu. Read the memos."

"I can't keep track," I tell her. She's trying her best to ignore me, that's obvious, but she's more gorgeous than any girl I've ever met—and she's tough and secretive—and I want to get to know her even if she doesn't want to get to know me. I want to touch her. And I want her to touch me back. "I don't know about all these vaccines. Sometimes I think it would be better to get one of these colorful diseases," I ramble on, hoping I can keep her engaged. And I do.

Her eyes dart from side to side, and she whispers, "The vaccines are poisonous." She wipes her mouth with the back of her hand.

I nod as though I agree, but really I'm trying to understand why she'd say something so weird. And instead of thinking through a cool response, I blurt out the first thing that comes into my head. "Do you have a phobia of needles or something?"

"No, I don't hate needles." She sighs. Maybe she thinks

I'm not taking her seriously, but I don't know how to claw my way back into her favor and I have no idea why she doesn't like the jabs, so I simply sit there staring at her. She turns away and eats her toast.

"I might try the line again in a minute. You?" I ask.

"I don't think so. I want Nurse Kelly to do it. She's gentle. You should try to see her. Whenever you can." She stands up.

"What's your name?" I ask.

"Why?" For once she isn't being rude. I think she really wants to know what I plan on doing with her name.

"Just . . ." I shrug.

"I'm Alina," she says, and walks off, leaving her tray on the table.

There's no point in following her as she's clearly decided she isn't interested, so I polish off the toast, from her plate as well as my own, and go back to the vaccination line. Ferris and Riley are right up front by the nurse's office. I make my way toward them, past the other kids who've been waiting all lunch period, and squeeze into the line.

"You're not pushing in, are you?" Riley sneers.

"Get the hell out of my way," I say, and elbow him aside to make room for myself.

"We just saw Bea," he tells me.

Ferris sniffs and raises his eyebrows. "Nice, tight shirt she had on," he says. "I don't know why you've never gone for a piece of that." He covers his mouth with his hand and snorts, so without thinking too much about it, I punch Ferris in the gut.

He doubles over. "It was a joke," he groans.

"Cool it, Quinn," Riley says, patting Ferris on the back.

I look around to see if Bea's still within sight, but she isn't. I stand for a minute staring at the frosty glass in the door to the nurse's office, then change my mind about getting the vaccination and walk away.

4
ALINA

Silas beat me home from school. I watch him through the glass balcony doors, crouching to examine some sprouting lavender. He pats the earth around the plant and stands up. He cocks his head to one side, pleased, and moves to another plant. Six large boxes are arranged in rows on the balcony, all containing different cuttings. Silas is so absorbed in them, he doesn't hear the beep as the inner and outer doors open and I step outside. When I tap his shoulder, he jumps, turns, and shouts, "Damn it, Alina, what are you creeping around for?"

"I'm not creeping anywhere."

Silas looks from side to side and up and down at the grid of empty balconies surrounding our own and gestures for me to follow him inside.

"Sit down," he says. This is something I've only ever

heard people say in films, so I don't know what to do. Silas uses the remote to turn on the screen and flip to a music channel. It's playing toxic dance music, which he hates. Even so, he turns up the volume and falls back into the couch. I sit next to him. "Abel's missing," he whispers.

"What?" I ask, though I've heard him.

"Abel. He's missing," he snaps. "He hasn't been in school. I thought he was sick or something. I didn't really get too worried until I stopped by his place today, to see what was going on. There was no one in. A neighbor told me she hasn't seen him in a while. Did you know he lives alone?"

"No."

"Anyway, the neighbor said she'll file a missing person's report. For all the good it'll do."

"I saw him the day after the mission and we arranged to meet for lunch today," I say, not mentioning that I was angry and jealous when he didn't show up, not mentioning that I left school early because I couldn't cope with listening to Mr. Banbury droning on about algorithms when all I could concentrate on was the feeling of rejection. "Maybe he left the pod," I say.

"I hoped as much myself. I went down to Border Control and checked the departure roster. He wasn't on it. He's vanished, Alina. Gone. Not only that, but they didn't even have his name in the system. It's like he doesn't exist."

"What about the school directory?"

"I tried that, too. He isn't registered for any classes."

I sit back into the couch and watch the half-naked dancers on the screen. The music is too loud. I can't think. I want to turn it off and sit in complete silence. But we can't risk turning down the music and anyone overhearing. I know better than most what it means for people to go missing in the pod. Missing means gone forever. Missing means dead.

We sit for a long time without speaking. Occasionally Silas looks at me, but I keep my eyes on the screen and my mouth straight. I look like I am concentrating, and I am. But I am concentrating on not remembering my parents and how the same thing happened to them last year, how they simply disappeared and were never heard from again. Obviously we didn't believe that they'd run away, that they'd somehow managed to bypass Border Control, but that was the story the Ministry gave the press, and so that's what we had to say when anyone asked, if we didn't want to end up missing too. Is Silas telling me that Abel is dead? "They've wiped him from the system?" I say.

Silas sighs and rubs the back of his neck. "It doesn't make sense. Abel doesn't know anything. He just joined up." He looks out at the balcony and I know he is thinking about whether or not he should destroy the plants. We don't have a permit to keep them. Not only that, but they would want to know where we got them and there is no good answer to this question. At eighteen, two years older than me, my cousin, Silas, seems practically a man. If he has to destroy the plants he will. But he'll look for an alternative first. He's spent too long with this last set to let them go without a fight.

"What will they do to him?" I ask. I am imagining Abel bound to a chair, being beaten until he bleeds. I am imagining him hanging upside down. Having pins driven up his fingernails. And naturally, I am imagining the obvious—Abel being pushed from the pod and starving of oxygen. Suffocating.

I turn to Silas and must look petrified because he pats my arm and smiles. "We just have to be more careful," he says. "We've been skipping too much school. We have to be as inconspicuous as possible. We can continue to meditate, but no more night training, it's too dangerous."

"We have to help Abel. This is my fault. We should have abandoned the mission when the first rock failed."

"What first rock?"

"The retrieval didn't go exactly according to plan," I admit.

"Why didn't you say something sooner?" He moves closer to me.

"We thought we got away with it."

"Damn it, Alina! We follow procedure or we get out,"

he snaps. He doesn't need to be angry with me. I feel bad enough. "Let's think about this."

"We *have* to get to Petra," I say.

"If we leave the pod so soon after our last trip, we'll be flagged."

"We can't do this alone. We're all at risk and we need help, Silas."

"Calm down. For all we know, Abel's just fine. Let's lie low for a couple more days and see how this thing pans out. Agreed?"

"Silas . . ." I try.

"Agreed?" he repeats, more sternly.

"Fine," I say, but I'm not so sure the plan is a good one: we're protecting ourselves, but what about Abel? The Resistance is a family and when one member gets cut down, we all feel it. But even if Silas is wrong, what can I do to help Abel? I don't even know where he is.

Silas nods to the balcony and we go outside again, where I look up at the ceiling of the glass pod. Silas bends down to rub one of the leaves on the lavender plant he's been tending to and brings his fingers to his nose. "It's gorgeous. Smell," he says. He puts his fingers up to my nose. I inhale deeply, to distract myself if for no other reason. I need to get the picture of Abel out of my head.

"What if the neighbors see the boxes?" I ask.

"They'll think they're as fake as theirs." Many of our neighbors have plastic plants on their balconies, and there's no reason for anyone to suspect that ours are any different.

"Just don't let anyone see you watering them," I say.

"What? Old Watson waters his plants. When I asked about it, he said he did it to remind himself of how things had been. Poor guy. He started choking up." Silas stands and brushes some soil from his trousers as a speed camera momentarily lights up the street below. Someone's been caught.

I peer down into the shadows. A tram clanks along its rails and the pedestrians on the pavement shuffle along. It's illegal to run in the pod without an airtank. It's illegal to walk faster than three miles per hour. The speed cameras track movement. As do the stewards. That's why Silas and I train at night, in alleyways and under bridges where no one can see us, where no one is monitoring the excess oxygen we use. Not that we want to be using excess oxygen; we'd prefer it if they turned the oxygen levels right down.

There have been a few close calls when a steward has wandered down an alley and come upon us, and then we've really had to run, balaclavas covering our faces so the cameras can't identify us even as the speed cameras flash and whistle.

"Let's go inside," Silas says.

The lights are on in the apartment and Uncle Gideon and Aunt Harriet are in the hall kicking off their shoes. They hug us both before collapsing onto the couch, exhausted from working twelve hours at the agriculture unit of the biosphere. This is a good placement compared to some jobs. At least they get to spend their days breathing in natural air and sometimes they manage to smuggle fruit or vegetables out so we can taste real food. Only Premiums can afford food that's grown; the rest of us survive on vitamin-heavy synthetic breads and smoothies. Today their uniforms are covered in red splotches that can only mean one thing.

"Berry picking?" I ask.

"Dessert," Uncle Gideon says. He delves into the front pocket of his trousers and pulls out a handful of ripe raspberries. Silas looks annoyed. He keeps his eyes on my aunt and uncle, tapping his foot impatiently, expectantly.

"Especially for you," my aunt says, and pulls from her bag a small raspberry plant cutting and three more raspberries. "Are there enough seeds in those to keep you happy?" she asks Silas.

"Perfect," he says.

"God, what are you two listening to?" Aunt Harriet asks. She rubs her temples.

Uncle Gideon reaches for the remote and turns off the screen. "What I need is a cold drink and some grub," he says, looking at Silas. Silas wanders into the kitchen. I follow him, open the freezer, and take out a slab of frozen dinner cake. The apartment is quiet as my aunt and uncle doze on the couch.

"Why didn't you tell them?" I whisper.

"They have enough to worry about. If it looks like the Ministry is on to us, we'll say something. Until then . . ." He runs two fingers across his lips as though zipping them together. "Got it?"

I nod and unwrap the dinner cake from its waxy paper. There's no use grieving over Abel when, for all I know, he's fine. This is the lie I feed myself.

5
BEA

The hailstorm and heavy rain sound like a giant is drumming his fingers against the glass pod. After school, I'm waiting on a narrow bench at a tram station for Quinn, but suddenly wish I were at the world-viewing station, as I was yesterday, watching what the weather does to the world, how it creates puddles in the dips of the earth and rivulets where it's hilly. No matter what happens outside, we are sheltered here: no rain or snow in the winter, no humidity or heat in the summer. The temperature is always perfect and the air always clear; the pod protects us from every element, saves us from suffocation.

Quinn shows up a few minutes late. I see him before he notices me, nudging his way along the crowded platform. When he gets to my bench, he hurls his bag to the ground and plonks down next to me. Before I have a chance to ask him what's wrong, he starts ranting.

"Can you tell me why I need to be injected for the green flu when I don't even know anyone with the green flu. Has anyone *you* know got it?"

"Did you read the memo?" I ask. He pushes up the sleeves of his shirt and crosses his arms.

"You're the second person to say that to me today. No, I didn't. And even if I did, they never explain why we need vaccines for illnesses no one has." He has a point. The vaccines are mandatory, yet I've never met anyone with any of the things we're constantly being protected from. Still, I'm not sure it's worth taking the chance.

"The green flu could kill you and it's airborne, so unless you plan on living out there"—I point up at the roof of the pod—"you've got to deal with it." When the tram pulls into the station, we hustle our way to some back seats with a view of the screen a couple of rows ahead. A woman jumps into the carriage just before the doors slurp shut.

"Is this a clockwise service?" she asks.

"Anti," someone tells her.

"Oh." She sighs and slumps against a luggage rack as the tram races out of the station.

"Where've you been all day, anyway? I sent you a million messages," Quinn says.

"I haven't looked at my pad. What's wrong? Did you hear from Professor Felling?" I ask. I know he can't really be upset about the routine vaccinations, so maybe he's heard that he failed the exam and that's why he's stewing. I elbow him when he doesn't answer. "Quinn?" He stares out at the smudged rows of apartment blocks as we speed along.

"I haven't heard a thing yet. You?" He looks at me, his anger momentarily diluted.

"I failed. So . . ." I trail off. I don't need to explain what failing means for me and my family.

"What? There's no way. Bea, I'm sorry." He squeezes my knee and leaves his hand resting there. My stomach tightens as I wait for something else, something more to happen between us. But it doesn't. He sits quite still with his hand on my knee and stares at me. This is all that happens today and this is all that will ever happen. "It has to be some kind of clerical error. We'll go down to the Scholastic Institute and ask to see the professor. We can go *now*. Or I'll speak to my dad. Don't worry."

"It isn't a mistake, Quinn."

"It has to be. Your arguments were flippin' flawless."

"Well, obviously they weren't. It seems like we've both had a bad day," I say.

Quinn crosses his arms. "Tell me what the message said."

"I don't want to go into it. I'll just get upset. Do you mind?"

He shakes his head. "Of course I don't mind." He pauses. "I guess that means I didn't pass either." He shrugs, trying to act as though he isn't concerned about himself when I know that this was something he really wanted to do; he wanted to show his dad he could make the cut on his own merit.

"If you haven't had a message, there's a good chance you passed," I say. I don't say what I'm thinking, which is that his father has influence and maybe his chances were always better than mine anyway.

"It hardly matters. I don't want to leave school and join the Scholastic Institute on my own. I'd never see you. The plan was that we *both* get into the program. Are you okay?"

I press my lips together and nod. "I'm fine. Let's change the subject. What happened to *you* today?"

"Nothing," he says. "But these vaccines . . . I can't stand them."

I swallow and take a guess. "A girl?"

He sighs and laughs at himself. "I don't know what happens, but every time I meet someone, I turn into a cartoon." I try smiling, but I actually wish we could talk about the debate again. Anything but Quinn's love life. "You can't imagine how stunning she is."

"You said that about Tilly, and it turned out she was of goblin proportions."

"Tilly *was* short." He laughs again.

"Admit she was a goblin," I say, though I know it's cruel.

"And she's got these eyes." He pauses and shakes his head disbelievingly.

"She has *eyes*? Wow!"

"No, really. She has these piercing green eyes. Now who do you know with green eyes?" It's hard to believe. He's looking right at me. He's looking right into my eyes and he doesn't notice their color. "Anyway, Alina thinks I'm an idiot," he goes on. Alina. The name sounds familiar. I try to retrieve an image of this girl in my mind, but I can't. Our school serves a couple thousand students, and it would be impossible to know every one of them.

"Sometimes you *are* an idiot," I say. I am trying to tease him, maybe I'm trying to flirt, but he's so dejected all he does is nod in agreement.

"It was Ferris and Riley. They're never around when you need them, and when you don't want to be bothered by them, they show up. God, I'm glad I didn't invite them camping."

"You were going to invite them camping?"

"Ferris never shuts up about you. Why don't you give him a chance?" Now he's the one teasing. Last week Ferris tried to put his hand up my skirt, and it was all I could do to stop Quinn from pulling Ferris's arms from their sockets.

"Give Ferris a chance to what? Humiliate and ridicule me?"

"Poor Ferris," Quinn says with a laugh. "He's just so—"

"He's a pervert and an ignoramus," I interrupt.

"That's harsh," he says, but he's still snickering, so I know he doesn't mean it. He's as repulsed by Ferris as I am.

"What about the time he snuck into your house so he could do whatever he wanted with that girl without his family getting an excess oxygen charge? I don't even want to think about *that*," I say, though I am already thinking far too much about it.

"Don't be jealous. You can use my room any time you like." He winks playfully and I blush, not sure what he means.

"Quinn!" I slap him gently. He holds his stomach like he's mortally injured and begins to moan. Then we both crack up and only stop tittering when a woman in the seat in front turns and shushes us.

"I'm trying to listen to the news," she complains, nodding at the screen. We both look up. It's another terrorist report. Someone has been caught trying to interfere with the air-recycling system. This is the worst thing anyone can imagine. If the pod ran out of air, we'd be stuck, and we'd be dead. I shiver.

The news report continues:

"Suspected terrorist Abel Boone, a member of the Rebel Army Terrorist Sect, was found dead today. It is believed he ran out of air attempting to cut through the rubber tubing that connects

the Air Recycling Station East to the pod. Various RATS arrests are expected to be carried out within the coming days. The Pod Minister has asked for calm."

Right on cue, a solemn Pod Minister appears on the screen with a journalist beside him. "Luckily we avoided a major tragedy, and I am grateful to the stewards for their haste in dealing with this matter. The Ministry will continue to work around the clock to provide safety for *all* people. We will not allow mindless acts of terrorism against tens of thousands of innocent civilians to go unpunished. I urge all citizens to remain alert."

"And your message to the terrorists, Pod Minister?"

"To the terrorists, I say run. Run." He looks straight into the camera and grins because a running citizen is an arrested citizen, unless the runner is a Premium with a tank, of course, and the journalist laughs, too, and even the woman sitting in front of us laughs. But I do not. I do not like the joke.

With that the screen goes black before a typically interminable commercial break begins.

When the tram reaches our stop, Quinn stays in his seat. "Are you sure you wouldn't rather go speak with the professor?" he says.

"I'm sure," I say, knowing it would be pointless to speak to anyone: once academic decisions have been made, they are impossible to reverse. We get off the tram, walk up to the camping shop, and choose a bright blue tent and two extra-warm sleeping bags for our trip. Quinn tells me I'll need boots, a coat, a hat, a scarf, and gloves, and he insists I choose from a Premium selection hanging in the women's department. I can't look at Quinn as he pays for everything, as the simpering cashier swipes his father's card.

"I'm nervous about leaving the pod. I didn't think I would be," I admit on our way back to the station. "No air? It'll be so strange."

"Don't worry. Look, with all these terrorist attacks, we might find we're better off out there anyway. And if we're going to suffocate, wouldn't it be fun to suffocate together?" He pinches me lightly, trying to put some humor between me and my fear. But what he doesn't realize is that I *would* want to be with him at the end. If I were to die, I'd rather die out there with him than in the pod with anyone else.

6
QUINN

"My clever boy!" my mother announces, throwing her arms around me as soon as I get home. I pull away, embarrassed.

"Hey," I manage. My father steps forward and claps me on the back. "I'm here!" I say, knowing my homecoming can't possibly be the reason for their sudden interest in me.

As I walk into the living room, I see immediately what's going on: standing with one hand behind his back and one holding a glass of something is the Pod Minister, Cain Knavery. During the interview on the tram screen a couple of hours ago, he'd looked serious and purposeful. Now he looks jolly. Jolly-well drunk. He's standing next to the mantelpiece where, I notice, my parents have taken down our old oil painting of a seascape and put up a portrait of the Pod Minister in its place, so that Cain Knavery looks like he is standing next to himself. They replace the artwork, as well as their personalities, whenever he visits.

"Ha-ha! He has arrived. Well now, Caffrey Junior," the Pod Minister says, and stretches out a hand. He has at least one gold ring on every hairy finger. "Congratulations. You are a credit to your parents." He points at my mother and father, like I might not know who they are.

"Thank you," I say, and shake his clammy, jeweled hand.

"How old are you now?" the Pod Minister asks, still squeezing my hand.

"I'm sixteen, sir," I say.

"Sixteen! Ha! Well, you're a fine specimen. You could be twenty-one. Jude, get this man a drink," he says, finally letting go of me and gesturing to the whiskey bottle on the sideboard. My father scurries over and pours a little of the amber liquid into a clean tumbler. "Is that it? Ha! Don't be a miser, Jude," the Pod Minister says, and laughs through his nose. My father chuckles, too, and fills my glass to the top. My father is usually gruff and stoic, so seeing him grovel for the Pod Minister is always fascinating. In fact, the whole scene is sort of preposterous, but why not take advantage of it? I swipe the whiskey from my father and take a large gulp. That's when I notice the twins, Lennon and Keane, both ten, sitting on the gray couch holding their own measures of whiskey and giggling. Lennon raises his tumbler and mouths the word *Cheers!*

If Bea were here, she'd probably sidle over to the twins and, with a stern look, grab their drinks from them, though she'd definitely take a sip herself. She won't believe it when I tell her about it later.

The Pod Minister clears his throat and my father hurries to refill his empty glass.

"Good man. Ha!" the Pod Minister says. "And your wife? Cynthia, you won't have a tipple?" I wonder how drunk the Pod Minister must be not to notice that my mother looks like she's swallowed a balloon.

"A little one on the way, Cain." My mother rubs her belly. I have to turn away. I can't look at her at all now that she's pregnant. Whenever I do, a picture of my parents comes to mind, and it's not a picture I like. "Anyway, this is Quinn's day," my mother says, coming toward me.

"I don't think he knows. Why don't you tell him, Cain. Go on, do the honors," my father says, delighted. He is smiling so hard I can see his back teeth. The ass-kissing is too much. I take another gulp of whiskey.

"What's new?" I ask no one in particular. They're all *so* happy they must have something unreal to tell me, like I'm pregnant, too.

"Well, young man, I'm happy to report that you got through round one of the Leadership Program, and you did so well, Professor Felling is promoting you to the final exam without making you go through the other four stages first," the Pod Minister says. I'm sipping as he's speaking and can't help spitting out what I have in my mouth. What am I going to tell Bea? She was so upset today she couldn't even talk about it.

"My carpet!" my mother yelps, and rushes into the kitchen.

"Well, what do you say, Quinn, my young protégé," the Pod Minister asks, clapping me on the back so hard I stumble forward and spill even more whiskey as my mother waddles back into the room.

"Oh, for goodness sake," she says, and kneels down in front of me to soak up the mess.

As I look into my father's beaming face and my brothers' grins and the Pod Minister's bloodshot eyes, I know they are all waiting for me to throw up my arms and hoot. They'd probably be thrilled if I performed a one-man cancan routine.

"I think there's been a mistake," I manage to say. My mother gasps. My father's smile vanishes.

"Excuse me?" the Pod Minister says, his eyes narrowing.

"I was *okay*. But Bea Whitcraft was better. And she failed. So I can't have passed."

"There has been no mistake," my father says slowly. My brothers peel themselves off the couch and sneak into the hall. Even my mother backs out of the room.

"Scruples! Ha-ha!" the Pod Minister shouts, and slams me on the back again. I catch hold of the mantelpiece to steady myself. "I love a man with scruples!" I look at the Pod Minister and try again.

"Bea deserves this. I think there was a miscalculation."

My father strides across the room and has me by the collar before I can defend myself. "Did you hear what I said? There. Was. No. Error." It isn't easy to breathe with my father holding my neck. I wrangle with him for a moment until I realize he's not looking for a fight—he's looking for my assent, that's all, so I nod and he lets go. "The mistake may have been your friend's," he says.

"We want leaders we can trust," the Pod Minister says, ignoring the ruckus going on between my father and me. "And, well, when we looked at the footage of the debate, we had to conclude that the Whitcraft girl is not necessarily a person to trust." Bea can't be trusted? Have they forgotten that I was in the debate, too? I heard everything she said. I'd tell them that, too, if my father wasn't giving me the stink eye. "Your friend is what we affectionately call a 'tree hugger,'" the Pod Minister says. "Although tree huggers have also been called less affectionate names. Ha!"

"Like RATS," my father says.

"You think Bea's a terrorist because she argued for the

trees?" I say. The idea is ridiculous; Bea is so moralistic, it's like doing the right thing has been programed into her. The Pod Minister and my father exchange knowing looks and I begin to feel nervous. Is it possible Bea has been added to a suspect list?

My mother tiptoes back into the room. She stands rubbing her swollen tummy again. "Would you like another drink, Cain?" She picks up the whiskey bottle and moves toward the Pod Minister.

"I would love another. Sadly my children are expecting me and I'll be whipped if I don't make it home soon." He laughs. "So, I'll wish you all a good night. Especially you," he says, addressing me. "You have a bright future ahead, Quinn." He is smiling and then he is not. He moves closer to me, takes me by the elbow, and hisses, "Tree huggers beware. Ha!" I stand back and stare at him. I don't want to be his enemy, and I don't want Bea to be his enemy. I nod. "And I'll see *you* tomorrow." He points his two index fingers, like guns, at my father.

My parents send him off and I'm alone in the living room, still holding the glass of whiskey. I sip some more, then set the glass on the coffee table, hoping to make it up to my bedroom before my parents get back from the front doors. But when I look up, they're both standing there, and they're both scowling.

"He got fat," I say. It's obviously a joke, but it's not funny and pretty much irrelevant. My father settles himself into an armchair and gestures for me to sit down, too. I collapse onto the couch.

"You don't seem happy," my father says.

My mother balances herself on the arm of my father's chair. "He doesn't seem grateful, either," she says. Why should I be grateful? If anything, I should be furious. I only passed because my father is a director at Breathe. Bea needed this. She deserved it. Yet her failure and my success were both fixed. As usual, I can't be allowed to achieve anything on my own.

My father is scrutinizing me, and when I look directly at him he smiles and dips his head, ever so slightly, as though to say *You're welcome*. "I don't want this. I want to pass because I'm good enough, not because you threatened some examiner." And I wanted to attend the Scholastic Institute with Bea, I think, but I don't say it.

"Oh, grow up, Quinn. I watched the footage. That friend of yours completely thrashed you," my father says. He seems mildly jubilant, as though my inadequacies are cause for celebration.

"So why would the Pod Minister want me to train with the leaders? Why would *you* want me to do that?" I never know what my father wants from me. Sometimes he ignores me completely, so I assume he doesn't care what I do, and at other times he won't get off my case. I think what he really wants is to create a miniature, muffled version of himself.

"Oh, my lovely boy," my mother says, and comes to sit next to me on the couch. I hate the feel of her dry hand against my face. I brush her away. I'm not a child anymore. She can save the stroking for the baby.

My father continues. "You are my son and connections matter. This is life, Quinn. You can't help it that your father knows the Pod Minister, and Bea can't help it that her parents are subs."

"Father!" I shout. I've never heard him use this slur before. I shake my head and jump to my feet.

"Don't be so dramatic, son."

"Sir, I—"

"You may go," he says, and abruptly stands up. So I leave the room, bumping him with my shoulder as I storm out. Lennon and Keane are sitting cross-legged at the foot of the stone staircase. They aren't drunk, but they're not what you'd call sober either.

"Poor Bea," Lennon says.

"I love Bea," Keane adds. This is true. Keane's loved Bea since he was a toddler. And she loves him. "What are you gonna say to her?" he wants to know. I shrug. "She'll cry," he says.

"For certain, she'll cry," Lennon agrees. I imagine Bea as they do: her lips pinched together, her nostrils twitching as she listens, too proud to cry in front of me.

I don't even need to make the Leadership Program; whether or not I succeed in politics or business or anything else doesn't affect anyone, whereas Bea's success could save her whole family. I'm ashamed. I pat the tops of my brothers' heads, warn them to go easy on the whiskey, and head upstairs to my room.

I lie on my bed, turn on my pad, and flick to the tracking menu. Bea's active and I can see that she's at home. I want to call her, tell her everything and tell her I'm sorry. Instead, I lie awake worrying about it.

On cue, a message comes through from her: *You heard from the professor yet?* I lie staring at my pad, wondering how to respond. After several minutes, I tap out the words *No, not yet.* This is the truth: I haven't heard from the professor.

I turn off the pad and toss it onto the floor. Then, still fully clothed, shoes and all, I pull the covers over me, ease into the alcohol, and go to sleep.

7
ALINA

The apartment is silent. The lights are out. And in the living room Silas is on the couch with his head in his hands. My aunt and uncle are in there, too, sitting on either side of him. Something so awful has happened that no one is screaming. No one is shouting. All they can do is sit.

"Silas," I murmur. I'm afraid of upsetting the stillness. My aunt looks up and dashes toward me.

"Where in hell's name have you been?" She hugs me then stands back to check I'm okay. "They found Abel," she whispers. Though I know I've heard her correctly, I can't believe it. My parents have been missing for a year, and there's been no news. I want to ask *where* they found him, as though he might have been hidden under his bed, or in the bathroom taking a shower. But I know that what I'm really asking is how he died because if he were alive, no one would need to whisper.

So I say, "*When* did they find him?"

"This morning," Aunt Harriet says. "It's been all over the news. The poor boy was found between the pod and the recycling station. They say he was cutting the tubing."

"Yeah. With no airtank. He ran half a mile holding his breath," Silas mutters.

"So they scratched him from the system, then found him again just so they could kill him? Why?" I ask. Silas shrugs.

Uncle Gideon stands up. "Silas told us what happened at the biosphere. He must have been flagged."

No one is looking at me now. Do they think it was my fault? It was my decision to bring him along on the mission. And I forced him to throw the second rock. He didn't want to. He didn't even want to throw the first one. Was it worth it? How can working for the Resistance be more important than our lives? So we'll manage to steal a few tree cuttings, smuggle them out, and replant them somewhere—it hardly constitutes saving the planet. When the trees make a comeback, Abel will still be dead. We'll *all* be dead.

I must be shaking because Uncle Gideon and Aunt Harriet are standing on either side of me holding me up. If I hadn't liked Abel so much, he would still be alive. *Don't get involved with each other,* Petra warned us. She warned us again and again. Why didn't I follow the rules?

Silas is watching me. It's possible he guessed how I felt about Abel a long time ago. He won't say anything though; he won't put Abel's death on me. He turns on the screen, turns up the volume, and jumps up from the couch. "You have to leave the pod. Even if you weren't spotted, we can't be sure he didn't betray you—in the end. You have to go to Petra."

My breath quickens. I have no airtank to help me breathe outside the pod and even if I did, I'd never make it through Border Control with the Ministry after me. Silas sees my panic. "Pack a bag, Alina. They'll be coming for you." He marches into his own bedroom. "Now!"

My aunt and uncle look at each other frantically and then, without speaking, spring into action. Uncle Gideon dives into the recesses of a kitchen cupboard and pulls out a large airtank and facemask. "For emergencies," he says. Aunt Harriet is packing a bag with food and water.

Only two days ago I was celebrating with Abel, and now Abel is dead and I'm going on the run. My gut turns and suddenly I am on my hands and knees retching. I can't stop myself. Aunt Harriet rushes to me and holds my hair out of the way.

"You'll be fine," she says, smiling as though she really believes it.

"Alina, get moving!" Silas hollers.

"I'll clean it up," I tell my aunt.

"Just hurry," she says. And then we hear it. The thudding on the apartment door that can only mean one thing: the Ministry has arrived.

"The plants," my uncle whispers. Silas runs to the balcony and throws open the door.

"Come," he says. I take the bag Aunt Harriet has half filled for me and dash out onto the balcony with him. We both stand there for a moment, terrified, desperately looking at the plants and then at the street ten stories below. It's time to dump the plants.

"Over here," comes a crackling voice. Silas and I turn with a start to see Old Watson leaning on the railings of his balcony, gazing at us. I turn to Silas. I don't know that we can trust him, but what choice do we have? Either I jump and fall to my death, or I climb over his balcony and risk betrayal. Old Watson sees us hesitate. "You didn't really believe the story about why I water my plants, did you? Pass them over here," he says. Inside the apartment, Aunt Harriet and Uncle Gideon are trying to stall the stewards who are banging on the door. "Get a move on," Old Watson clucks.

I glance up at the apartment buildings and balconies crowding in on us, but to check for people watching is ridiculous when so many probably are. I throw my small backpack onto his balcony and climb over myself. When I get to his side, I look down at his plants and see he wasn't lying: everything is real—some of them are even flowering.

"Pass the boxes," I tell Silas, and he does, heaving them up and laying them in my open arms as carefully as a person might hand over a baby. As I put the final box safely on Old Watson's balcony, we hear a scream.

"They're in," Silas says. A glance I can't read passes between Old Watson and Silas. Then Silas is gone, the balcony doors beeping as they shut firmly behind him.

Old Watson leads me into his apartment and I gasp. His entire living room is filled with plants. "Magnificent, aren't they," Old Watson says. "You steal from them, I steal from you," he confesses.

"I have to escape," I tell him. "If I stay in the pod, they'll find me."

"Yes," he says. Something crashing in my apartment causes the wall to vibrate. I shudder and consider climbing back across the balcony. If I surrender, they might leave my family alone. Old Watson leads me to the front doors. "Go while they're busy," he says. With a beep we step onto the porch. Old Watson looks through the peephole in the outer door. "It's clear. Now, is there anything you need?"

"Where do I go?" I ask.

"Get to the Border. Find a group of Premiums and cross

with them. They always get through." He's right. My only chance is with a Premium. "Quickly," he whispers. He pushes me into the empty corridor. Muffled noises, like someone is being strangled, filter through my own front doors. "Get out of here, you stupid girl," Old Watson snaps. "Go on! Go!"

I push open the emergency door to the stairwell and scamper down ten flights of stairs, following the routine Silas and I have when we train. I come out in the alleyway between our apartment building and the monstrous construction next door. It is silent and dark. I pause to get my breath and plan a route. I need to run and I can't do that in the open. I know all the alleyways in Zone Three, but I haven't explored the ones in Zones One and Two. I'll have to do my best when I get there.

As I turn the first corner, I come upon a couple panting and pulling at each other. I start for a moment but then relax. It isn't unusual to see this kind of thing; it takes a lot of oxygen to be in love, and if they stay at home they'll get taxed for the excess air. I keep running and the half-naked couple doesn't even notice me.

I think of Abel as I run. I knew he wasn't quite ready for the mission. I wanted him with me because I wanted an excuse to be alone with him. And now he is dead and I will never get the chance to be alone with him ever again. Abel is dead because I liked him.

I can't allow myself time to grieve because up ahead I spot a lone man with long thin hair standing in the shadows. Illegal exercise and sex aren't the only reasons people dwell in alleyways; this is where criminals hide, too. I pause, and when the man in the shadows hears me, he looks up and licks his lips. He drags himself toward me pulling a bad leg behind him. Screaming would be too dangerous. And he seems to know it. He snickers and pulls out a short, sharp blade. I've run almost twenty blocks and hate to turn back, but he'll cut me for sure. So I turn around and run. Behind me he calls out, "I wasn't going to hurt a delicious thing like you. Come back, my tasty."

Natural dawn light from outside starts to fill up the pod. The night has been so long. I haven't slept or stopped. At least I've made it safely to Zone One. I walk up the main street toward the border. The air is burbling with excitement. Packs of giddy travelers check their backpacks one last time.

I have nothing. A few scraps of food, some water, and an airtank. I didn't even bring warm clothes.

I have no idea how I'm going to get across. And even if I do, how will I survive out there?

8
BEA

Mom taps on my bedroom door before popping her head into the room. "Quinn's here, love. Shall I send him in?" I shake my head and follow her into the hall, where Quinn is standing holding not only his own backpack but the bag with the tent in it and both our sleeping bags. His hair has fallen over one of his clay-colored eyes. When he sees me, he smiles.

"Let me carry some of that," I say.

"You can't." He peers at the floor. He's right; I haven't the strength, or a permit for carrying heavy loads. Mom is standing between us smirking.

"I saw the things you bought for my Bea, Quinn. That was very kind of you." She touches him gently on the arm.

"It's nothing," he says, pushing his hair out of his eyes. "Bea, are we going?"

"Stay for breakfast," Mom says.

Quinn shakes his head. "Thanks, Mrs. Whitcraft, but we want to get to the border before the crowds." He always does that, addresses my mom as *Mrs.* Whitcraft even though he's a Premium and within his rights to use her first name. My mom blushes.

"It must be nice to have a father who works for Breathe. All those airtanks," she says. She looks at me, at Quinn, then back at me. I have to get out of this house and away from my mother's suggestive smile. I kiss her on the cheek and move to the front doors just as Dad strolls out of the bedroom toward the kitchen wearing only a pair of baggy orange underpants. When he sees us in the hall he shuffles over, rubbing his hairy belly. He yawns. I'm close enough to be able to smell that he hasn't brushed his teeth.

"Quinn Caffrey," he says, shaking hands with Quinn, who is staring, stunned, at my father. "Every time I see you, you look more like a man." He pats Quinn's cheek. If I'd tried to imagine the most embarrassing situation possible, I don't think I'd have put my dad in a pair of old orange underpants. I love my mom and dad, but this is too much. They are outdoing themselves.

"And a handsome man at that. He's taking Bea out of the pod for a day or two. What a treat," Mom says.

Dad frowns. "An overnight?"

"Oh, goodness, Cooper, I *told* you."

"I'll take care of her, Mr. Whitcraft. I promise," Quinn says.

"You better," Dad says.

We take the tram to Zone One, and when we disembark, Quinn lugs our bags through the station and down onto the packed street. Everyone is loaded up, as we are, with tents and sleeping bags, airtanks hanging from their backpacks. We're hounded every few steps by children selling cookies, old-fashioned compasses, paper maps, and airtanks. "Can you believe how many people buy oxygen from street sellers," Quinn scoffs. "They mess with the gauge, so you can't tell how much oxygen they really have in them. Usually they're empty." He pats the airtanks he's brought from home.

At the border there are five lines: four short ones devoted to Premiums, and one for auxiliaries, which is about ten times longer than the others. "Where are you going? I got you a Premium pass," Quinn says as I edge toward the auxiliary gate.

"Save the pass. I can wait there." I don't want to be even more indebted; I want us to be equals.

"Oh please, there's no need to get all principled—I didn't buy the pass for you; I bought it for me. I want to get out of here *now*," he says, pulling me by the arm toward a Premium line. This is something I love about Quinn: he always knows how to do something nice yet make it seem like really he's being completely selfish, so it never feels like charity.

As we join the line, a girl with long tangled hair rushes up to Quinn and throws her arms around him. She's disheveled and out of breath. I check her earlobes: no tattoo. I glance around to see if a steward has spotted her rushing, but they're all up at the border trying to manage the exodus. I've never met this girl before, though I do recognize her from school, from my advanced biology class last year. Apart from me, she was the only person I knew who had skipped a year. I haven't seen her much since.

"It's you," she tells Quinn, who doesn't seem to know what to do. He stares at me, his arms by his sides, while she squeezes him. I shrug and he mouths the word *Sorry*. Then he gently unties himself from her hold.

"Alina?" he says.

Alina.

"You remember." She glances at me, but I look away. Quinn's latest crush is the last person I want to see. "I need your help," she says.

We step out of line and thread our way through the crowd to a bench. "What's happened?" Quinn asks. He sits down next to her, and I sit on her other side. The smell of breakfast loaf from a food cart opposite drifts over. Alina looks at it and swallows.

"I have to get across," she says, nodding at the border.

"Are you hurt?" Quinn asks. He is frowning, concerned, but secretly he must be delighted; what better way to win this girl's favor than to save her?

"I'm in trouble. I can't explain. If I go through with the auxiliaries, I'll be stopped for certain."

"What have you done?" he asks.

"Would you believe me if I said I've been saving the world?" Quinn shakes his head at the absurdity of it. "Can you help? Will you?"

"Are you a terrorist?" I ask. Quinn glares at me, but we've got a right to know. Alina turns away from Quinn and, taking my hands, draws me toward her. Quinn wasn't wrong about her looks—she's beautiful, even with all the sweat and panic.

"You don't know me. You have no reason to trust me. But if you help me cross the border, you'll never see me again. I promise." Even though there are alarm bells ringing and my gut is telling me to steer clear of her, she is so earnest I don't know how to refuse. Besides, if we help her do this one thing, she'll disappear; it will be Quinn and me alone again, and he won't have any reason to resent me.

9
QUINN

I only have one Premium pass and it would take days to apply for another, so Bea's standing in the auxiliary line after all. Alina is next to me. "We should try to look like a couple," she whispers, holding my hand. This is fine by me.

I know I should be worried about Alina and a bit afraid for myself, too, but even though this is dangerous, it's also the most interesting thing that's happened to me in ages. It isn't every day the girl of your dreams asks you to rescue her.

Alina looks like any other tourist making her way out of the pod. She's even smiling a bit. I probably look more nervous than she does. I push back my shoulders and stand tall as the line narrows.

When we finally step up to the first gate, the official looks at my ear and nods, then down at the pass I hand him. He eyeballs Alina, then waves us reluctantly through the giant, metal gate to the scanning station.

I take out my pad and am about to scan when Alina touches my wrist. "Oh God, I've completely forgotten my pad," she says. Of course. If she's on the run, there's no way she can scan her pad. She'll be pulled aside and God-knows-what.

"Seriously?" I shout, attracting the attention of the stewards nearest us. "Well, there's no way we're going back. No way!" I'm not exactly keeping things low key. I just don't know how else to play it, so I do my best impression of Ferris.

A male steward approaches and stands before us with a hand on his baton. "Is there a problem here?" he asks.

"Yes, there is a problem, actually. My halfwit girlfriend has gone and forgotten her pad!" I glance at Alina, hoping I'm on the right track. She wipes her eyes with the back of her hand and sniffles. "I mean, how hard can it be? Look at the size of her bag and look at mine. I've got everything and all she needed to remember was her ID. Typical." I throw up my arms in frustration and the steward grins. It's at that moment I notice his wedding ring. "We're meant to be getting engaged out there. All planned. And now . . . well, you can say good-bye to any kind of proposal, love." The steward stops smiling and takes me by the elbow.

"There's no need for that, sir," he soothes.

"No need at all," a lady behind us mutters.

"So you'll let us out?"

"I'm sorry, but if your girlfriend has forgotten her pad, she'll have to step out of the line. She can't leave unless we can identify her."

"Do you know who my father is?" I say. I've heard other people use this, but when it comes out of my mouth it doesn't sound real. "If I'm not through this gate within five minutes I'll be calling my father and then the Pod Minister. I'd like you to explain to *him* why you've stopped us."

"The Pod Minister?" the steward says, and takes a step back.

"Exactly! I'll let *you* speak to Cain Knavery and explain why you've stopped his protégé at the border for no good reason!" I'm shouting so loudly that six or seven stewards come forward and surround us. One steward pulls out his baton and waves it in our direction. Alina gives me a look that says *I hope you know what you're doing*. I don't, of course.

My pad vibrates as the stewards huddle together to discuss the situation. It's a message from Bea. With all the commotion I'm causing, I'm not surprised they're able to hear us way over in the auxiliary line. I open the message and it reads *Is she worth it?* Alina is standing by the scanner, her hands hugging her own body. Her hair falls in untidy ripples down her face. I remember the first time I saw her, angry and zealous in the vaccination line. Back then all I wanted to do was kiss her. And now I look at her, blotchy and red-eyed, and I want to help her. She is doing something. And she must believe in it to put up with all this, and me. I look again at Bea's message and I think *Yes! Yes, this girl is definitely worth it!*

A steward steps forward. He has a long mustache covering his top lip and his eyebrows join in the middle, making his face look like it's been driven over by a buggy. "Give me your pad," he says. I quickly flip to the ID display. The steward looks down at the pad then back at me. Down at the pad. Back at me. He scans the pad. A digital voice responds: "*Quinn Bartleby Caffrey—authorized.*" "Your dad a director for Breathe?" he asks.

"Can't you read?" I sound arrogant and impatient, a lot like my father.

"Doesn't say anything about the Pod Minister. What relation did you say you was?" I glare as though I'm really getting tired of their nonsense and grab my pad from him.

"That's it. I'm calling Cain." I bang around on my pad for no more than a couple of seconds when the steward tips his baton against my hand.

"No need for that. I have an idea. We let you and your girl through, you do something for us." *Anything*, I want to say. *I'll do anything.*

"You must be mad. If you think you're going to bribe a Premium's son. A friend of the Ministry—"

"Air," the steward interrupts. His hands are joined so he looks like he's praying. He no longer looks threatening at all, but sad and desperate. "Can you get us tanks?" He is keeping his voice low so the crowd of tourists filing through the other lanes and queuing behind can't hear him. "Not a bribe. A gift." The other stewards are watching intently and their faces are no longer clenched. Each one has his eyebrows raised in expectation.

"My wife and I haven't . . . danced together in years," he says. We stare at each other for a long time. It's quite possible he knows I'm lying.

"I can get you five tanks," I say, looking at each of the stewards in turn.

"Ten tanks to be delivered here within seventy-two hours."

"Eight. And you'll get them in a week." I won't be a pushover.

"Open the gate!" the steward hollers.

And that's it.

Alina and I are through the second steel gate and making our way along a glass tunnel. Other tourists saunter alongside us. We lean against the curved glass to wait for Bea.

"Do you have oxygen?" I ask Alina. Shaking a little, she pulls an airtank from her backpack, then attaches the cylinder to her hip using the belt. Once she pulls the transparent silicone mask over her mouth and nose, she tightens the straps at the back to ensure it is airtight. I take out my own tank and do the same.

When Bea gets through, she runs to us, though she shouldn't, and before I get a chance to speak, she throws herself at me. She presses into me so tightly it pinches. "Don't break my ribs!" I say. I know she was worried. I don't want to dwell on it. "I'll help you with your mask," I say. "We have to get going."

We walk down the sun-drenched glass tunnel—Bea, Alina, and me. We push open the revolving doors at the end. And we step, as one, into the airless planet.

PART II

THE OUTLANDS

10
BEA

Without speaking or even looking at each other, we've somehow agreed to stick with Alina for a while longer; it would seem too strange if she wandered off alone. And we've also decided to get as far away from the pod and day tourists as we can. Most of the other tourists are as silent as we are—focused on breathing, avoiding panic as they move farther and farther from guaranteed air.

We could talk if we wanted to—it's easy to be heard through the holes in our blowoff valves; it's just that we aren't used to having our faces covered. The masks keep us alive, but mine is also keeping my nose warm. I gave Alina my scarf. What else could I do? Watch her shivering and ignore it? Quinn gave her a spare sweater and tried to give her his green gloves, too, but she refused. They finally agreed to one glove each. And so now they look a little like two parts of the same person.

I had hoped that once rigged out in her mask, Alina wouldn't look so pretty, but her round eyes and sharp eyebrows stand out even more. And she was smart enough to fit the straps under her hair so that it falls down over them at the sides. I stupidly pulled mine tight over my black bob, so my head must be the shape of a mushroom.

The only other time I visited The Outlands was for a school trip when I was around seven. We were all being offered a chance to try breathing without a mask, taking turns as the teacher slowly drew it from our faces and cheerfully told us to inhale. It was like drinking fire. The teacher watched as I gasped. She smiled, nodded, kept the facemask away from my nose and mouth, and then, when I began to stagger, she snapped the mask back into place and tightened the straps. "Wasn't that an experience?" was all she said. I always wondered what the purpose of that trip was. Were we being taught how desperately we needed the pod? It was certainly a way to ensure I never tried to defect. So I have to wonder what is happening to Alina to make her flee like this.

Behind us, the sunrise is pink. The light hits the pod in such a way that it could be a beautiful glimmering mountain if it weren't for the four recycling stations steaming next to it. There is nothing else close to the pod. All debris was cleared a long time ago. It's only now that we are at a distance that we come upon the rubble of the world as it was before The Switch. There are rows of tumbledown houses along cracked, warped roads, and everywhere the remains of old vehicles covered in what looks like ivy. Even though it's winter and the frost is probably freezing the roots off everything, the earth is not as barren as I imagined. Besides the ivy, tufts of wild grasses and moss eat away at the ruins. I carefully sidestep anything living, anything growing, though now and again I bend down to brush the greenery with my hand.

What I love most is the dirt. Everything is so clean in the pod. Even the streets in Zone Three are spotless. In the short time we've been walking, my boots are scuffed and brown. The old roads are often impassable. The paths we are using are muddy, worn tracks made by the tourists, spreading out erratically from the pod like veins. I take off my gloves and reach down to dig up a handful of cold, hard, pebbled soil. I rub it between my fingers so that it crumbles, until I'm left with only one small blue stone. I pinch it between my thumb and forefinger. Alina is by my side, between Quinn and me, and she is watching. Her eyes squint so I know she's smiling. But I don't know what her smile means—maybe she is laughing at me. I throw the blue stone back onto the ground and brush my hands against my pants. And I notice Alina's laces are undone. I consider not mentioning it. But I don't. I point down at her feet. She nods and bends to tie her shoelaces. When she stands up again I smile at her, too. I think I might be trying to prove how nice I am, so she'll be on my side. If I'm kind to her, maybe she won't take Quinn away from me.

Within half an hour, we pass The Cenotaph. A crowd has already gathered to weep and read the names of their dead loved ones from a mammoth pentagonal stone. The actual burial places are many miles from the pod to prevent the spread of disease, too far for people to travel to. So the Ministry erected this monument to give the grief-stricken a place to remember. Not that many auxiliaries can afford the air to get here. When my grandmother died, we had to hold a small vigil at home instead. "Are there names of people you know engraved on The Cenotaph?" Quinn asks Alina.

She turns to him and her eyelids flutter closed for a moment. "No," she says. "My parents' names aren't on it."

He opens his mouth to respond, but I pinch him. It isn't his business. Whatever it is. Then he says, "Can you imagine how big that thing would have to be if they made a monument to everyone lost in The Switch?" We all look at The Cenotaph but quickly turn away. The truth is, it's impossible to imagine how far it would have to stretch.

Eventually the hundreds of armed stewards who guard the pod in concentric circles thin out, and after another hour of walking, there is no one ahead of us and only a scattering of ambling day-trippers almost a mile behind—shifting dots in the distance.

We cut through an old school yard, past rotting wooden benches and a capsized basketball hoop. At the edge of the yard, garbage cans lie on their sides, bottles spilling out of them, the plastic ones intact. We reach a wide road, climb a set of stairs, and cross a concrete bridge to the other side. When we get there, Alina stops and stands with her hands on her hips. "This is as far as we go together," she says. I look at Quinn.

"You won't be safe on your own," he says.

"I've enough air to get me to where I'm going." She knocks on her tank with her knuckles and gives us the thumbs-up. "I don't need as much as you. I've already tightened my valve."

"Where exactly are you going?" Quinn wants to know.

"West," she tells him.

"You'll die before you even make it to the city, you know."

"I'm going to a safe place."

"You have to tell us what's going on. Do you know what kind of hassle I'm going to get when my father hears I helped the RATS?"

"We prefer to call ourselves the Resistance," Alina says.

Quinn's neck blushes. "I mean, I know you can't be as bad as they say. It's just that . . . well, my father will ground me for a month. Two months, maybe. But if you explain what this is about, he might be able to help." Alina grimaces. If Quinn is trying to impress her, he's doing a terrible job; she's being tracked by the Ministry, but he's in trouble with his dad—the two don't quite hold the same weight. And the chances of Quinn's father being on her side are slim.

"Quinn—" I begin, but he waves me away.

"Thank you for helping me. But you can't come any farther. It isn't safe." Alina looks at me. Why? Do I seem weak? Surely she's as weak as I am, if she's an auxiliary, too.

"You know, you haven't even asked us our names," Quinn says. "It would be nice to think you want to know our names." He sounds hurt.

"You're Quinn Caffrey. I found that out at the border."

"This is Bea," he says, and places a hand on my shoulder.

"Nice to meet you," she says formally. She shakes our hands and turns to leave. "Thank you again for the clothes. I would have frozen." She stares at the eddying clouds and clusters of derelict buildings on the horizon. The landscape changes quickly—one minute it's a huge expense of wasteland, ground that was once used for mass farming, the next it's tight knots of rubble.

As she starts to walk away, Quinn calls after her. "You don't trust us." He looks at me for support. I shrug. Why should she trust us? I don't trust her. I don't even know her.

Alina stops and turns. "This is a decent place to camp," she says, ignoring Quinn and gesturing to the land surrounding us. "If you go any farther it's sort of depressing and quite dangerous, unless you brought hard hats." She tries a smile. "A little north of here was a forest once. The whole area. Monk Wood." I roll my eyes to show her that she needn't think we're stupid; we know about Monk Wood. Everyone knows. And that was exactly where we planned to camp all along, though we didn't plan on getting to it so quickly. We were going to wind our way through some of the old villages rather than cutting right across the country. The route Alina chose bypassed most traces of the old civilizations.

"Fine," Quinn says, defeated.

"Good luck," I mumble, and then, "Have you any food?" because even though I don't want Alina sticking around, I don't want her to starve. She shakes her head. I reach into my backpack and pull out a box of crackers. When I hand them to her she smiles, and with her empty hand she waves, though she is no more than three paces from us.

Quinn and I watch her hike toward the rows of crumbling houses in the distance. She seems to know exactly where she's going.

The sun has fully risen and is now high in the murky sky. When I look around, I can't see any other people at all—not even moving dots. Quinn and I are completely alone. We sit on an unsteady stone wall and eat a couple of coco protein bars. Eating isn't easy: with one hand we pull the lower half of our masks away from our faces and awkwardly slip pieces of food into our mouths, and with the other hand we make sure our noses stay completely covered.

Quinn has been brooding ever since Alina dissolved into the horizon. For a while I ignore his scowl, hoping he'll come around, but he's probably going to be in a grump our entire trip unless I let him talk about it.

"She must have broken the law," I say. I can't bring myself to use her name.

"Whatever she did, she's in big trouble. I hope we helped her."

"Come on, Quinn, she didn't seem lost. She knows exactly what she's doing. Anyway, what do you want to do? Stalk her?" Quinn continues to stare at the derelict buildings in the distance. Suddenly he stops chewing, lightly slaps himself across the side of the head, and stares at me. I stare back. He puckers his lips and bumps his facemask against mine, making a loud kissing sound with his lips. I feel my face getting warm and fiddle with the zipper on my jacket so he won't notice.

"What is it?" I say, pulling at the hair pinched by the straps of my facemask. It feels constrictive and uncomfortable; I adjust the rubber strap at the back of my head.

"You're right, we have to follow her. If we don't, she's all alone. She could die. There are drifters, and look at that sky—the weather is only going to get worse, and she isn't ready for it. You know what we'll be, if anything happens to her? Killers, that's what."

"How will we be killers? When she needed our help, she asked for it. She doesn't want our help anymore because she's got people out here, Quinn. People way tougher than us, I'm guessing. We aren't her friends. She told us to get lost." As I say it, Quinn bites the insides of his mouth, hurt.

"Don't you want adventure, Bea? Here it is. A real adventure. Not some game we've invented like when we were little kids. Don't you feel alive?"

"I actually feel very alive. But if we try tracking that girl, I might not feel alive for long. This oxygen won't last forever." I rap my fingers against the tank.

"We have plenty of air. We brought enough for two full days. And anyway, she as good as told us that where she's going, there'll be plenty of the stuff. So we'll get a refuel."

"Oh, Quinn." I want to cry. I want to tell him that none of this is fair; we'd planned a trip together, the two of us, and I hoped he'd discover *me* out here, not another girl. But if I refuse I'll only have one choice, and that will be to trudge back to the pod on my own. And then what will he think of me?

"I know you're afraid," he says. This makes me feel a little better. At least he's thinking about my feelings. "We need weapons. Did you bring a weapon?" He jumps down from the wall.

"Why would I bring a weapon?" I ask.

"I have a knife I was planning to use for preparing food and stuff." He pulls out a knife with a long, thick blade and passes it to me. The hilt of the knife is heavy and the blade is sharp. "You keep that," he says, and hands me its sheath. "I have rope, too. Oh, and I have a hammer for the tent pegs."

"Exactly how mad do you think she'll be that we followed her?" I tease.

"The weapons are for the drifters," he says without smiling, and bends down to tighten the laces on his boots. Then he tightens my laces, too. "Ready?" he asks, standing up.

"Drifters?" We've all heard stories about the drifters, old pod prisoners and lunatics who managed to escape and set up rudimentary air systems to keep themselves alive. They lie in wait to terrorize tourists who venture too far from the pod. They live in the gray nooks and crannies of the city. But how can this be true? Even if the drifters managed to escape and found a way to breathe, they'd certainly starve to death. It has to be a rumor—a legend. "I'd be too scared to use this," I admit, and hand back the knife, which Quinn slips through a loop in the band of his pants.

"Wanna get going?" he asks. He starts to pack away lunch, puts on his one green glove, and wipes his forehead with it. "If we wait much longer she'll be too far ahead and we'll never find her." So that's it. I'm going to follow Quinn, who's following Alina, and we are all going to march willingly into the pit of this forgotten city.

11
ALINA

I didn't want to take the old tarmacked roads and be visible from a distance. I would prefer to forge my own route into the city. But it would be hard to find a way through without having to climb dozens of dicey walls and fences. And it's started to rain. Hardly a downpour, but enough to make mud of the fields. I pull the scarf Bea gave me over my head and tie a knot to keep it in place. And so I walk along the deserted, warped road instead of taking a rougher, safer track.

Tourists can walk for miles without being reminded of the carnage out here, and in the pod we all try to forget what The Outlands really look like. The farther from the pod I get, the worse the devastation. There is rubble and garbage everywhere—evidence of the chaos at the end: hundreds of rusted-out cars and buses and vans and shopping carts and blanched tree stumps and collapsed telephone poles. Every now and again I spot something simple and ordinary—like toothbrush. What happened to its owner? The old billboards remain in place but their messages have long since faded away. It is eerily quiet. My own footsteps are the only sounds I can hear. I can no longer make out the hum of the pod's recycling stations. There are no trams rattling along. And there are no people, of course. No one to reclaim all the spoons, trays, sunglasses, kites, wheelbarrows, bowls, and everything else.

There *were* people. Many years ago. There were millions across this country until The Switch, when the population dwindled to half a percent of what it had been, not merely here, but everywhere. Across the whole planet, the bulk of humanity was annihilated within a few years. I shudder to think of all the bodies that must be buried in the yards around me. Because that's what people had to resort to, eventually, when the graveyards started to overflow. Then even the mass graves couldn't take the numbers, so they stopped burying the people. They burned them instead. And when the only ones left were weak and choking, they stopped doing even that; they simply left the bodies to rot wherever they fell.

I recall the video footage from history class of decaying bodies in beds and baths. Bodies on the roads next to abandoned cars or in them. People were still sitting up—bodies large and small, adults and babies, some bodies with the flesh decomposing, some already stripped leaving nothing but an arrangement of bones. The animals had gone long before that, destroyed in droves as soon as people figured out what was happening. Used for food when the farmers quit farming. Even the domestic animals were eaten up. No one entertained the idea that the creatures might have had just as much right to the air as the people. Then again, no one thought the trees of much value either.

In the distance, thunder rumbles, and it starts to rain. As I gaze upward I imagine that a crooked telephone pole is really a branchless, leafless tree. The thought makes me angry. I know why they cut the trees down. I know the problem: the world's population was soaring and people needed to eat. And the solution was to log all remaining forests and use the land for farming. But how could everyone have been so stupid as to imagine that the oceans alone could provide the planet with the oxygen it needed to survive? And they didn't care what they used to grow food. The trees, the soil—nothing was safe. No one predicted the havoc billions of gallons of toxic runoff from agriculture would cause the oceans. No one imagined the oceans could die. And not so quickly. But that's how things usually go. We always think we have time. We didn't. Within years the oxygen level in the atmosphere plummeted to four percent.

This isn't the version we get at school. There we're told it was China's fault—all those factories. It was India's fault—all those babies. It was America's fault—all those shoppers. The rain begins to come down harder. I open my mouth to the sky.

I'm meant to think of myself as one of the lucky ones—a descendent of someone who managed to survive. And how did humanity survive? We have Breathe to thank for that. I look over my shoulder, but the pod is well and truly out of sight. Breathe managed to concoct a solution, working away in their laboratories using scuba-diving airtanks to keep themselves alive. The tanks were filled and handed out to the deserving in society first—the doctors, judges, politicians. The artists didn't stand a chance—what use could they be? And the homeless? The sick? They were the first ones to rot.

But the government ran a lottery, too; half the tanks and pod passports were given to randomly selected citizens under thirty years old. And so my grandparents, who were young and fit, both won places and were given tanks while they waited for the pod to be built.

My grandparents didn't know each other at that time. They met in the pod, when they worked together in one of the recycling stations. They both died when I was small, but they never could believe they'd spent most of their lives under a glass dome. The pod was meant to be a short-term solution while the trees and plankton replenished themselves. But that was just a fairy tale: anyone with half an ounce of sense knew they'd never again live in the outside world or taste organic air. The planet needs a lot more time to heal itself. More years than we can imagine. Even now, so many years after The Switch, the oxygen level in the atmosphere is only up to six percent.

The Ministry works hard to ensure that its citizens hold out no hope of ever living beyond the pod, but maybe it was worse for my grandparents because they knew what they were missing. And they'd witnessed The Switch firsthand. They never got over it.

All four of my grandparents have their names engraved on The Cenotaph, but there was no point in telling Bea and Quinn that or stopping to look. I have no interest in seeing lists of the dead.

I pass dilapidated buildings, most of which are old houses, crumbling now and enveloped in moss. Many of them are piles of rubble. The silence is beautiful.

I notice a stack of bones on the pavement. A whole skeleton perfectly decayed—white and dry—pulled together into a neat pile, the skull balancing on top. Who did this? And when? Could these bones belong to Abel? No sooner do I think this than I realize it's a ludicrous idea. How would he have made it all the way out here? Plus he's been dead no longer than a couple of days. There's no way he could be all bones yet. Is there? Which stage of decay is he in? Is he oozing and bloated? Is he filling with maggots?

I try to picture Abel as I last saw him: waving good-bye from the entrance to my building; giving me a theatrical wink when I tightened the straps on my backpack containing the tree clippings; congratulating me. He had no idea he was as good as dead.

And *I* might be dead if I'd stayed in the pod. If I'd been held at the border. If Quinn and Bea hadn't saved me. Quinn looked so hurt when I left them. He'll probably head back home and tell his father all about it. I'm sure he wants to be a good guy, but at the end of the day he's Premium, and Premiums are not to be trusted. They have too much to lose. And I couldn't bring Bea along; people in love are the most dangerous of all, the most likely to do something rash. *I* proved that. I wanted to love Abel. Now that he's dead I almost feel that I did love him even though nothing happened between us. Since when does someone being dead make you feel more affection for him?

I'm doing it again, thinking about Abel when I should be focused. I could be ambushed at any time if I don't watch out. The place appears to be deserted, but that doesn't mean it is. There could be drifters anywhere. And Breathe could be out here, too.

Suddenly there is a rumble, like an old wheel lumbering toward me. I spin around and drop to the ground. I see nothing suspicious. The road is clear. Then the rumble sounds again and I see it's coming from a lamppost that has fallen against a building. The wind is rolling the lamppost back and forth on a window ledge, creating the deep echo.

The last time I was out of the pod Silas was with me. He had a gun, and I had a knife. No one came near us. We didn't see one drifter. Why couldn't I have remembered to bring a weapon? I need to protect myself. But with what? I scan the street. There's nothing I could use except rocks and broken bricks. But if someone gets too close to me, rocks will be useless. I need something to swing.

Though most of the street is lined with piles of rubble, some of the houses *are* still standing. And if I'm lucky, there will be kitchens in these houses, and knives in the kitchens, whole drawers filled with blades and skewers. And I'm cold, despite the one green glove and sweater Quinn gave me. The rain has turned to sleet now and the scarf around my head is completely sodden. I've nothing waterproof with me at all.

The nearest houses have had their doors kicked in and windows broken, which means they've probably been pillaged already. I pass a gas station with several cars rusting in the lot. One car even has the gas pump sticking out of its tank. On the other side of the road is a small hospital.

I could definitely try in there. But I'm scared of what I'd find—how many stacks of old bones, how many beds of bodies. Up ahead are more houses, big ones with heavy wooden doors, and not all of them look like they've been ransacked. Apart from the moss covering them, they could very well be inhabited. That's not possible though; I banish the thought because it's actually scarier than imagining the houses empty.

My teeth are chattering. I decide to take shelter in one of the grander-looking houses.

I climb a low stone wall and make my way through a front garden, trying not to slip on the slick, mossy stones.

I wish I hadn't left Quinn and Bea. It would be better to be with people. Any people, so long as they are alive. I am not afraid of ghosts, usually. But something about The Outlands makes hauntings seem almost plausible.

I push on the heavy, peeling door and it opens with a sour creak.

12
QUINN

"What is she up to?" I ask, taking Bea by the arm as we watch Alina, who is several hundred feet in front of us, mounting a wall and making her way toward a pretty dodgy-looking house. "We're going in after her." Bea shakes her head and pulls up her hood.

"I would, but . . . no, I don't think so." Sometimes I want to shake her, tell her to stand up straighter and fight back, but I know that wouldn't be fair. What right do I have to tell her to get her act together? She'd think I was being an insensitive moron, a Premium who didn't understand, and she'd be right.

"What do you suggest we do?" I ask.

"Maybe she's meeting someone. For all we know, that's the Resistance hideout. And if it is, she'll be safe and *we'll* be in danger."

"If she's marching in to the safety of her own people, why's she so jumpy?"

"Aren't terrorists usually edgy, Quinn?"

"It doesn't look safe. She may need help."

"Follow her then. Go and save the day, why don't you. I'm sure she'll appreciate the fact that we've been creeping after her."

"What's eating you?" We don't have time for this.

"Nothing. Nothing. I'm. Absolutely. Fine," she says, just like that, as though each word is followed by a period. Why do girls do that?

"I'm sorry," I say.

"Really? What are you sorry for?"

"I don't know."

"Well then don't say sorry," she snaps. We don't have time to argue; Alina is already inside the house and we're outside getting drenched.

"You know, I thought you had more integrity," I say.

"Integrity? What are you talking about? I haven't done anything wrong. Tell me what I did wrong?"

"You won't help Alina."

"We're following her, aren't we, even though I'm pretty sure she doesn't want us to. What more do you want? If we hear something, we'll go in, otherwise. . ." She trails off and crosses her arms in front of her chest to show me she isn't moving, that she's resolute, that she'd rather stand out in this clawing sleet than go into that house. If I rush in to protect Alina, will Bea come with me? I can't exactly leave her out on the road. I pull at the strings of my hood and sigh. Bea isn't looking at me and scowling anymore; she's staring at the road ahead like she is mesmerized by it.

"Quinn," she whispers.

"What?"

"Look." She clutches my sleeve with one hand and with the other slowly extends her arm to point at something in the distance. Her eyes are wide and her grip tightens. I spin around, ready to throw a punch if I have to, but I can't see anything threatening at all.

"What is it?"

"Look up," she says, and I do, right into the cloudburst. "No. At the house. The window." A thin figure is standing at the upstairs window of the house Alina went into.

We are being watched.

"Now what?" Bea is still clinging to me with one hand, her other hand on her facemask as her breathing quickens.

When I thought about protecting Alina from dangers in that house, I have to admit, I didn't really think there would be anything particularly menacing to protect her from. I just thought it would be a brilliant opportunity to seem brave without really having to do very much. So now what? I poke the ground with the toe of my boot.

"Quinn," Bea presses. I could wrestle a man to the ground if I had to, but what if the house is full of drifters? What if the house is full of dead tourists and empty airtanks?

"Let me think," I say.

"We're going in," Bea announces all of a sudden, pulling the knife from the loop in my pants and unsheathing it. "The hammer," she reminds me. I throw my backpack to the ground and rummage around until I find it. The hammer is smaller than I'd like it to be. "We need a plan," she says.

I stare up at the window as the figure slowly draws the curtains and disappears. "I suppose we should try not to get killed," I suggest.

13
ALINA

Each strip of yellow paisley wallpaper in the hallway is unfurling. The beige carpeted floor is stained and moldy in most places. To the right, a large set of open double doors leads to a grand sitting room, and at the end of the hall is a kitchen. I start by taking off my soaked outer layers and leaving them in a pile by the front door. The house is cold, but at least the wind and rain can't get to me in here. Even so, I won't stick around for long. Just in case. I'll look for something to wear, find a weapon, and leave. I need to get into the city before nightfall. I don't want to be out walking the roads when it's dark.

The sitting room is furnished with dust and patches of green damp. But this was once a fine house: a red marble fireplace faces the double doors; a grand piano nestles in the corner; at the far end of the room hangs a huge, cracked entertainment screen.

I leave the sitting room and move down to the kitchen, which has been ransacked. The back windows are smashed and the garden strewn with rotten furniture—chairs and a table, an ornate headboard, a broken high chair lying on its side. During The Switch people went crazy; with no hope they took to destroying things, anything they could find. I'm surprised the piano is in one piece.

The floor of the kitchen is a mess of broken dishes and glasses. I sift through the debris with my feet in search of a knife. The one I find is completely rusted and sticky with grime, but the blade is long, about twelve inches, and still quite sharp. I keep it in my hand as I walk back along the hallway and up the creaking stairs to the bedrooms. When I get to the landing I pause. Do I hear something? The house is so still, any noise at all startles me. "The dead can't hurt me," I say aloud.

The carpets upstairs are moldy, too, and even mossy in places. I continue along the landing, avoiding the trickles of rain coming through the ceiling, and push open the door to a small pink bedroom, the walls plastered with pictures of unicorns and fairies. I move to the door opposite, which must have been the parents' room. The roof in here is undamaged and so is most of the furniture. I place the knife on a large dresser and open one of the drawers. There are piles of clothes in the drawer—thick sweaters and dry socks. Quickly I choose a few items, strip down to my underwear, which is damp but bearable, and change into the clothes I've found.

I go to the wardrobe because I still need a waterproof jacket. The wardrobe is heavy with clothes—all kinds of sparkling dresses and sharp suits and shelves of pointy shoes and belts and hats. The double bed is unmade, as though the couple who shared the room jumped up and rushed off to work, and for a moment I wonder when they'll be home again, and if they'll be upset when they catch me pillaging. This is senseless: even if they survived The Switch, they'd be old and withered by now. I can't find a waterproof jacket, so I grab a black cap and heavy duffel coat instead. Then I pick up the knife from the dresser and make my way back to the hallway, passing by the bathroom, which, even through the facemask, I can smell is disgusting, like the toilet was used a hundred times and never flushed. I have everything I need, and I should leave, but curiosity makes me check the last door in the hallway, which is slightly ajar.

This room is dark because the curtains are drawn and a draft blows the door shut as I step inside.

I wait for my eyes to adjust, holding the knife out in front of me just in case. There is a low gurgling noise in the room, like water trickling through a pipe. The roof must be leaking in here, too. I see a mound of clothes in the corner of the room and not much else except a few boxes and piles of dishes here and there. I'm about to leave when, slowly, the pile of clothes begins to move toward the door, toward me. I gasp. It's an old drifter with long, matted hair. She can't move too quickly because she is attached to something—a large, cumbersome box, a solar respirator, which she is dragging behind her.

"If you come any nearer I'll use this," I say, wielding the knife. I turn to flee and stumble in the gloom.

"No need to be afraid of lil' ol' me, treasure," she rasps. "Let me touch your face. Let me get near to you now." When I turn around she is still sliding toward me, gurgling and huffing.

I can smell her—a sweet dirt, like candied urine. How many years has she been in this house? It's possible she's a hundred years old. She looks like she must be. She looks like she is already decaying and she isn't even dead yet. I feel my stomach start to heave.

"Get away from me!" I yell, holding out the blade and backing myself into the corner. The woman stops and in a moment of surprising vigor, throws off the layers of blankets. She is wearing a light nightdress thin enough to reveal her scraggy, withered frame.

I don't want her to touch me. I flatten myself against the wall hoping it will swallow me up.

"Ain't no need to be scared," she croaks, shuffling across the moldy carpet. "Maude Blue wants to take a gander, that's all."

"Who's Maude?" I manage.

"Who's Maude? Ain't I got no reputation?" She coughs, brings up something, and spits it onto the carpet. My stomach turns again.

"Naughty Maude Blue," she shrieks. Maybe she managed to escape from the pod's Mental Sanitation Unit and is foraging in deserted kitchens to keep herself alive.

"Let me out. I won't tell anyone I saw you," I say.

"I know you won't," she chortles. I have never seen a breathing apparatus like the one she's attached to, though I've heard of them. It looks like a small refrigerator.

"I'm leaving," I say, groping for the door handle. All I feel is damp wallpaper.

"Don't leave me," she whines. When she is close enough that I can see the grime in her few remaining teeth, she strokes my arm. I scream and swing my knife. "She's a wild one, all right," she wheezes, and laughs again before lunging at me. With one hand she tries to rip the mask from my face and with the other begins unbuckling my tank from the belt. I kick and push her away.

"Think you'll hurt Maude Blue and get away with it?" she shrieks, and charges at me again. I duck as her hands reach for my throat and run to the other side of the room. This is stupid. Now I'm even farther from the door. "I'm gettin' outta this house. Gimme your portable air," she crows.

"Get away, you witch! Get away!" I scream.

"Get away," she mimics. "Get away." She laughs. I swing again as she comes toward me, but this time, as she shoves me the knife slips from my fingers, and she snatches it up from the carpet. She slices the air with the blade, so I protect my head with my hands, but as I do the rusty knife slices right down my arm. I'm too shocked to feel any pain and simply hold the gash with my hand and watch as blood seeps between my fingers. As it drips onto the carpet, Maude Blue bends down and dips her finger in it.

"How fragile we are," she says. She looks up with her narrow eyes. She holds the knife in front of my face.

I have to get out of this room, even if it means throwing myself from the window, but Maude Blue seems to have other ideas. She holds the knife to my throat and removes my airtank. I close my eyes as she unfastens my facemask. "I'm sorry, treasure," she whispers, running a bony, dry finger from my forehead down to my chin. I try to breathe, but unlike the Resistance members who live at The Grove, I'm not ready to cope with such limited oxygen. In an instant, I feel nauseous.

Maude pulls off her own breathing apparatus and slips mine over her mouth and nose. She drops the knife, but I don't think I can even stand up much longer. I lean against the wall and slide down onto the dank carpet.

"It'll expire in a day or two," I croak. Maude Blue looks at my tank and strokes it. She crawls over to me and attaches her old mask to my face. I should be glad of this, but the smell is so foul I don't know if I can bear it. I'm probably losing so much blood I'll die anyway.

I wonder how it happened to Abel. I wonder whether he thought of me at the end, whether he blamed me. He had every right to.

Then I hear a noise out on the landing. Does Maude have backup, a smelly old lover who has been out prowling and is now back to finish me off? She jumps up and grabs the knife again, so I know she's not expecting anyone. My next thought is Breathe; they must have followed me. Either way I'm doomed. But then Bea bursts into the room swinging a knife. Quinn too, and he's also brandishing something. It appears to be a small mallet that he is whirling above his head. He is so serious, so tall and strong, and the weapon is so inadequate, that even in my condition, I have an urge to giggle.

"Get away from her," Quinn hollers.

"She has a knife," I warn them.

"We have a knife, too. And there are two of us," Bea says. "Three," she adds, looking at me.

Maude frantically waves the knife at Bea and Quinn. "Come get me, kids!" she screeches.

"You grab her arm!" Bea tells Quinn.

It doesn't take much for the three of us to grab Maude, take the knife from her, and retrieve my tank. Maude hurriedly reclaims her own stinking mask and slinks into a corner of the room, muttering to herself.

Quinn stuffs the hammer into a pocket of his backpack and Bea hands her knife to him before rushing over to examine my arm. "Did you follow me?" I ask, and it comes out more accusingly than I want it to.

"We'll need to clean that and wrap it," she says. She stands and opens the curtains to let the light in, then digs through her backpack and pulls out an antiseptic spray and bandage. Quinn moves to guard Maude.

"You came prepared," I say as Bea pushes back my sleeve and starts to clean and dress my injury.

"We've been planning this trip for a few days. We weren't on the run." I don't know whether she's admonishing me or being kind.

"What do you want to do with *her*?" Quinn asks, pointing at Maude. I don't have any idea what to do with her; I haven't been trained for this, but common sense tells me we should just leave her here.

"Take me wiv ya," Maude whines. "I'll die if you leave us

here. Why do you think I wanted that airtank? I'm too old to be hauling this thing about." She gives the respirator a weak kick. "How am I meant to scavenge for berries or search in old houses for cans of tasties when I can't even get anywhere anymore? Don't leave me 'ere. I'm too old for this life."

"We can't trust her," I say. "We have to leave her here." Bea flinches but continues to bind the bandage.

"You're gonna let me waste away?" Maude says. Quinn rubs his temples and tries to attract Bea's attention by nudging her with his foot. She doesn't look up.

Bea uses a safety pin to fix my bandage in place, stands up, and moves to the window. "She's just an old lady," she says. Her voice is calm but lined with indignation. "We can't abandon her to die slowly of starvation."

I look at Maude, who stares back at me. Even if she hadn't attacked me, I couldn't help her escape this place. I need to move quickly and she'd slow me down. They all would. She has to stay here where we found her, but negotiating with Bea and Quinn won't be easy; I need them to believe I'm merciless and that leaving Maude would be a gift. So I say, "It would be mean just to let her starve. Maybe . . . maybe it would be kinder to kill her."

14
BEA

They're talking about murder as though they're talking about the weather. Quinn can't possibly agree with what Alina's saying; he's trying to be ruthless because he doesn't want her to think he's weak. But killing someone? She's an old woman.

They've spent the last ten minutes trying to decide what to do. Should they leave her here to die alone, take away her respirator and let her suffocate, or put her out of her misery by stabbing her? Stabbing her! Why doesn't Quinn just use his mallet to bludgeon her to death? I stand by the window watching them. They're doing an excellent job of pretending that they're perfectly resolved to end this old woman's life. Finally Quinn says, "What do you think, Bea?"

"You know what I think," I say, which he does. And this is the reason he hasn't been able to look at me.

"What?" Alina asks Quinn, as though I need an interpreter, as though she can't speak to me directly.

"Bea thinks we should help her," he says. Alina laughs, and I hate the sound of it because it means it's Alina and Quinn now, not Quinn and Bea.

"Why are you in The Outlands anyway?" I say, looking at Maude.

"Don't talk to her," Quinn says.

"She's helpless, Quinn, look at the state of her." Maude is muttering uncontrollably. "What are you doing so far from the pod?" I ask again.

"She'll probably kill the next person who comes along. We should make sure that doesn't happen," Alina says.

"Please stop talking like that," I beg, and the old woman squawks. "It's murder," I whisper. I don't know why I'm not screaming, urging them not to do this. And if they decide to go ahead anyway, then what will I do?

"Back in the pod it may have been murder. Different laws apply here. My main concern is protecting the Resistance," Alina says.

"I don't care about the law. I care about what's right," I say.

"And how can you know what's right? How can any of us know that what they taught us is true? Everything's a lie. You don't even know the half of it."

"It has nothing to do with what I've been taught. It has to do with how I *feel*," I say. Alina stares at me.

"How you gonna argue with that now, huh?" Maude mumbles.

"Shut up!" Alina shouts. Quinn watches her closely, hoping, I know, that she's changing her mind. Why doesn't he say how he feels? Is he really prepared to let her stop him from saving a person's life?

"Maybe we *should* talk to her," he says at last.

Alina is rubbing her chin. When she looks at Quinn she stops, and they gaze at each other: Alina staring into Quinn's eyes, Quinn looking into hers. And me, off to the side.

"Okay, Maude Blue . . ." Alina advances on the old woman, who has curled herself tight into the corner of the room, where she is scratching her groin. "Tell us why you tried to hurt me. This better be good, for your sake." Maude pulls her matted hair into her mouth and begins to chew. "Maude Blue, I'm talking to you!" Alina shouts, and I think she's about to kick her, but she stomps on a cracked plate on the floor next to her instead.

Maude raises her head. "I chose a house with large bay windows. I chose a room that gets the sun. First time I closed the curtains was when I saw yous coming along." I don't understand. She pats the respirator.

"It's solar powered," Alina says, "I know that. So why steal *my* air? As long as you stay in the light, you'll have enough in that thing to keep you going forever."

"I thought you wanted to kill me, you little brat." Maude coughs into her hand, then wipes it on a dirty blanket.

"I still might."

"The Ministry gives you a choice: Mental Sanitation Unit or The Outlands. Well, we all chose The Outlands thinking it'd be a lot better than some loony ward, until they handed us these things." She taps the respirator again. "Solar powered and portable, all right, which is jolly when you're a young'un, but look at me. I'm too worn out to be lugging that thing around looking for grub. So even if the air keeps tick-tick-ticking along, I'd not have lasted more than another week if yous lot hadn't come in 'ere."

"Why did you get expelled?" Quinn asks. He squats down in front of Maude so he's eye level with her. There's a softness to his voice at last.

"We know too much and that's dangerous to 'em. We all gets expelled eventually, but they don't tell you that when you sign up. Unless you're a bigwig, you don't never escape the cut. They thinks it's a gift, letting us live. A gift for all the service we've given 'em."

"What do you mean, 'they'?" Quinn asks.

"You know exactly who I mean. And by the look of your

sweet purple lobe, you're one of 'em, too." When I look closer at Maude, I see that she has a circular tattoo on her earlobe.

"You were a Premium?" I ask. I thought drifters were lunatics and criminals. Surely Premiums could never be degraded like this.

"The drifters are all ex-Breathe," Alina says impatiently, as though I should know this already.

The solar respirator clanks and Maude elbows it. "Tha's right. But we was dubbed the Hope Hitmen back in the old days. If we found anything living, we sprayed it and whoosh—gone—jus' like that. Trees means hope. So they've always wanted rid of 'em."

Alina doesn't look surprised, and I try not to seem too shocked either, but I am. Breathe destroy trees? "The Switch was an accident and now the trees won't grow back because there's so much lightning," I say, fearing I'll be contradicted.

Maude sniffs. "Yeah, The Switch were an accident. But everything else is a load of old poppycock. Lightnin'? Pah! I bet they're still pretending they're working on replanting the earth and cleaning up the seas."

"I know all this already," Alina says. "You're useless to me."

"But if there's no clean-up, we'll never get out of the pod," I say.

Alina moves toward the window and peers out at the drizzle. "I have to go," she says.

"I should come along with yous," Maude suggests, ignoring me completely and looking sideways at Alina. "I know the whole area, dun' I? There's about a gazillion drifters and I know where they're at and . . . and . . ." She runs out of ideas.

"*And* you tried to kill me, you witch." Alina rolls up her sleeves like she's preparing to fight. I stand between her and Maude.

"Why wouldn't they replant the earth? They're growing trees in the biosphere," I whisper.

"Tokens!" Maude barks, pointing a twisted finger at me.

Alina sighs. "They pretend they're the only ones who can grow anything. That the earth is so scary, even the trees would rather be in the pod."

"Bring me along. I ain't useless," Maude whines.

"And they kill the trees on purpose?" I keep my voice even, but inside I'm coming apart, and I realize suddenly that there was never any way I was going to make it into the Leadership Program, not after what I said in the debates about the trees and how much they matter.

"They've capitalized on a very ugly reality," Alina says.

Quinn puts up a hand in protest. "Okay, but Breathe didn't cause *this*." He tugs on his facemask. Then he gives me a pleading look like there's something I could do that would stop what they're saying from being true.

"They're after you because you did something," I say to Alina.

"I need to keep moving," she replies. "Stay here, if you like. I'm off." She moves toward the door.

Quinn's face is pale. He jumps in front of the door, barring Alina's way out. "What did you do?" he asks.

"I stole cuttings from the biosphere. That's what I did. And they'll do anything to stop the Resistance from replanting the earth. That's why I have to get out of here." She pushes Quinn easily aside but doesn't leave.

"They don't want the world to get better because then we'd be free," I say.

Alina nods sadly, like she's full of pity for my lost innocence. "People are dying. People who try to grow things are being killed. If I'd stayed—" She pauses. "It's a long story." She reaches for the doorknob.

"Maude will die if we leave her," I say. "We need to get her somewhere safe, at least. Maybe find other drifters who can feed her." Alina turns around, looks at the old woman and then at me. Her eyes have lost some of their fury.

"Leave me 'ere and I'll holler up a hurricane as soon as the first Breathe convoy rolls by," Maude says. No one responds. It isn't a serious threat.

"She'll attack us on the road. It's too dangerous."

"Not if we're with you," Quinn suggests. "We want to

help." I have little interest in helping Alina, but how can I go back to the pod when there's so much I don't know? I need to know everything. About the pod. About the Ministry. And about what the alternatives are to it all.

"We're coming," I tell Alina. "If you say no, we'll simply follow you." I keep my chin up, trying to look tougher than I feel. "And we're bringing Maude Blue."

15
QUINN

We've been walking for more than two hours, and I think I've spent one hour looking at Alina's ass and another hour trying *not* to look at it. I have to be careful though, when Alina glances around, not to let her see me staring. She's the kind of girl who'd be likely to sock me if she caught me.

Old Maude Blue with her stench and knotty hair is gasping in her mask, but Alina won't slow down, and Maude has to keep up with her because the airtank she's now wearing, my spare, is tied to Alina's wrist. I was pretty impressed when Bea came up with the idea: there's no way the old woman's going to bolt and then turn up and attack us later when her air supply is attached to Alina. Compared to the soggy air she's been breathing, the stuff in my airtank probably feels golden, but even so, she's old and not used to walking. I feel sorry for her, in a way.

But I feel more sorry for Bea because she's not used to a lot of exercise either. I am because my father can afford it. "All right?" I ask, tapping her on the shoulder. She steps over a prostrate parking meter and nods. The rain has eased, but Bea still has the hood of her rain jacket up to protect her face from the scorching wind.

Bea doesn't seem to notice me and turns toward Alina. "We're basically prisoners?" she asks. I should, if I want to get anywhere with her, give Alina a chance to answer. I don't.

"No way," I say, even though I know firsthand about the corruption in the pod. There's no guessing how far the Ministry would go to retain power. Yet I find myself defending them. "If my father knew, he'd do something to stop it. Maybe we should be going back to the pod to tell him. He knows the Pod Minister. You should be taking this to the top instead of running away." Maude chuckles and Alina sniffs. Bea shrugs. They don't buy it. And neither do I. "Why would they want to breathe in chemically manufactured air when they could breathe in the real stuff?" I try desperately.

"Breathe would be ruined. Everyone would leave and rebuild their lives. What would the directors and politicians do with themselves?" Alina says. "Their way of life depends on you being unable to survive without them. And to make sure you can't ever leave, they pump the pod with more oxygen than is needed. "

"Well, that's obviously not true. They charge for extra oxygen consumption. Oxygen is expensive," I say.

"That's right. It is. But they give us enough for free to get us hooked. Before The Switch, the earth's air was twenty-one percent oxygen. In the pod they give us almost thirty percent. Why? So that when we come outside and have to suck in only six percent, we won't be able to cope. But we *can* cope. We would cope if they only taught us how."

"What about the other countries?" Bea asks. "Every country can't be corrupt."

"Coastline Division," Maude wheezes. "I had a pal who was a member of that unit for a couple of years. Yes. Yes. Nice little number, that was." She pauses, puts her hands on her knees, coughs, and continues. "They don't want no one coming and they don't want no one going. They caught a few tourists in a makeshift boat once. Trying to make their way to France, they was." She picks her nose with one of her long black fingernails.

"They say Russia is managing to subsist on thin air," Alina says. "They've trained many of their people to exist on lower levels so they can be free. The pods in Russia are almost empty."

"No they ain't. They have pods. *Everyone* has pods.

Pods, pods everywhere. Breathe sold the oxygen formula to the whole world," Maude snarls. For a moment Alina looks unsure but quickly restores her composure.

"The point is, it's possible. Do you know why we keep having to be vaccinated? It has nothing to do with diseases. They're lowering our levels of red blood cells, so we'll need more oxygen. Everyone, even the poorest auxiliaries, will feel the need to buy more air. We have a nurse on the inside who injects people with a saline solution instead. I make sure I see her and no one else."

"So that's why you were so mad when Riley and Ferris pushed in," I say.

"The nurse's shift ended at one."

"It's beyond belief. I mean, I do believe *you* . . . I can't believe *it*," I say.

"They'll have absolute control until the trees take it back. With a little help from the Resistance. Here's hoping we survive long enough to make a difference." Alina looks straight at me when she says this. I don't know what else I have to do to prove to her I'm not like all the other Premiums she's ever met. "And talking about survival, take the batteries out of your pads or they'll use them to track you," Alina says.

Bea nods and pulls her pad from her backpack. She takes out the battery and hands it to Alina. I do the same thing.

"You sure you're all right?" I ask Bea. She nods. "Are you hungry? I've got snacks." She shakes her head. I glance down at my watch. Almost four o'clock. It'll be dark soon.

"We'll need to find a safe place to camp for the night," I mutter, looking at Maude's ass now because she's stepped behind Alina. I could look at Bea's instead, but that would be weird.

"What?" Alina turns but keeps walking. Her bandage is coming loose and there's blood seeping through it. Her cheeks are red from the cold.

"It's getting dark. We should find a place to sleep. And maybe Bea could fix up your arm again. Looks sore."

"*I'm* walking through the night. You do whatever you want," she says, marching on so quickly she almost rips Maude's mask off, and the old woman has to scurry after her. Bea has slowed and is next to me now.

"You all right?" I try one more time.

"I'm *fine*," she grumbles. I don't blame her for being fed up. I mean, our trip hasn't exactly turned out as planned. She whispers something so Alina won't hear. But I can't hear her either and move my ear next to the holes in the blowoff valve of her mask. "We're in deep," she whispers. Alina spins around.

"I didn't ask you to come," she says, "and I'll actually have a lot of explaining to do if you're with me. I really don't want to get you into something you aren't ready for. Go home. I don't want another death on my conscience."

"*Another* death?" we all respond in unison.

"Who's dead?" Bea asks.

"You should go back," she repeats. I'm starting to wonder whether we *should*. I took a fancy to a girl, so I helped her escape the pod. After that I saved her from a crazy drifter. Now I'm following her to God-knows-where to see God-knows-who, and all she can do is give me the evil eye and tell me to get lost when really she should be applauding my audacity. I've managed to make Bea hate me, and if Alina kind of despises me, despite my best efforts to impress her, why on earth am I using up my oxygen and vacation time to trek into the city with her? I think about saying this, but I don't because the truth is, I like her.

"We can't go back while you have *her* tied to you," I say, pointing at Maude, who grimaces. "You said yourself she'd attack you."

"Oh, don't you fret about me. I'll be as good as gold," Maude cackles. I'm about to tell Alina that we won't leave her unprotected when Bea speaks up.

"It's got nothing to do with protecting anyone, Quinn. I'm not going back to the pod to spend the rest of my life being an underling. Maybe if we go with Alina we can help change things. Or at least learn the truth." She glares at me.

"I still think we should take a rest," I say. "What harm would a few minutes do?"

"Not 'ere," Maude says sharply, scurrying forward and signaling with her thumb to a building on our right with broken stained-glass windows and a tall, crooked spire. Up in the bell tower, I make out the shape of a person. A man whose face is covered in hair. He's waving. "That there's Larry," she says. "He ain't dangerous but he's got scabies or somethin' like that in his skin. Contagious for sure." The man waves and waves. Maude doesn't look up. We keep moving.

After another mile or so, Bea begins to slow down. "We're resting," I announce. This isn't a request. I stop walking and grab Bea's arm to make her stop, too.

"Five minutes. Then we move on," Alina says.

"Yeah, five or ten minutes should be good," I say. Alina frowns at me. I look away.

Mountains of rubble are everywhere now, and the buildings still standing on either side of the road are twice the height of those we passed before we found Maude. If any of these buildings spontaneously crumble, we'll all be dead for sure, buried beneath tons of concrete blocks and steel rods. Alina takes out an old-fashioned compass and starts to turn it this way and that. "Where are we?" Bea asks.

"Blackhorse Road," Alina says.

"And where exactly are we going?"

"The Grove. It's an old stadium."

"A soccer stadium from before? Where is it?" I ask. I take out my pad again, to show them pictures of our school soccer team, when I remember there's no battery in the thing. "By some fluke, my team won the league last year."

"How wonderful for you," Alina says.

Bea and Maude are sitting on a red plastic bench beneath a transparent structure. It looks like a miniature tram stop although there is no evidence of tracks on the road or tram lines overhead. Next to it is a tall sign with faded numbers printed on it: 123, 230, 158, N73. Maude sees me examining the sign. "Bus stop," she wheezes. "*Brum-brum*. Like a big buggy." Bea reaches into her backpack and pulls out her water flask, which she holds to Maude's lips while the old woman keeps the facemask in place over her nose. I'm not thirsty, but I've been bursting to pee for over an hour. I've only managed to keep my mind off it by, well, looking at things I shouldn't.

"I'm off to take care of some business," I say.

"What kind of business?" Alina asks.

"*Private* business," I say slowly, so she gets the point and I don't have to say *I'm going to pull my trooper out and take a piss.*

"Oh. I actually need to go, too," Alina says.

Bea is still watering Maude but looks at me, then back at Alina, and she must be thinking what I'm thinking: *Is Alina planning on coming with me*? I like her, I do, but I don't think I'd manage to go at all with her watching me, even with her just listening. I'm one of those people who need complete peace to go. Like in school, I can't bear it when I'm standing there, about to pee, and another guy comes in and stands next to me. Especially when he starts talking. Who wants to have a conversation when you're trying to avoid peeing on yourself?

"Maybe I'll go first and you afterwards?" I say.

"Oh, Quinn," Bea sighs.

"You thought I wanted to go with you? How was that going to work?" Alina asks. The two girls look at each other and grin. I try to explain myself, but everything I say makes them smile even more. By the time I manage to slink away, even Maude Blue is tittering.

"Sure you don't need no one to hold your hand? Or was it something else you needed help holding?" Maude calls after me.

I give Bea a look, one that says *you're supposed to be my friend*, or something like that. She stifles a laugh. Maude starts blowing me kisses and that sets Alina off. I turn and march back in the direction we've come from. I'm looking for a large car or a wall—anything I can hide behind.

Once I've taken a piss, I don't feel like going straight back, so I take a look around. The farther into the city we walk, the more wretched everything is because every inch of space is piled high with crap. Any standing walls are smothered in blanched graffiti: SUFFOCATION IN HELL TO ALL WHO DO NOT BELIEVE, THE DEVIL AWAITS THE UNREPENTANT. In the years and months leading up to The Switch, people went crazy for God. What did God have to do with anything, that's what I want to know. *People* destroyed the forests. *People* poisoned the seas. And in the end, people saved themselves. No matter what Alina thinks of Breathe, no one would be alive now without them.

I hear a low rumbling and look up. The clouds are definitely gearing up for a downpour, and if we don't find a shelter, we're going to get another drenching.

As I walk back, I can hear the sky again. This time it's less of a low rumble and more of a tremor that I can actually feel through the ground. But the tremor doesn't stop like normal thunder does—it's more of a continuous quake, like some kind of drill. It can't be coming from the sky. I look up to be sure. And then I look back over my shoulder and I see it, a black tank pointing its gun in my direction.

A soldier is waving at me from the tank's turret and I have no idea what to do. Should I run? He's obviously seen me, and that would only make me seem suspect. Was he looking for me? He was probably after Alina and she's only around the corner. I stay where I am and put my hands up. The waving figure now has a megaphone in front of his face. "Stay precisely where you are," he commands. I do as he says. "We are Ministry Officials. Stay where you are. We will dismount the vehicle. Stay where you are." I haven't moved a muscle, but he keeps repeating himself as though I'm ignoring the simplest of instructions. I hope Bea and Alina have heard and taken off already.

The tank stops and two soldiers clamber out of the hatch. They stretch their arms and look around like they're glad of the freedom. They amble toward me. They're a lot more frightening-looking than the stewards in the pod, even the ones on Border Control. These guys have heavy black helmets covering their faces, which must have built-in air, and as they walk, they swing steel batons. They also have guns tucked into their belts.

"You're very far from home," one of them says.

"I'm lost," I say, and I shrug.

"You're Premium?" the other asks.

"Yep" I say.

"Let me see your ear," he says, and moves closer. He pushes back my hair and clears his throat. "Fine. We also need to scan your pad. It's not all that difficult to get a counterfeit tattoo," he adds.

"Yeah, I get it. My pad? Ah . . ." I scratch my head. "I have no idea what happened to it," I say, hoping they don't search me and find it in my coat.

"If we can't identify you, we'll have to take you in. Ministry orders are to sweep the area."

"Sure, sure. I'm glad you found me, to be honest, I was running out of air." I tug on my tank, not showing them the gauge, which would reveal that the tank is far from being empty.

"Who you traveling with?"

"Me? Oh, I'm alone. I'm kind of a loner, you know. Not many friends. Alone *a lot* . . ."

"Really."

"Really." I'm sure they know I'm lying. But they don't seem that interested in me.

"Let's go," they say.

"Can I grab my stuff? I left everything in there," I say, looking at a ramshackle building that might once have been a store. They look at each other, and though I have no idea how they can communicate with their faces covered, they turn to me simultaneously and nod. "Great. Wicked. Awesome," I say, probably overdoing it; I'm not exactly what you'd call a trained anarchist.

I turn away from the soldiers, making my way toward the old store. "Get a move on, mate," one of them growls.

When I'm inside, I see it was never a store at all; it must have been a barbershop. A whole wall is covered in cracked mirrors and in front of them is a row of black swivel chairs.

The pictures on the walls are peeling, but each one is a headshot of a slick model. I look out at the soldiers. One is nonchalantly leaning up against the tank. The other one has decided to follow me. I could sacrifice myself and go with them—Alina can protect herself—but I can't leave Bea; she wouldn't be able to run if she had to. Plus, I have no idea what those goons will do with me once they get me back to the pod and find out I was the one who helped a fugitive cross the border.

I bolt to the back of the barbershop and an open door leads me outside into a narrow alleyway. Left would take me back toward the others, and if the soldiers caught me, they might catch them, too, so I hurtle right instead.

I run past doors leading into the backs of stores and dash through one of them. This one is piled high with old screens and computers. I go to the windows and peek out. Both soldiers are clambering up the tank and through the hatch. One of them pops his head back up and hollers through the megaphone.

"If you do not come out, we will fire. Come out with your hands up. NOW!" I run out the back door and, trapped by stores on one side and a towering brick wall on the other, I decide I only have one choice, and that's to climb. The wall looks ready to crumble, but I find a few grooves to slip my fingers into and start scrambling up to the top.

I can see three small figures, Bea, Alina and Maude,

shuffling along, covering their heads with their hands. And I'm not sure why they're doing this until I hear a violent explosion and feel rocks and glass shattering against my back. I cover my head, too. Before I can jump, the wall sways, throwing me back to the ground. I stare at it, unable to move as it finally cracks and comes crashing down on top of me.

16
ALINA

I'm not sure whether or not we were spotted. But we keep moving. There's nothing else we can do. The buildings around us are exploding and showering us in concrete. If we stay where we are, we'll be killed.

There's an underground station up ahead, its entrance yawning like a hungry animal. The entrance is cordoned off by a flimsy wire fence that was ripped apart a long time ago. As we approach it Maude stops, and even when I move forward and yank her mask from her face, she stays where she is. The tank is still firing and the sky is a mosaic of rubble. Bea grabs Maude's arm, half drags her toward me, picks up the facemask from the ground and reattaches it so the old woman can breathe. "Not in there," Maude screeches above the explosions, jabbing her knotted finger in the direction of the station. "Never in the ground."

"Let's go, Bea," I yell.

"Not without her," she says, trying to pull Maude into the station. The old woman is strong—I know this. I run back and help Bea drag Maude in with us.

"No!" Maude screams, as though we're trying to kill her.

"We have to go down. They could bomb the entrance," I tell them.

"Quinn's still out there," Bea says.

"When the firing stops, we'll come up and find him. We can't help him now. We have to go." Bea hesitates for a moment then starts down the motionless escalator. Maude is frozen in place and staring into the pit of the station.

"You dunno what's d-down there," she stutters.

"Well, there isn't any sun down there, so at least I know it'll be free of drifters," I say, and follow Bea.

It's pitch-black at the bottom. I hear Bea rummaging around in her backpack and eventually she produces a flashlight and shines it into the darkness. The underground station has escaped a lot of destruction: the walls are dirty but perfectly intact and the floor tiles are even. Bea balances the flashlight on the escalator handrail.

"We'll give it a while and then we'll go back up," I say, knowing she's worried. And I feel a bit worried, too. And guilty. We shouldn't have teased him so much. We made him look silly and *of course* he went off to sulk.

"He isn't very worldly," Bea tells me, as though I hadn't figured it out already.

"No," I say.

"But he's a good person," she goes on.

"I didn't say he wasn't."

"Just because he's Premium doesn't mean he's like all the others. He doesn't ever act like he's better than me."

"That's because he isn't," I tell her. She goes quiet and when she does, we hear a thundering aboveground. They must know Quinn isn't alone. Did he tell them we were with him? Did he tell them about me?

Bea is crouching on the ground next to Maude. The old woman is whining like a broken alarm. "Get her up," I snap. I'm starting to feel mildly sorry for Maude, who is so old and obviously sick and unhappy, but I won't let her know it.

"Come on, Maude," Bea soothes, lifting her up and setting her on the last step of the escalator. Then, without speaking, without asking me if it's okay, she comes to me, unties Maude's airtank, and hands it to the old woman. I think about snatching it back, reminding Bea of the deal we struck: we let Maude live, but we give her a reason not to run or attack any of us. I think about this and realize there isn't anywhere for Maude to go.

"If she's getting the tank, you'll need to tie her hands. She could still attack us."

"She won't," Bea says.

"She might. Tie her hands." Bea shakes her head, refusing, and I don't argue. Maude groans and points in the direction of the platform.

"You can't make me," she wheezes. I stand up and move toward the platform. "Don't!" she shouts.

"What's gotten into you? People walk through the tunnels all the time." The underground has always provided our safest passage into and out of the city, mainly because there are no drifters.

"What about the bodies?" she asks.

"The bodies rotted a long time ago," I tell her. I don't say that the smell remains; she can probably smell it herself.

"This is a Death Station," she whispers. Bea stands up and holds out the flashlight as though she expects something to attack her.

The station shudders as it takes another hit aboveground. "It's getting worse," Bea says, looking up. I nod. She's thinking of Quinn. I am, too.

"I were a nurse," Maude tells us. "I were a young nurse. Well, actually, I were a student. I were a student-nurse, you know. I hadn't passed all me exams when the universities shut down. But people needed nurses and there weren't enough, see, so even the students had to work. People needed us. We was needed. We did our best."

"But what could you do? You couldn't save anyone," Bea says.

"Nope. So we did the opposite. Right down 'ere."

"What do you mean?" Bea whispers.

"People came and waited on the platforms and the doctors and nurses walked through the tunnels from station to station doing what they could."

Bea is frowning and casting her eyes about looking for answers. "You killed people," I say. Maude hugs her knees into her chest.

"We put 'em out of their misery. No one else would. It were illegal."

"Death Stations," Bea says.

"It were the only way out in the end. And *they* came to *us*. All different types, they was, though usually they was poor. They knew they hadn't a chance of buying themselves a place in the pod."

"Death Stations," Bea repeats. She shudders as another blast rocks the station.

"I helped deliver a baby down here," Maude continues, "and the first thing the mother said when I told her she'd had a boy was 'do it.' I knew what she meant. We all knew. But how could I?" Maude is speaking quickly now, more to herself than to us.

Bea is watching her, hypnotized. "What happened to the

baby?" she asks. She has tears in her eyes.

"I freed the mother. Freed—that's what we called it, freedom. I took the baby and left it on the doorstep of the biggest house I could find."

"And after all your mercy you went and took a job with Breathe?" I'm not buying her remorse.

"*They* recruited *us*. They promised us places in the pods. They found out what we was doing here and chose us because they thought we was merciless. And maybe we was. Anyway, killing the last of the trees was better than killing people."

"You sicken me," I tell Maude, and I mean it. I should never have listened to Bea's bleeding heart. I should have left her back in the house to rot. Maude mumbles something I don't hear. "What did you say?" My voice reverberates and comes back at me, bitterly hollow.

"I said, I—sicken—myself." And what can I say to that? It shuts me up at least. Bea nods and moves closer to Maude. She doesn't hug her, perhaps because the old woman is so filthy and decayed, but pats her hand gently. I don't know where she finds the compassion.

Suddenly the ground quakes, and a noise like thousands of boulders being hurled at the station from the sky reminds us where we are.

As quickly as it began, the pounding stops and we hear what must be the tank rumble away. We stand in stunned silence for a moment. If Quinn hasn't been captured, he is probably hurt. "Leave her here and bring the flashlight," I tell Bea.

"Don't leave me down here in the bloody dark," Maude mewls as I bound back up the escalator two steps at a time.

"We won't be long," Bea says over her shoulder as she follows me.

For some reason the light doesn't change and the only reason I can see is because Bea is behind me with the flashlight. When I get to the top, I stop and look around.

"Did we come down two levels?" I ask Bea when she catches up.

"No, the exit should be right there." She directs her light at a pile of bricks.

She looks at me horrified.

"Quinn's out there. We have to help him," she cries. She runs toward the exit and frantically starts to throw rocks in all directions. But it's pointless: the whole roof has caved in. It would take twenty of us days to safely move everything and forge a way through. I let her attack the bricks for a while. Then I go to her.

"We won't get out this way. We'll have to walk through the tunnels," I say.

She isn't listening. "I think I can hear him. What if he's under *here*? Help me, will you? Help me!" I rest a hand on her shoulder while she tries to dislodge a metal pole from the pile.

"Bea," I say softly.

"Quinn could be dead," she says. "Quinn," she repeats his name quietly. She loves him, that much is obvious. But he's so oblivious he can't see it. And maybe now he'll never know how she feels. Does *she* even know how she feels?

"He probably got picked up," I tell her, though I don't believe it. They wouldn't have been endlessly firing if they were giving Quinn a friendly ride back to the pod. "He's Premium. Nothing ever happens to Premiums. And his dad works for Breathe. It wouldn't be worth it to them to hurt him."

"He ran. We saw him running. They started shooting. Why are you lying?"

"He's fast. He's probably halfway to The Grove by now. Don't you think?"

"He doesn't know the way to The Grove. How would he know the way?"

"He'll find it. He'll worry about you, and he'll make it his business to find it."

"No. No, he won't. And anyway, he wants *you*. He'll worry about *you*. He's besotted with *you*. You know that already though, don't you?" Bea looks at me searchingly, and I can see that she wants me to tell her he doesn't like me, and that I haven't noticed anything.

"He doesn't even know me, Bea," I say, which is true. An image of Abel comes into my mind: his square shoulders, the curl of a smile when he teased me. If Quinn is alive, I will tell him to stop looking at me. I don't want anyone to look at me in that way again. "We won't get through that," I tell Bea, pointing at the wreckage.

After Quinn came back from peeing, I was going to pretend to do the same, but give them all the slip. Even as the tank began to fire at us, I thought about running in the opposite direction from Bea and Maude rather than trying to explain to Petra why I'd dragged along refugees. I couldn't though, not with Maude tied to me. And now it seems that I'm stuck with them.

"It's pointless staying here," I say. Bea picks up a loose rock and throws it from one hand to the other. Then she lobs the rock as hard as she can against an old ticket machine.

"If he doesn't make it, I'll blame you," she says. And so whether I like it or not I have to accept it: I now have Quinn Caffrey's blood on my hands, too.

17
QUINN

It takes me a second, like a good second, and when I come to, I know I'm buried in bricks. I have a bloody mouthful of mud and dust, which must have somehow penetrated the mask. I'm so thirsty, I'd drink anything.

Luckily I can breathe—the explosions didn't puncture my tank—but can't see a thing. I blink. Nothing changes—everything is blackness.

I push rubble away from my face and manage to wriggle my body free, though the pain in every limb is searing. What feels like a large, flat slab of concrete is right above me. I lie on my back again and try using my feet to dislodge it. It doesn't shift an inch. It's prevented me from being completely crushed, but now it's trapping me, and I can't even be sure how deep I'm buried because it's so dark.

I lie on my back and wiggle my legs again just to be sure I can feel them. Although, maybe I *am* paralyzed. I've seen it in films—soldiers losing their legs in war and they're in so much pain they can't even tell when they've been maimed; they start talking about their wives and stuff. In fact, the calmer they are, the more likely it is they're dead—legless or headless or whatever.

It might even be possible that I'm dead. I haven't thought about death very much, but if I try to imagine it, I think it would be exactly like this: a tight, lonely darkness.

I hope Bea got away. I saw her running. I saw Alina, Maude, and Bea running. I hope Alina got away, too. I try calling out Bea's name, but my voice is blanketed by the dust and I start to cough. I must be alive if I'm coughing, right?

18
BEA

I don't *want* to love Quinn. If I could love someone who loved me back, my life would be calmer and I'd be happier. I don't want to ache for him every minute of the day. And now that he's missing, that aching I feel for him in my chest has swollen up so that my whole body feels like it's filled with poison.

I don't love him in the way my parents love each other—sweetly, almost wearily. When I'm with him I feel each nerve within me awakening so that when he touches me, when he brushes my arm accidentally, I shiver and I have to bite back an urge to cry out. I feel the ache everywhere: in my neck, in my belly, between my legs.

But he'll never know any of this because I'm too much of a coward to tell him the truth. I don't want to have to see his expression as he tries to work out how to tell me he doesn't love me in return. I would rather walk along next to him hoping he'll turn and see me, one day, than be told once and for all that my love is hopeless.

I try not to remember that he could be dying.

I try not to remember that if he is dying somewhere, he'll be thinking of Alina, while I'm thinking of him.

19
QUINN

How long have I been buried? It's hard to get a handle on time when you have no sense of space and when all light has been pinched out. The pain has started now: a dull ache in my back and in my legs.

I've been coughing since I was buried and I'm pretty sure I heard the armored tank rumble away a long time ago. If anyone was searching for me, surely they would have discovered me by now; they'd have heard the coughing. Wouldn't they? Maybe they wouldn't have heard anything at all because it's so dark in here it's possible I've been covered up by tens of thousands of bricks and cement blocks.

I could rot away underneath this rubble. I might be a dry jumble of bones by the time anyone clears the devastation. I try to shout.

"Bea!" It comes out as a chalky whisper. "Bea!" I try again, but my voice has been crushed, too. I cough and this time the cough is loud as my lungs try to clear themselves of dust. I cough and cough and before long the cough turns into panicked pants. I'll die here. My airtank will expire before I do, and I suppose that'll be for the best; I wouldn't want to actually die of hunger or thirst. "Bea!" I call again. "Bea!" She must have hidden when the explosions started. Now she's either trapped, looking for me, or dead. There's no way she'd leave without looking for me, is there?

"Bea?" I call, and then I cough. "Bea?"

20
BEA

I have to keep reminding myself that the voices I hear are the echoes coming from connecting tunnels, that the muttering up ahead actually belongs to us. When I hear Quinn calling out, I have to remember that we are one hundred feet below ground and even if he were calling out, I wouldn't hear him. Yet, I can't stop imagining Quinn in trouble. What if he *is* calling me? What if he's dying?

I see Alina watching me as I dry my eyes and wipe my nose on my sleeve. Occasionally she asks me how I am. Sometimes she touches my back or squeezes my arm. "He'll be fine," she says, and after a while repeats, "he *will* be fine," even though I haven't contradicted her.

And poor Maude is convinced the spirits of the dead live in the tunnels and she can feel them brushing by. "Serves you right," Alina snaps. "You shouldn't have murdered them." Maude struggles to move forward as we follow the metal rails through the dank capillaries of the underground system. The brown water we are sloshing through is flavored with floating bones and covers our ankles so that even in boots our feet are ice.

Maude wants to tell us about some of the people she "freed." "I want to confess," she says, but Alina won't let her talk.

"Save your air for breathing, old woman. No one wants to know about it." Alina's right. I don't want to hear about all the people who chose death. I don't want to hear about the despair. I need to believe. Without hope, what do we have?

Finally we get to the next station. "Where are we?" Maude asks. I shine the light back and forth to get a look at the place. The walls are gray, but I can almost make out broken lettering surrounded by a large red circle. "Tottinghan ale?"

Maude looks up at the shattered signage and groans. I guess this too must have been a Death Station. Alina is way ahead of us, still on the rails and almost at the mouth of the tunnel at the far end of the platform. "Alina!" I call out. She turns and shakes her head. "Alina, let's go up," I yell. It's taken a long time to get through the tunnel and I wonder how long it will take to pick our way back to Quinn. Alina clambers onto the platform and disappears under an arch. I boost

Maude and climb up, too. We sit down on a bench tucked into the wall and Maude awkwardly starts to unlace her rotting, wet boots.

Eventually Alina reappears. She moves toward us slowly and leans against the wall next to the bench. "Alina?"

"I'm sorry, Bea, I really am. I honestly didn't remember," she says.

"What's going on?" I nudge her with the flashlight. "Listen, if you don't want to come with me, I understand. I'll go alone," I say, hoping she won't make me.

"It isn't that. Look around you." I shine the flashlight on the walls again. "Don't you see?"

"What?"

"Fire," Maude croaks. I look at the walls. They are thick with black grime.

"The staircases and escalators are gone. There's no way up," Alina says.

"But we can get up through the next station," I say. Alina looks away. "Well?" She takes the flashlight from me and shines it on the gauge of my tank. Then she shines it on her own tank.

"It would take several hours to get back to Quinn. And then we'd have to find him. We need to refuel. We won't make it otherwise."

"We have enough," I say. "We could move more quickly.

We can run." I know that it's a stupid plan, that we'll use up even more air if we hurry. Alina takes me by the arm and we walk along the platform away from Maude.

"There is a way you could do it," she whispers. "If we had an extra tank of air, maybe we could find him." When I turn to look at Maude, she is tipping her boots upside down to get the water out. "It's her or Quinn, Bea. And it's your choice." I am too stunned to speak.

Maude looks over at us. "I'm hungry," she says, so I move back to where she's sitting and open my backpack.

"Here's a nutrition bar." She snatches it from me, tears it open, and stuffs half the bar into her mouth.

"Take my tank," Maude whispers.

"Maude, I—"

"Yeah, I'd be happy kicking around for another few years, but I know what you two was muttering about. And I know there ain't enough air for us all to get out of here alive *and* save your boyfriend."

I don't know what to say. So I say the first thing that comes into my head. "He isn't my boyfriend." Maude blinks and stuffs the other half of the nutrition bar into her mouth.

"Last meal. I would've enjoyed a glass of bubbly and a plateful of chocolate truffles, but, oh, this will do." She unhooks the tank from her side. "Go and find him. If you like him, he must be all right." She pulls off her facemask and hands it to me. I am amazed. I am amazed and I am broken by Maude's kindness. But I haven't the right to swap her life for someone else's, even if that person is someone I love.

I push the mask back onto her face and without thinking, throw my arms around her.

"Get off me," Maude mutters.

"Are you out of your mind?" Alina shouts and runs to pull me away from Maude who, despite her protest, is clinging to me as tightly as I am to her. "Who knows what she's got living in her skin. What the *hell* are you doing?" Alina screams. She looks at Maude with disgust, until gradually, her face changes and her look turns from hateful to sad. And when I let go of Maude, I see why: she is crying inconsolably, and in the dim light looks so human, so beautiful and vulnerable with her tank still held out as an offering, that it would take a monster not to pity her.

21
QUINN

I'm pretty sure no one's searching, or if they are, they must be giving up the search by now. There's no point in calling out, so I've stopped. And I've stopped trying to find a way out. It only uses up more air.

I never really thought much about my life before, and it's kind of sad that the first time I am actually thinking about it is probably the last time I ever will; it's likely I won't survive more than a day, and all the regret and gratitude I have churning around in my head will be wasted because there's going to be nothing I can do about any of it.

I can't stop thinking about my brothers—Lennon and Keane—and even though they do drive me up the wall sometimes, I love them. And I love my parents, too. I don't like thinking about it, how much I love everyone and how

I won't see any of them again, to tell them that I love them. I wish I'd been nicer, you know, like actually talked to my family from time to time.

I don't know why Bea didn't tell me to get lost ages ago. The number of times I blew her off because I got a better offer from some girl I'd met an hour earlier. And later, when I realized that girl was as boring to kiss as she was to talk to, I'd be on the pad to Bea complaining about my disaster of a life. *My* life? And there she was with two parents who couldn't afford to let her breathe too much, let alone make out with someone. If I survive, the first thing I'm going to do is apologize to Bea. I imagine her face, forgiving me. I imagine her eyes blinking away tears as she comes toward me and we embrace.

22
BEA

Maude, Alina, and I are all sitting on the dirty platform with our legs dangling over the edge. I open another nutrition bar, which Alina and I share, taking turns so that we can keep each other's masks on.

"If I gave you *my* tank would you go back for him?" I ask Alina.

"You know I wouldn't," she says, and I do know that, but I have to ask anyway, to be sure.

I try to tell myself that he's okay, that he'll be waiting for us when we emerge from whichever station Alina intends to use to get us out of the underground. I tell myself all this, though I know it's more likely that Quinn is dead or that he will be soon.

I make a promise to myself that if Quinn *is* dead, I'll find a way to avenge his murder. I'll find a way to make the Ministry pay.

23
Quinn

I've given up all hope and am falling in and out of consciousness when a voice brings me back. Someone calls out. "Al-ala?" I wonder if it's my imagination, if I'm so low on air that I'm delirious and starting to hear things. I cough. Then the voice rings again. "Al-aaala?"

I try to shout, but my throat is so dry, all that comes out is another cough. I cough and cough and as I do, the bricks shift slightly around me and dust sprinkles into my eyes.

"Hello!" I say, and it sounds like a real word. "I'm here!" I call, louder this time.

"I'm coming!" Above me there's a sound that reminds me of a tram pulling into a station. The voice disappears, but a crunching and thudding sound replaces it. After what feels like an hour, a gray sliver of light punctures the gloom and the concrete slab is at last hauled away, and a face peers down at me in the moonlight.

"You're not Alina," he says.

"I'm Quinn," I tell him.

"Okay," he says, and continues to shift the wreckage so I can move. He frowns, his eyes dark and hard. And another figure appears over his shoulder wearing an even fiercer look. He helps to dig me out. "Can you stand?" the first guy asks when I'm free. I manage to sit up, but when I try to stand, my legs buckle and I fall. "Here," he says, and takes a water canister from his companion. I adjust my facemask, take a long gulp, and hand it back. "I'm looking for someone," he says. "I'm looking for a girl."

"Who are you?" I ask. They don't look like they should be trifled with. The first of the two, the talker with the hard eyes, hands the canister back to the blond, who puts it into his backpack without speaking and looks up at the moon. It is full in the sky and there is a fierce wind whipping our faces. The blond pulls his hat down as a few flakes of snow start to float to earth.

"You're a Premium," the first says. It's amazing how quickly everyone spots this, like it's the one thing they need to know in order to fully understand a person.

"My name's Quinn," I tell him again, holding out my

bruised and bloody hand. He looks at it for a moment and finally puts out his hand, too.

"I'm Silas," he says, taking my hand and gripping it tightly. "And this is Inger. We're looking for my cousin."

PART III
THE RESISTANCE

24
QUINN

"So what you're saying is that you met Alina?" Silas asks, looking down at me warily. "You were traveling companions and you helped her? *You?*" Maybe this isn't easy for him to believe. I'm covered from head to foot in dirt, my body is still sort of shivering from the shock of being buried alive, and I'm holding an old T-shirt to my face to staunch the blood coming from a gash above my eyebrow.

"The drifter would've killed her if we hadn't come along," I croak, dust still lining my throat.

"We?" Silas looks at Inger, who still hasn't spoken. He is standing behind Silas with his hands on his hips.

"My friend Bea," I say. "She's with Alina now. At least, I think she is. I hope she is."

Silas rubs his mouth and stubbly chin. He's got the same

unflinching frown as Alina, giving him the look of someone who's lived a very long time. He's eighteen or nineteen maybe, twenty at most. But unlike Alina, Silas doesn't look like he's about to punch me in the face when I speak.

"So, why exactly did Alina decide to drag along the drifter?" he asks. "They're dangerous." Inger nods in agreement and folds his arms across his broad chest. I'm unnerved by Inger's silence and explain everything again, right from when I met Alina in the vaccination line and then again at Border Control, and they listen carefully. When I'm done, and they're just about satisfied I'm not lying, Silas throws my arm over his shoulder and hauls me up. "Can you walk?" he asks.

"I think so," I say. Pain runs across my abdomen. I hunch over and groan, but it only makes the pain more intense. I gasp. I can't help it.

"You must have cracked some ribs," Silas says. "Nothing a doctor could do about that anyway. They'll heal. You'll be fine."

Silas and Inger look like they'd keep walking even if they lost their limbs—they'd try, anyway, and wouldn't complain about it. So I pull the straps on my facemask tight and take a deep breath. Even doing this is so painful I have an urge to howl. I take small, shallow breaths and try to focus on the moon, shining as brightly as a new coin, and on the silvery angular shapes on the horizon. I try not to look at the buildings pressing in on us, their windows shattered, their roofs caved in at the corners.

"How did you find out Alina was on the run?" I ask.

"Alina lives with me and my parents." Silas grunts and puts his arms through the straps of his backpack.

"Why?"

"Since her parents disappeared, she's been like a sister to me," he says.

"Like a sister. Huh." Silas doesn't respond. "So, where we headed?" I ask.

Silas frowns. "You're going back to the pod," he says.

Inger nods and finally speaks, his voice a low growl. "You would be in our way," he says. Because Silas has done all the talking until now, my initial impression was that Inger was something of a sidekick, but hearing him I know that can't be true. There is a strength and authority to his voice.

"Breathe will probably come hunting again tomorrow and you can hitch a ride with them. Flash that tattoo," Silas says.

"My best friend is heading into the city, and I'm responsible for her, so I'm coming with you," I say.

Inger sniffs and puts his hands in his pockets. "She's *your* cousin," he tells Silas.

Silas, who has been holding my backpack, throws it at me and pulls up the hood on his jacket. "We found your stuff over there," he says, pointing to the spot where I last saw Bea, Alina, and Maude. He looks up at the sky, clears his throat, and then, like he's just seen his fate in the clouds says, "All right, you can come." He manages a smile. "But we won't get far tonight through this mess. There's no road we can follow. Let's find somewhere to get a bit of shut-eye until dawn."

"I have a tent," I tell them. "Really easy to put up: all you have to do is shake it."

"You have a tent? Where did you get a tent?" Silas wants to know.

"I bought it."

"'Course," he snorts.

"Well, my dad bought it," I add, and then wish I hadn't.

We walk until we find a solid-looking house with a front garden. Inger and Silas stop, shrug off the bags, and kick the remnants of an old bicycle and some broken bottles aside while I slowly unravel the tent. Within a few minutes it's ready.

"I have these," I say, pulling out the sleeping bags and tossing them onto the ground.

"That must be the smallest thing I've ever seen." Silas stares at the tent. He hasn't said it, but what he really means is, *We'll have to lie really close to each other.*

"Oh well," I say, trying to sound blasé but really, I'm

weirded out too: I hardly know these guys and it *is* a small tent, even for two.

"It'll keep us dry," Inger says, crouching down and crawling inside. Silas and I crawl in after him with the sleeping bags. We unzip them the whole way and use one as padding for the ground and the other one as a kind of blanket. We lie down, me in the middle. Inger and Silas turn their backs on me, so even though I usually sleep on my side, I can't do this without spooning one of them. I lie looking up at the shadows, making sure I keep my feet together and hands on my chest.

After a few minutes Silas says, "You're sure Alina's all right?"

I know that what I need to say is, *Yes, Alina's fine, don't worry*, but the reasonable part of my brain shuts down momentarily as the concussed part kicks in. What I end up saying is, "Do you have a crush on her too, Silas?"

"Really?" Inger exclaims, stifling a laugh.

"What in hell's name is wrong with him?" Silas says. I have no idea how to respond because I know that Silas is her cousin and I sound like some wacko. I pull the sleeping bag up under my chin.

"I'm sixteen," I say, like that's an explanation. Silas laughs, thank God, instead of hitting me.

"He's sixteen," Inger repeats.

"He's an idiot," Silas says. "Go to sleep."

25
BEA

When we emerge from the underground into the dawn, I have to squint to protect my eyes from the light. The cold bites me, too. There are little flurries of white frost circling in the morning air and silently settling on the ground. "Beautiful," Alina says, holding out her hand to catch some snowflakes and pulling away her facemask so she can taste them.

I haven't spoken for hours; none of us has, we're saving our energy. And I have nothing to say.

We walk in single file down a narrow road leading to an even narrower one, more like an alleyway than a road really. I have no idea where we are. I need a map. I don't have one—Quinn had everything in his bags, so I wouldn't have to carry anything and wear myself out—and my pad has no battery.

Maude and I have been struggling to keep up with Alina.

How she managed to maintain her fitness without ever getting caught by a steward or one of the Ministry's cameras is astounding. I'm jealous and angry I didn't try to break the law myself. I've been virtuous my whole life, practically saintly, and where did it get me?

We've been walking through the night. When Maude needed to pee we all found nooks to get a minute's privacy, but that was the longest break we took. We have to keep moving at exactly the right pace to ensure our air supplies last, though Alina's will last longer because she's trained herself to subsist on lower densities of oxygen.

Alina keeps her head down and marches onward, turning left, then turning right, rarely looking up to check she's on the correct road. She points occasionally, warning us to avoid glass or cracked skulls.

I wonder whether or not Alina is thinking of Quinn. Maybe it feels better to be the one filled with desire than the one desired. I wouldn't know. Maybe I'll never know.

Maude grabs my arm again. "How are you holding up?" I ask. She nods rather than making the effort to speak. She doesn't disgust me anymore, old Maude Blue. I pity her, that's all. "Be careful in the snow. It could get icy."

Alina turns. "Soon," she tells us, "you'll see what's possible." I don't ask. I was curious for a while, but now I don't care. As she walks, Alina continues to reach out now and again to allow snowflakes to settle on her palm. I watch her and am about to reach out too when a low murmuring sound, impossible to mistake, stops me.

"Tank!" I shout. Alina reacts quickly. She points at a solid building with faces carved into its stonework. We all pound our way through the heavy door.

"Do you think they saw us?" Alina wonders aloud. "We have to stay hidden." She glances at the gauge on her airtank and looks at me seriously.

"You're low on fuel," I guess. Alina shrugs.

"We all must be," she says. I look at my own gauge and see she's right. Our air is running out. When I turn to check Maude's gauge she isn't there. She's somehow managed to scoot to the other side of the room where she is looking up at the walls.

"Amazing!" she calls out. "Amazing and horrible." I move to where she is standing and look up, too.

"Are they real?" I ask.

"Books," Maude says. "Books and books and books. Paper." She laughs and reaches out to touch them. She pulls one from the shelf and opens it. The pages are black and moldy in the corners. A few Premiums own books, but most paper products were left in The Outlands to rot, and I've only ever seen pictures and videos of them.

"'In a word, I was too cowardly to do what I knew to be

right, as I had been too cowardly to avoid doing what I knew to be wrong.' It sounds different reading from paper, doesn't it?" she says. I don't recognize the words Maude is reading, but I can hear the difference in her voice: it is tender now, and light. "I'm keeping this one," she says, slipping the book into her coat. "Choose one," she demands. "Go on." I run my hand along the spines.

"What's this one?" I ask.

"*Pride and Prejudice*. Don't you know it? What *are* they teaching you in school?"

"Shakespeare, mainly. Our teacher says all literature is in Shakespeare."

"Yes, well, maybe it is. Anyway, I'll take that one." She grabs *Pride and Prejudice* from my hands and slips it into her coat before retrieving the first book and tossing it to me. "*Great Expectations* would be better for you. Pip would be right up your alley." I slip the book into my own jacket, letting the hard edges rest against my stomach.

Alina has climbed onto a table and is peering outside. "They're getting closer," she warns. The rumbling is louder and the ground beneath us starts to tremble. I stand next to Alina on the table. The tank is almost outside the building. Gradually the treads stop turning and the engine lulls to a complete silence. A figure emerges from the tank holding a rifle that he points into the air and fires.

"What's he doing?" I whisper.

"I have no idea," she says.

"They're playing," Maude says, despite the fact that she can't see what we're seeing. "They're bored, so they're playing. That's what we did. Bang-bang-bang. Fun and games."

"Are you sure?" Alina asks. Maude doesn't answer. She is busy reading. When I look back at the tank, the soldiers are climbing out of the hatch. They start to saunter down the street, gazing up at the sky as they go.

"They've stopped to enjoy the snow," I tell Alina. A smile of relief appears as she sees I'm right: the soldiers are crouching down to touch the snow. They both push up the black visors of their helmets. One of the soldiers is a woman with a pointy chin, while the other is a man with a thin beard. In a strange way, they look alike. They are younger than I would have expected: no more than twenty. They gaze back up at the sky again and laugh before moving toward each other.

"They're normal. They look like completely normal people," Alina says. "How's that possible?"

"They're in love," I add. I look at Maude, who is scratching the nape of her neck and muttering as she reads.

The soldiers continue to laugh, but now they are apart, backing away from each other. They gather up handfuls of snow and pat it into tight, cold bullets. Still laughing, they throw the balls of snow at each other. The female soldier screams and runs. Around and around the tank they run, screaming and laughing and throwing snow. The female soldier abruptly stops running, and when the male soldier catches her, she points toward the building opposite and the two of them make a dash for it.

We continue to watch for several minutes. Alina looks at me and raises her eyebrows. "Well, that's one way to keep warm," she says. I laugh. Alina checks her gauge. "Right. That's it. We're taking the tank." I stare at her. She has to be joking.

"No way!" I say.

"No way what?" Maude calls, interested now there's a dispute.

"You're helping me to steal that tank," Alina tells her.

"You're damn right I am!" Maude yells, throwing the book she's holding high into the air and letting it fall, with a crash, right back down on top of her own head.

26
ALINA

It's ridiculously easy. Maude clambers through the hatch and starts to power up the tank. I'm in front of the door the two soldiers disappeared through, and I'm wielding a knife, which I'll use if either of the lovebirds come sauntering out of the building early. Bea is sitting on the turret; her job is to grab me and pull me aboard when the time's right. I'm not sure that Bea even has the strength to haul me up, but I wasn't going to give *her* the knife: if one of the soldiers appeared she'd likely collapse with guilt and slit her own throat.

The tank hums to life and Bea calls out. "She's ready. Come on! Come on!" I run and she grabs my hands. "They're coming. Oh. My. God. They're coming!" I look back. The soldiers are scrambling down an external fire exit several steps at a time. Bea pulls me up and within seconds we are both tumbling into the tank.

It's not as sophisticated as I'd expected—rudimentary knobs and levers, the space cramped and dirty. I peer through the periscope. The two soldiers are on the street and running hard, fighting to get back into their jackets, slipping on the snow as they charge toward us. "Fire!" Maude shouts, pointing to some levers she can't reach and wielding Quinn's tiny mallet.

"Get that thing!" I shout at Bea, who quickly grabs it.

"Fire at the scoundrels! Fire the guns!" Maude shouts again, looking for a way to control the guns herself.

"Stop it," Bea demands, slapping Maude's hand away. The tank is rolling forward but the soldiers are close. Could they climb aboard with the tank moving? They don't appear too keen to try, edging away as we growl forward. They are screaming at each other and waving. One of them pulls out a radio, pushes a few buttons, and yells something.

"Why are we stealing it?" Bea wants to know.

"Oh, it's a clever move, girlies. Now that lot really know they have a war on their hands," Maude declares. I shake my head, about to say no, that we need to move faster and save air, that's all. But as I think about what Maude's just said, it dawns on me that she's right: I've started a war.

27
QUINN

You know those films where a guy wakes up next to some girl, then creeps out of bed and kind of skulks off because he doesn't want to have to have an awkward conversation? Well, it's not exactly the same thing, but I still have that awkward feeling when I wake up next to Silas and Inger. Anything I say, even if I try and say it casually, is going to sound all weird and forced, so I get up and crawl out of the tent, trying not to wake them.

Everything is covered in a thick layer of white. "Come and look," I say, poking my head back into the tent. Silas sits up and yawns. Inger is still on his side, asleep.

"Oh God, it's completely light. Wake up, Inger," Silas grumbles. He crawls out of the tent. "Wow," he says when he sees the snow. "Wow."

The fine sheet of sparkling whiteness makes the ruins around us look less like mounds of destruction and more like spectacular monuments. If Bea were here, I could say something like that without feeling embarrassed. But I stay quiet.

"The world doesn't seem so bad when it looks like this, does it?" Silas says, looking at me. I don't know if he wants me to respond. I sigh, which could mean anything. "You know what I mean?" he says. I look at him carefully. He rolls his eyes and crouches down, skimming his hand across the surface of the snow.

Before long, Inger materializes. "Time to go," he says.

The roads are even worse today. The snow isn't simply hiding the danger but making everything slick, too. Inger and Silas trek ahead, scrabbling over mounds of rubble, using their hands as well as their feet. It's embarrassing: they're ten times fitter than I am, yet I've had more air than them my whole life.

After a few hours, I stop. I can't walk any farther without eating. I take a few bites of a nutrition bar, then split the rest and hand the pieces to Silas and Inger. Silas pushes it into his mouth without saying thank you. Inger nods gratefully at least.

"How much farther?" I ask.

"You worried about your air?" Silas asks. He checks the

display. "Two hours, if that gauge is accurate. Are you an efficient breather?"

I don't know what he means by "efficient breather." I breathe in and out and that usually works fine: I'm still alive.

"I'm efficient," I say, finding myself inhaling deeply and exhaling a long breath.

"Hey," Silas warns. "Enough of the heavy breathing." Before I get a chance to answer, Inger puts his fingers to his lips.

"Can you hear that?" he whispers.

"What?" I whisper back.

Silas holds up his hand and scans the road behind us. Then he looks up at the sky and squints through the snow.

"Zips," Inger hisses. "Damn it."

"We need a building. A tall building," Silas says. He darts across the road and pushes through a revolving door. After a moment he reappears, opens his coat, and fills it with snow before going back into the building again.

"Let's go," Inger says. "Bring snow." He opens his backpack, shovels snow into it, and bolts through the revolving doors behind Silas. I gaze up at the towering structure. If it's a tank they've heard and it starts firing, none of us will survive being buried alive by this building. Silas's face appears in a second-floor window. "Quinn! Get in here. Now!" he shouts.

"I don't want to get buried alive, Silas!" I yell. "You can call me a wimp if you like, I don't care." Rusted cars line the street, many abandoned right in the middle of it. I'll hide in one of those.

"*I'll* bury you alive if you don't quit your sniveling and get your backside in here. Use the stairs."

I don't know why, but I race after them, into the building and up the stairs. I run and run, expecting to meet Silas and Inger, but I'm met with more stairs. "Not far now!" Silas calls from somewhere above. I keep climbing and eventually there he is, staring at me.

"Come on," he says. We dash along a darkening corridor past empty offices, the desks and chairs overturned, some with the computer screens smashed. "Inger?" he calls out.

"I'm fine! Don't worry!" Inger shouts.

"Right," Silas says when we are in almost complete darkness. "Take off your clothes," he says. I stare at him as he starts to pull his coat and sweater over his head. He rips off his boots and socks and hurls them down the corridor. "Oi! Did you hear me or what?" His facemask has come loose and he struggles to refit it, holding the airtank under his arm.

"Silas, I think . . ." I begin.

"You're too warm. They'll detect the body heat. You need to get cold. Take off your bloody clothes or we *will* get buried alive," he shouts, which he has to, because I can hear it now—not the low murmur of tank treads but the slicing of the air around us. Close to us. In the sky. I get out of my clothes. Silas throws snow at me and then tips his water bottle over my head. I cry out. Silas is already dripping wet. When I look down I see that he's kept on his underpants whereas I'm stark naked. I cover myself with one hand and with the other keep a tight hold of the airtank.

"You told me to strip," I say.

Silas shakes his head and turns away. The noise is deafening. I wrap one arm around my head to protect my ears and feel myself start to shrivel up from the cold—I'm glad Silas has his back to me.

When the noise dissipates, I lower my hands and put on my underpants. Silas turns around.

"There'll be more," Silas says. He's right. Within a minute, the sky is thundering again, and all we can do is stand shivering and wait. I don't want to look at Silas's body, but I can't help noticing how strong he is. I look down at myself. I'm lean and muscular, girls have never complained, but Silas is huge. He's got the kind of body women want. He looks like a man. And this is what I'm thinking as life-threatening zips whir overhead. It's stupid. I'm standing freezing and half naked and close to death, and all I can think about are Silas's muscles.

"That's probably the last of them," Silas says, retrieving his clothes from the floor.

"We're going to get hypothermia."

"Dry off your hair and you'll be fine," he says, climbing back into his clothes as I pull on my pants. When I'm fully dressed, he says, "Come and look." We walk along the corridor into an office with a window. In the distance two fat aircraft with long overhead rotor blades pummel through the sky.

"What are they?" I ask.

"Ministry zips. Classified. Those things are serious. They don't get those babies out unless something big is going down. Their thermo-detectors are more advanced than ever. They can see right into most buildings. We had to be cold and at the center of the biggest structure possible or our body heat would have drawn them right to us." He moves away from the window and I follow him back out of the building. Inger is on the street getting into his coat and looking into the sky. He too has wet hair. "You all right?" Silas asks him. Inger nods.

"What about the others?" I ask, thinking about Bea.

"Alina's trained," Silas says.

"But what if they can't make it to a building in time? What if—"

"Let's get going," he says. "I'm not sharing air with you. And by the looks of it, you're almost out."

28
BEA

My eyelids feel heavy, but I am determined to stay awake for Alina. She took over the driving from Maude an hour ago, and even though she must be exhausted, she's managing to keep her eyes wide and unblinking and fixed firmly on the road ahead.

"Where are we going to park this thing so no one sees it?" I ask.

"I have a place in mind," she says, smiling without showing her teeth. Occasionally she mumbles an assurance to herself about stealing the tank, though no one is doubting her, at least not out loud.

How has my life gone from being simple and sensible to completely anarchic? I'm rumbling along in a stolen tank and on the run from the Ministry with two people I don't really know, and Quinn is missing. I focus on Maude, whose breathing has slowed as she slinks into sleep. Alina notices and gently kicks her. Maude swears, swipes the air with her fingers, and jiggles herself awake.

"When did you learn to drive one of these things? When you worked for the Ministry?" Alina asks Maude.

"I was naval. Boats and hovercrafts," she says, puffing up a little.

"Were there trackers?" Alina asks.

"Trackers . . ." Maude murmurs, remembering. "Trackers. Yes. In case we got lost. Not that they cared a jot about us—the boats are worth a fortune. They couldn't afford to lose a boat."

"Or a tank," I suggest. The penny drops and Maude's eyes widen.

"They'll find us if we stay in this thing," she says. "We've gotta dump this galumphing tin can and get away as fast as possible. They'll send zips. We ain't got long."

"Can you find the tracker, Maude?" I ask calmly.

"Can I find it?" Maude wonders aloud. "The tracker. . . the tracker."

"Was it hidden in the boats?"

"In the boats it were under the driver's seat. But that were in the boats."

Alina stands up, still driving, and I twist the seat until I feel it come loose. It unscrews easier than I imagined it would and after a couple of seconds I've got the seat in my hands. There's nothing on the underside, so I pass it to Maude and look into the wide cylinder the seat was attached to. Inside is a tiny black box. I reach in and remove it.

"Did it look like this?" I ask Maude.

"That's it!" she says.

"Well, I thought it would be harder than that to find. Maybe our luck is turning," Alina says, but as soon as she's spoken, I wish she hadn't; it gives me a feeling that something awful is about to happen.

"What do you want me to do with it?" I ask Alina.

"Swallow it," she says, and laughs.

"Seriously, Alina. We need to get rid of it," I say.

"Open the hatch and chuck the damn thing out," she says. So I climb the ladder, push open the heavy hatch, and throw the tracker as far as I can.

Alina and Maude are quiet. They haven't much to say to each other when they aren't arguing. I screw the seat back in place so Alina can sit down. She doesn't thank me—she doesn't even look at me—and I don't think she'd even consider thanking Maude for knowing where to find the tracker.

We power on for another half hour before Alina says, "We're here." She slows the tank and parks it. Then she jumps from her seat and scurries up the ladder. We follow, climbing out and into a wide building with a high tin roof. The tank fits without any problem, but the structure looks flimsy and unsafe. "It's an old bus station," Alina says.

She grabs my arm. "Did your stomach just rumble?" she asks, squeezing. I put my free hand to my stomach, wondering whether it did or not.

"It were probably me. I'm so hungry I could eat a fat teenager," Maude announces.

"Shhh," Alina says, putting her fingers to her lips.

"Don't you shush me," Maude warns, raising her fists as though she's about to get into a boxing match.

"I think it's zips," Alina gasps. Maude listens. We all do.

"You're right. Mercy me," Maude says.

"Oh God, I've led them right to Petra." Alina's voice is a whisper. "They'll see everything from up there. I'm going to get everyone killed." She is paralyzed, staring up at the roof as though expecting fire to rain on top of her. I turn to Maude.

"What do we do?" I ask.

"We need to be cold," Maude says. She grabs what looks like an old traffic cone, runs out into the open, and fills it with snow. As she's hobbling back toward us she shouts, "Now we hide. They'll be over us in a minute. The tank should be safe. Get that hatch open." Alina comes to her senses and we all crawl back down into the belly of the tank. I have no idea why we have to do this until Maude explains that the zips have body-heat sensors. Within seconds we are all in our underwear and rubbing ourselves with snow.

We sit shivering in the tank, listening to the drone of the zips overhead and our own teeth chattering. "Are tanks thermo-detector-proof?" Alina asks.

"'Course not," Maude snaps. "But it's the best we've got." Maude reaches into the cone, scoops out another handful of snow, and launches it at Alina. And rather than leaping for Maude's neck, Alina rubs the snow into her skin.

"Thank God for the weather," she says.

Once the roaring has subsided, Maude says, "We're clear, ladies," and, smiling, pulls her gnawed sweater over her head. "Now, Alina, what is it they say in the movies? *Take me to your leader?*" Alina doesn't laugh; she scrambles into her clothes and clambers back up the ladder, mumbling something under her breath.

When we emerge from the hatch, we straighten our clothes and airtanks and stand looking at one another for what feels like a very long time. Alina is scowling and shifting from one foot to another. Maude is humming.

"Do you think Quinn's dead?" I ask. Silence is the only possible response. "Do you?" I repeat quietly, so they know I'm not about to collapse into a fit of hysteria. Maude stops humming and touches my face. Her scrawny fingers rest on my cheek for a moment and then she pulls her hand away.

"I'm about to take you into the hub of the Resistance," Alina says, without answering me: she is brave, but even she hasn't the courage to pronounce Quinn dead. "You are never, *ever* to reveal this location to anyone. You need to know that if you betray the Resistance, Petra *will* have you killed. In fact, I will probably kill you myself. Now let's move." She buttons up her coat and marches out of the garage.

"She's so mean," Maude says, rattling along after Alina, a thick thread of mockery in her tone.

"You better watch your smart mouth from now on," I warn Maude. "I'm worried about Petra."

"Pah!" she snorts.

"Seriously," I say.

We turn right at the first road, left at the next, and eventually come face-to-face with a colossal, frosted glass building: the RATS headquarters. My legs feel shaky as we approach the steps. I can't help wondering whether or not I should have turned back and gone home a long time ago. I lean on Maude to steady myself.

Alina turns, sees me, and stops. "Everything good?"

"It's icy," I say. Alina nods and continues walking.

"Don't let anyone see you're afraid," Maude whispers.

I release her and reach for the balustrade at the bottom of the steps. Then I swallow hard and start climbing.

29
QUINN

I don't want to be paranoid or anything, but Inger and Silas have been hunched together in serious debate for the last mile or so, and now, even though they saved my life, I'm wondering whether they're planning to murder me. "We don't really have a choice," Inger says, nodding in my direction. Inger stops, takes out a tattered paper map peppered with small green crosses, and points to one of them. "Here," he says.

Silas stops, too. "Where did you get that?" he asks, taking the map from Inger and examining it. I peer over Silas's shoulder to see if I can work out where we are, but I can't.

"I made it. Petra's orders. Almost finished," Inger says.

"You made this? And all these crosses are solar respirators?" he asks.

"Yep," Inger says. He glances at me and then away.

"But what about the . . ." Silas begins.

"Most of them were dead already," Inger says.

"And the ones who weren't?" Silas asks. "You didn't, did you?" Silas suddenly steps away from Inger.

"Of course I didn't. It's a map. Petra wanted a list of locations for emergencies. When I found one alive, I didn't mark it down because we can't be sure they won't relocate." He looks at me. "His canister's parched. Tighten his valve," Inger commands. Silas steps toward me and twists the valve of my airtank. For a moment I'm sure he's going to twist it three hundred and sixty degrees and leave me a puddle of choking bones on the road, but he doesn't.

"I'm reducing the density. Breathe normally," he says. I feel the air start to thin, and I try to do as he says, but the drop in oxygen makes me panic and I begin to hyperventilate. "Calm down, will you?" Silas shakes me, making me feel even dizzier. I stagger backward and he has to catch me. He readjusts the valve on my tank, and once I can breathe again, I nod.

Silas and Inger give each other a look, then Inger grunts. "We don't have a choice," he says. "Let's go."

"What's wrong?" I ask. I try to sound nonchalant. "How much farther?"

Silas and Inger exchange a whisper and abruptly change direction. "Guys?" My voice is a croak. Suddenly Silas stops and stares up at a tall, red-brick building and rubs his forehead.

"We haven't seen zips for years, which means trouble. They're on the hunt and Petra will need us," Inger says. "If we try to share our air with you it will slow us down and we could be leaving The Grove in peril. Plus, we can't even be sure we have enough in our tanks to get us all there no matter what speed we travel at. You need a lot more oxygen than we do." Inger has taken on a military manner. He is even standing rigidly.

"In other words, if you come with us, you'll die," Silas says.

"We've reached an impasse." Inger is solemn. I think that means he plans to put me out of my misery. And maybe he'd be right to do it: I've heard that suffocation is the worst kind of death. I push my shoulders back. Silas is still staring at the red-brick building. "Maybe 'impasse' is too strong a word," Inger goes on, peering into the sky. "Come on," he says, leading me into the building Silas has been gawking at.

Inside the building is a steep set of stairs. "Get on my back," Silas says. "You're not going to make it to the top if you don't." I swallow my pride and do as he says. We climb up the stairs, passing the doors that declare FIRST FLOOR, SECOND FLOOR, all the way up to the TWELFTH FLOOR where Silas, now gasping himself, shrugs me off. It is only one more flight until we reach a door that says ROOFTOP. Inger pushes open the heavy fire door and we step into the sunlight again, onto a roof overlooking endless rows of tumbledown houses, apartment blocks, and twisting roads.

On the horizon are the outlines of huge buildings with domes and spires. I've seen them in pictures though I can't remember their names now. If only I could spot Bea or Alina, or even Maude, but the city and the snow obscure almost everything. Inger leads us to a far corner of the rooftop where we come upon a thick, clear tarpaulin covering a solar respirator. Inger yanks it off, turns a button, and shakes the respirator until it rattles to life. He removes his own facemask and presses the filthy one attached to the respirator to his face. He stays there for a few seconds, breathing in and out deeply, then hands the facemask to me.

"This is your lifeline. Take it." I pull off my mask and replace it with the one Inger is holding out. I breathe in. The air coming from the respirator is humid and the smell is enough to make me want to vomit.

"There's about three months' charge in this thing," Inger tells me. "But it isn't portable. It's an early model."

"How will I ever get back?" I ask. Silas looks pleased that I've figured out what's going on.

"I'll try to come for you, or I'll send someone."

"When?"

"Until we know what's happening at The Grove, I can't know for sure," Silas says.

"I'll starve," I tell them.

"You can survive on water for weeks," Inger informs me.

"I don't have any." I know I sound scared, and I no longer have any desire to hide it.

"It's going to snow for days. There are containers up here," Silas says. He points at some buckets and bins scattered across the rooftop. "You can fill them with snow and eat it."

"If a Ministry vehicle rolls by, throw something down to attract its attention. Or wave at the zips. You're Premium. You'll be safe. Tell them we kidnapped you or something," Inger says.

I want to promise not to betray the Resistance, but I can't. I want to promise to die for the cause, but who knows what I'll do at the end if I'm starving and desperate?

"I hope you find them," I say. "If you come across Bea, tell her—" I stop.

"We'll come back for you," Inger says.

"If it was true what you said, about saving Alina . . . well, thank you," Silas adds, speaking softly. Then, before I can think how to say good-bye, they've turned away and disappeared through the rooftop door, leaving me alone.

30
BEA

I am almost blinded by the sun reflecting off the glass panels and have to shield my eyes with my arm as we trudge up the seemingly endless stairs. If aliens ever land on Earth, I imagine they will arrive in a vessel shaped much like this building: it stretches out, seeming to have devoured everything beneath it in one clean gulp. On the side of the building is a large red crest with a picture of what looks like an old cannon.

"What was this place?" I ask.

"I told you. It's the stadium where they played soccer. There are colossal places like this all over the country."

"I didn't imagine it would be so big."

"Before The Switch, soccer was everyone's game. Thousands of people would go watch and teams were bigger back then, too."

"I can't imagine a time when auxiliaries had the same chances as Premiums. I wish we were that free." I stretch both my arms toward the stadium.

"Free? Ha!" Maude shouts. "What's free? Oh, we could breathe all right, yes, but there weren't never a time when we was free. Free don't mean nothing. Look back in history and all you'll see will be Elysian Fields. It weren't that way. It ain't never that way. People is people and greed is greed. There weren't never a time of true equality. Women didn't play in that stadium and get the same crowds as the men: no one cared how many goals a woman scored. Freedom and equality is myths, girls. Yous should learn that now. Freedom? Ha!"

"Are you finished?" Alina asks. Maude sticks out her tongue. It strikes me that Alina wouldn't want to know if the world as it existed before The Switch were ugly: the idea of a world with breathable air in it is the paradise she's fighting to rebuild. If that world were anything but perfect, it would make Alina's struggle less important somehow.

We trudge up the last few steps, but rather than heading for what looks like the entrance, we stop at a concrete wall. Alina turns to check that no one is watching, that we haven't been tailed, and gestures for us to follow. We make our way around the perimeter and along the concrete wall that is intermittently interrupted by steel doors. An old railroad comes into view, many of the train carriages windowless and lying on their sides.

Alina stops, approaches a door, and knocks. Three knocks, a pause, two knocks, another pause, and a final knock. Nothing happens. Alina glances at me, then tries the code again: three knocks, a pause, two knocks, a pause, a final knock. Still nothing happens.

I look down at the valve on my tank and take a liberal lungful of air. I only have a minute or two before it runs out. As though she's read my mind, Alina reaches over and tightens the valve. Instantly I feel lightheaded and have to lean against the wall to stay on my feet. Alina tries knocking again.

"Is there another way in? Maybe we're at the wrong door," I manage to say, finding my balance.

"We're at the right door."

"Maybe you should call out. Maybe you forgot the code."

"I didn't forget the code. It's an easy code." Alina stands frowning with her hands on her hips.

"Did they *change* the code?" I ask.

"They never change it!" Alina glares at the handle as though it might turn and the door magically open simply because she wills it to.

Maude eventually speaks up. "They're hiding. And they could be hiding for hours. Do you have a bunker?"

Alina looks at Maude and nods. I realize what it is they're saying: the Resistance had to hide from the thermo-detectors when the zips flew overhead and that means no one is aboveground to hear us knocking.

Alina leans her head against the sealed steel door and screams. Then she starts to pound on the door, first with her fists, but eventually with her head, too. She bangs her head again and again and again, until a thick streak of blood appears on her forehead. I grab her and pull her away. "It's me! It's Alina! If you don't want us to die out here, open the door!"

"They . . . can't . . . hear . . . you!" Maude shouts. She slides down onto the walkway, picks at a festering scab on her neck, and laughs.

"Open the door!" Alina hollers, my arms still wrapped around her. "OPEN THE DOOR!" Eventually she collapses against me. "I'm sorry I involved you in all this, Bea," she whispers. "You didn't want to be a part of it. You were a tourist. If I die, at least I'll have died for something."

"You did what you could to save us," I say, and squeeze Alina into me.

"But what does your death mean? It has to *mean* something," she says.

I should have an answer. Because though I didn't have to follow anyone, I did. So what *was* it for? Love? That was part of it. But it wasn't just Quinn I followed in the end, it was Alina, too. And Maude. I could have turned around at any moment, slipped back through Border Control and taken the tram home to my parents who will now never know what really happened. I want to cry, not for myself, but for my parents and what I am about to make them suffer.

I look into Alina's green eyes and say, "I will die because I knew there had to be a better way to live."

"You didn't find it," Alina says. "I wish you could've found it. I'm sorry."

"I did, Alina. I breathed freely for two days." This makes Alina hug me even tighter. Maude, who is staring at us, whispers something I can't hear.

"What did you say?" I want Maude to know that her last words are important, that she is important to someone. She pushes me away and starts to rub her scab again.

Even though Alina's fist is already rubbed raw, she tries again: three knocks, a pause, two knocks, a pause, one final knock. I try to take over, but she waves me away. "Save your energy," she says. I am about to turn the valve on my tank again when I realize it's too late; the air thins.

I tap my tank, trying to release any dregs of oxygen remaining in it, and the sound is diluted by a hollow thrumming in my ears and Alina's knocking.

My chest tightens and a blazing heat makes my lungs

shrivel up. I try not to inhale. I try to exist on whatever air is already in me. But I'm dizzy, everything around me dipping and diving as though I've just stepped off a merry-go-round. I think I'm going to pass out. Instead I feel a thick, sweet liquid in my throat and I let it dribble out of my mouth and onto the gray concrete.

I pull off my facemask to breathe in again, fighting for whatever oxygen remains in the atmosphere. Flames lick at my throat and in my lungs there's an explosion of fire.

I can hardly see. Maude and Alina appear like ghosts. Completely silent.

I hiss. I wheeze.

And I am out.

31
QUINN

I lean out over the edge of the roof and make out Silas and Inger on the street below. From this distance, and with all the snow everywhere, it looks like they are holding hands, and I can't quite tell them apart. One of them gestures wildly up the street in the direction we came from. Within a few seconds, they've set off, walking at a sharp pace without looking back. I want to call out, but what could I say? *Don't forget about me!* And if there are soldiers around, making noise will simply draw attention to them and put them in danger.

I slump down onto the wet rooftop, not caring that I'm sitting in a puddle of snow. Scattered around me are snow-coated chairs and upended tables and loads of buckets, most of them within reach. The tube connecting my facemask to the solar respirator is about four feet long, in no way long enough to allow me to take any leisurely strolls around the rooftop.

How did this happen? I've gone from rarely thinking about the air I breathe to spending most of my waking moments worrying about whether or not I'll have enough. This is how auxiliaries must feel all the time. This is how Bea feels. Until today I've never really understood what it must be like to crave air so desperately. I understand now, though.

"Keep calm, Quinn," I say aloud. "Chill out." But talking to myself doesn't help. It only makes me freak out even more. Doesn't talking to myself prove I'm on the road to madness?

The worst-case scenario is that Silas and Inger get killed before they ever have a chance to tell anyone where I am, and I die slowly and painfully of exposure, starvation, and dehydration. Or maybe not. The actual worst-case scenario is that Bea dies this way—alone and afraid. No. She's too clever to let something like this happen to her, and even if she were in my shoes, she'd stay calm and come up with a plan.

I pull a nutrient bar from my backpack and tear off the wrapping. Then I stuff the entire thing into my mouth and start chewing. It's the last one I've got, and maybe I should've taken a small nibble from it, but if I'm going to figure out a way to escape, I need to feed my brain.

I stand and take a look out across the city again. A convoy

of about twenty armored tanks is rolling down the buckled roads from the east—from the pod—in pairs. The tanks advance at some speed through the snow and rubble, crushing any obstacle along the road. I can see there are foot soldiers as well, hundreds of them. And they aren't marching in a troop but dividing, fanning out in small groups. They're looking for something. Or someone.

I can still see the tiny figures of Silas and Inger, heading straight for the soldiers. "Silas! Inger! Silas!" I holler. For a moment one of them stops and holds the other back. But then they are off again. "The Ministry's coming!" I shout. "SILAS! INGER!" Both of them seem to hear something this time and look in my direction. "It isn't safe! They're coming! SILAS!"

The soldiers are closing in on Silas and Inger, who have remained where they are, facing each other. "RUN!" I scream, not caring who else hears me. "RUN!" And they do. In opposite directions. Inger is coming my way, back toward this building. The soldiers must have heard or seen something because they are running now, too, darting down roads and alleyways. Inger is sprinting, weaving his way between buildings and leaping over mounds of rubble.

He slips in the snow and falls. He struggles to stand and starts to limp forward. The soldiers are very close to him and they aren't slowing down. I hold my breath. I don't call out.

He is right beneath me. He is so close I can see him rub his leg. He limps and limps and, just as the soldiers round the corner, he ducks into the building across the street for cover. Too late.

The soldiers stop outside the building. One of them pulls out a radio. Within a minute all the tanks and soldiers are speeding this way. The soldiers on foot merge into one troop again, and before long the entire unit is positioned below me. The tank engines shut down and instantly it is silent.

When Silas discarded my portable airtank, there was still a shred of oxygen left. I retrieve it from the ground, wipe away the snow, and refit it. Then I'm on my way downstairs. At the bottom, I crouch behind an old filing cabinet near a broken window where I can hear and see everything. If it looks like they plan to hurt him, I'll show myself. I'm a Premium. I must have some power. Surely they wouldn't hurt me.

Another soldier, tall and with perfect composure, emerges from a tank and climbs down. He is wearing the same hefty black helmet as the rest of them, but a different uniform. "Go in there and get him," he says, waving his hand casually as though retrieving Inger from the building is nothing but an inconvenience. "And bring him out alive," he adds. A team of twenty soldiers file into the building. I can hear their boots.

He approaches a soldier standing frighteningly close to

the window I'm peering through. "How many did you see, Captain?" the general asks. His voice is chilling and flat.

"Two, General. Two men, we think, sir," the captain responds.

"And are these the same men responsible for stealing our tank?"

"I doubt it, sir. The tank went missing five miles from here. We have zips looking for it, sir."

"I want that tank found, Captain. And the culprits, too."

"I understand, sir. We *are* going to find them."

"You'd better," the general says, moving away from the captain and talking into a radio. The general's voice, muffled though it is, is strangely familiar. My father is always bringing high-ranking ministers and officials to the house. Is it possible I've met this man before?

Inger is dragged from the building and made to kneel in front of the general, who kicks him in the chest. Inger shouts and falls backward. A soldier pulls him up again, and this time the general kicks him in the back of the head. I look away.

"That's me being kind," the general tells Inger. "If you want to know what I can do when I'm angry, you should lie to me. If you want to live, tell me where the other one is."

"What other one?" There is blood running down Inger's face and neck.

"I want to know who you were with and where he went. Does your family live in the pod? How about your friends? What have you been doing out here? Planting? Cultivating the earth?" The general laughs. "You people don't seem to realize that what you're doing is pointless. Do you know how long it would take to re-oxygenate the planet? A millennium. And by that time you'll be long dead."

"Then why are you chasing us?" Inger shouts. The general grabs a clump of Inger's hair in his hand and pulls his face toward him. That's when I spot the Breathe insignia on the general's jacket.

"Tell us where the Resistance is located or I will rip off your head, you sniveling little bastard." His voice is ice, and I have no doubt he means to do as he says.

"This war is on. We have Premiums on our side. And you're finished," Inger says. He spits into the general's face. The general releases Inger and knees him hard in the throat. Inger rolls and groans. The general climbs a pile of rubble and holds a loudspeaker to his face. "We have your friend. If you come out, we won't hurt him," he announces, though he's already beaten him to a pulp. "I repeat. We have your friend." I definitely recognize that voice, especially through the loudspeaker.

"Forget it," Inger says, "he's long gone by now."

"Captain, get the juice," the general demands. The

captain scurries to a tank nearby and comes back with a monster weapon that he points at a scrub of vegetation covered in snow. Black foam bursts from the nozzle, and the feeble grassy area is a withered mess by the time the captain has finished. "Even if you manage to grow anything," the general says, "well, I think the captain has illustrated what would happen."

"So it's true. Herbicide. What's the next formula you're working on? Toxic water?"

"Don't be dramatic, son," the general says, and laughs.

And that's when I know. There's no mistaking it. All my limbs twitch. It can't be. But it is. I wait for him to say something else, anything else to prove I'm wrong. Instead, he takes his helmet off and pulls a facemask and some tubing from his uniform, and when he turns around I go cold because the general is my father.

For a moment I can't breathe. I look at my tank and though the oxygen level is fatally low, it's not completely drained. I stare at my father and then press my fists into my eye sockets, taking shallow, even breaths. I stand up, about to run outside and save Inger, when a hand pulls me back down.

It's Silas. "What the hell are you doing? They'll kill you."

"That's my father," I croak. Silas doesn't understand.

"Shut up and stay down."

"That's my father," I say again. Silas stares at me. *That's my father,* I think. The man out there in charge. That's my father. I thought he pushed paper around a desk. I thought he did something useful but boring.

"What about Inger?" I whisper. Silas hunkers down next to me and he's so close I think I can feel him shaking. We peer over the lip of an old filing cabinet. Outside my father is pacing back and forth. This is what he does when he deliberates; I see it all the time. He stops and scratches his head, looking at Inger as if his prisoner might tell him what to do. Usually I'm frightened of my father when he has this look because it means bad news for me. Now I am terrified because I know it must mean terrible news for Inger.

"The Pod Minister made his instructions very clear," my father says in a low voice. "I can't save you. I doubt I could help you even if you were my own son." Silas looks at me in horror.

My father turns and climbs onto the turret of the tank. "Captain," he says, clicking his fingers, "take care of him." Then he vanishes.

The captain nods at the soldiers next to Inger, who pull him to his feet, remove his airtank, and throw it aside. Inger doesn't struggle. Even when his tank has been removed he stands rigid.

"Your last moments are free ones," the captain tells Inger, and the soldiers step aside so he can walk away, or run, or do whatever he pleases. Inger takes a few breathless steps and I expect him to run toward the building we are in, where he knows there is a solar respirator, but instead he turns and hobbles into the building they dragged him from not long ago.

"Attention!" the captain cries, and every soldier salutes before taking his place in line. Within a few minutes every tank and soldier is out of sight.

Silas jumps up and hurtles across the street. On his way he grabs Inger's tank. I've never seen a person run so fast and without thinking, I bolt after him.

We find Inger lying across the foyer. He is completely still. Silas pushes the mask into his face and opens the valve wide so Inger gets a high dose of oxygen. Inger doesn't move. Silas tries blowing air into his mouth. Then he shakes him. "Inger. Inger, you're safe now," he says. "Wake up." Inger is so still and looks so peaceful there can be no mistaking it: he is dead.

Silas hangs his head and presses his hands into Inger's chest. He sniffs and I look away. When I turn around again, Silas wipes the blood from Inger's face with the cuff of his sleeve. Then he buttons up Inger's coat and rearranges his limbs so that Inger is lying as straight as he would in a coffin. "Was that really your dad?" he asks.

I nod. I'm too numb to do anything else.

"What are you going to do?"

I shrug. I don't know what to do. I don't even know what my options are.

"I'm sorry," he says. We both look at Inger, and I don't have a desire to fill the silence with noise. Not even remotely. Maybe I'll never want to say anything pointless ever again. I just want to walk, to get out of here. Silas hands me Inger's airtank. "He doesn't need it. And I think you'll only be safe if you come with me. Did you leave anything on the roof?"

I shake my head. We both take one long, last look at Inger before venturing out into the dusk. I have no idea where we're heading, and I no longer care.

32
BEA

When I come around, I am breathing normally and being dragged along the ground. Maude is looking down at me, grinning. Alina is there, too.

"She's alive," a young man says, bolting the steel door. I try to sit up, but a lightheadedness rocks me back again. "Don't let her up for a minute," the young man continues. "Her brain's all out of whack. This'll be the worst hangover she's ever had." He crouches down and peers at me with stone-gray eyes. I smile. He pulls a few strands of hair from my mask. "There's plenty of air in that new cylinder I gave you. Are you feeling all right?" I nod and glance around; although we are inside, the cold is still piercing and I can hear the wind.

"Thank God you came to the door when you did,

Dorian," Alina says. He turns to Alina and they embrace. "I wasn't sure if my technique was working. I thought she was dead," she says.

"What technique?" I manage.

"One breath for you, one breath for me," she says, pointing to her own tank. She reaches into an open metal locker and takes two tanks from it. After Alina and Maude have been fitted with a fresh air supply, Dorian pulls me to my feet and helps me move along a wide walkway with them.

"I knew they wouldn't send out the zips for no reason. They had to be looking for someone," he says.

"Didn't Petra try to stop you?" Alina asks.

"Of course she did. Everyone else is in the bunker. She's locked up the entire stadium and threatened to slice my throat if I left the bunker."

"Thank you," Alina says.

"Oh, I can't wait to meet Petra. I think she's gonna just love me," Maude says.

"You haven't met Petra?" Dorian asks us. I shake my head. Dorian stops and turns to Alina. "Does she even know about them? Are they Resistance? I assume they're pod division. Alina?"

"They're civilians," Alina says.

"You brought civilians without authorization? And *I* let

them in? Someone might be getting his throat cut after all." He rubs his forehead.

"She can be trusted," Alina says pointing at me. "She saved my life."

"And the other one?"

Alina studies Maude carefully, trying to decide whether or not to offer her up as a sacrifice.

"The old woman, Alina. Can we trust her?"

"Yes," Alina says slowly. "I suppose we can."

Dorian lets out a long whistle. "We should go down into the bunker. The zips might still be swarming," he says.

"They went right over and kept going," Alina says. "Let's show them around first." She seems proud of this place. Dorian shrugs and we follow Alina down the wide concrete walkway, lined with kiosks.

Nothing could have prepared me for what I see when we turn and enter the stadium. I am expecting a gaping snow-filled pit. We are standing on a shallow set of steps next to rows and rows and rows of seats. There must be thousands of seats in this stadium. Tens of thousands of red plastic seats and on them, hundreds and hundreds of mismatched oblong boxes with makeshift lids.

"It can't be," I say, looking beyond the boxes to the soccer field. Dorian smiles. I stagger forward and he catches me.

In place of the players and goalposts, in place even of a carefully cropped lawn, the entire area is covered with sparkling, snow-laden trees.

More trees than I have ever seen in my life, and they are towering over us, climbing toward the sky.

There must be hundreds, all different shapes and sizes, some bare and spiky, others fully clothed in coats of leaves.

"Trees," I murmur. I blink to make sure I am not hallucinating. When I open my eyes the trees are still there and Maude is running down the steps toward them.

"Holy Mackerel!" she hollers. Alina and Dorian share a smile. I've never seen anything as splendid in my life. The trees are so strong and alive, even those without leaves, and they are driving their way up toward the sealed, slated roof of the stadium; I begin to run too, but my knees buckle and I fall.

"Oh my . . . " I sigh. Many of them almost reach the roof of the stadium. "How? And when? I mean . . . How?" I don't know where to begin. Alina pulls me off the floor. I lean against a seat to keep my balance. "Trees," I whisper. I have never prayed. I do not know how. But if I did, I would say a prayer now, in homage to the trees and to the Resistance for creating this place.

"She's obviously one of us," Dorian says, and that's when I become fully aware of the second wonder. We are in the open air and Dorian is without a facemask. Instinctively, and a little irrationally, I reach up and touch his chest to see whether or not he has a heart. He doesn't pull away and we stay there for a minute as I feel the rise and fall of his chest. "You can't be human," I whisper, getting to my feet.

"He is," Alina says, putting an arm around my waist.

"I don't understand. How do you live?"

"Slowly," he says. "And if you stick around long enough, we'll show you how to do it, too."

33
ALINA

Dorian keeps shooting me looks as we head toward the bunker. I shake my head because I'm afraid that if I speak, Dorian will hear the tangle in my voice. Coming alone wouldn't have been a problem—I had no choice but to flee the pod. But there is little excuse for bringing two unknowns with me, especially when one of them is ex-Breathe. Petra has strict rules. How else could she maintain security here? How else could she protect the trees? "What happened?" Dorian asks finally, pointing at my blood-stained bandage. I'd almost forgotten. I can't tell Dorian or anyone here what really happened, or Maude will be in for it.

"Long story," I say.

"So you fled," Dorian says. This is a question.

"Abel's dead," I tell him simply. I won't betray myself,

won't reveal that there's more to Abel's death than a comrade falling. Resistance members die all the time and there's a protocol for grief. We gather, we remember, we raise our arms in defiance of the Ministry, and we move on. Keep planting. This is a place of action: there is no time to mourn.

"Abel? I don't know him. Was he new? How did he die?" Dorian asks.

"He was a terrorist. Killed as he tried to destroy the pod. Apparently."

"How original. Poor guy."

"I don't know what to tell Petra," I say.

"Just tell her the truth," he says.

"I will, but listen—let me go in first and you hang back with these two while I talk to her. I'll soften her up a bit before I tell her I've compromised her life's work." I give Dorian a pleading look. We both know that if he agrees to hide them, even for a few minutes, he'll be complicit. He looks back at Maude and Bea.

They are still giddy. I don't blame them. When I first saw the trees I was in a state of euphoria for days. I don't usually go around grinning, but I couldn't help myself. After spending my entire life being told that any existence outside the pod was impossible, the idea that there could be something else was mind-blowing. That my parents had died for something was comforting, too.

"We missed you," Dorian says suddenly. He throws his arm around my shoulder and squeezes me. Dorian and I have flirted with each other at times, but I can't do it today.

"I wish I could come with better news," I say. I laugh, though I don't know why.

"When has anyone ever turned up here unexpectedly with good news, Alina?"

Bea joins us, first pointing to Dorian's mouth and then her own facemask. "How do you do that?" she asks.

"How about I show you the lab where we keep the seedlings and cuttings first? Later I'll explain all this. Let's go."

Bea stares at me. "Aren't you coming with us?"

I glance at Dorian. "I'm going to see Petra. Follow me down once you've had the tour. Show them the bunks, Dorian. And the showers. We have hot water here."

"Aye aye, cap'n!" Dorian salutes.

"What's going on, Alina?" Bea asks.

"Don't worry. Take a look around." I hurry along the wide corridor and down the stairs. The lower level is in absolute darkness, and I have to feel my way along the damp concrete wall to find the door to the bunker. I knock using the code. After a minute there is a click, a sucking sound, and the heavy door swings inward. I slip inside and push it closed behind me. "Alina," a voice whispers.

"Hey, Jazz!" I say, touching her spirally red hair. "Where is she?"

"Sleeping," Jazz says. "Why are you here?"

"The usual."

"Who died?" she asks.

I can't say his name. "A new recruit," I tell her.

"A new one? That's the worst," she says. "Do you want me to wake her?"

"You better not," I say.

"No. *You* better not. I can do what I like." Jazz bounces ahead of me into the dimly lit bunker. She is the youngest of us: a nine-year-old and the only person I know who was actually born in The Outlands. But her mother couldn't cope, gave up, and left the Resistance long before I ever joined. She abandoned Jazz, just a baby at the time, without leaving a note, and no one ever heard from her again. Jazz spends most of her days skipping through the corridors of The Grove and chattering with anyone who'll stop to smile at her. When she isn't playing, she's wherever Petra is.

I follow her. Every available bit of space is occupied by someone either lying on a bunk bed or sitting cross-legged on the hard floor: all two hundred or so Resistance members must be hunkering down here, and many of them are reading paper books. There are columns of salvaged books stacked up against one whole side of the bunker. "Alina!" a voice calls out. Then someone else calls my name. Within minutes I'm surrounded by twenty or more friends hugging me. No one is wearing supplemental oxygen and eventually Song, Dorian's cousin, unbuckles the mask from my face.

"You don't need that," he says, pointing up at the vents. "I've got it set to eighteen percent. That should be enough for you, shouldn't it?" I nod. Song is our biochemist, and once he'd helped the engineers install the camouflage blinds for the roof of the stadium, he quickly figured out a method for farming, storing, and transferring the oxygen from the trees and plants in the stadium to certain locations in the building. Even though most members can do what Dorian does, there are times when everyone indulges in higher levels of oxygen—just to keep their brains healthy. Song is an invaluable member of the Resistance and never released for missions. Petra keeps a close watch over her prized recruits.

"Thanks," I say, handing him my airtank.

Jazz elbows her way into the center of the group. "Hey, you've gotta come. Petra's up. She's in the back alcove. She's waiting." I follow Jazz into the recesses of the bunker and find Petra sitting on top of an elevated mattress covered in a plethora of multicolored blankets and pillows. Petra's legs are crossed, her eyes are shut, and she is humming. Her graying, waist-length dreadlocks, normally twisted into a thick chignon, are unfurled—snaking their way down her back and thin, bare arms. "She's meditating," Jazz whispers. "She's memorizing strength and endurance." I nod and we watch her. All Resistance members practice meditation with Petra. Jazz is pretty good at it. She climbs up onto the bed and sits cross-legged next to Petra, then closes her eyes, too. I study them for a few minutes, focusing in on Petra's right arm, which is covered with a sprawling tattoo. The spindly roots of a dark tree begin on her hands. The trunk climbs up her forearm and the branches and leaves fan out at her elbow and continue to spread up across her shoulders toward her chest. Jazz has a new tattoo of her own—a small cluster of orange flowers above one eyebrow.

Petra stops humming, opens an eye, and nods at me. She gets up and stands in front of me, close enough for a few loose strands of hair to tickle my face. I step back.

"Alina," Petra says, taking my hands and pressing them between her own. "There must be a fire of resistance burning in the pod for them to send out the zips. We heard tanks, too. What's the news? We didn't expect you so soon. Did you get the clippings?" She gazes intently at me.

"I did, Petra."

"Good." She lets go of my hands and turns to retrieve a full-length, long brown coat from a makeshift hook on the wall. It is patchy and worn—a relic from a bygone age. She starts to button it up.

"People are in danger."

"What happened?" Petra asks in a whisper so no one will overhear.

"The stewards came for me. They were armed and weren't going to leave without an arrest. I escaped, but Silas was there. And my aunt and uncle may be in serious trouble, too. I didn't know what else to do." I am rambling. Petra does this to me. "Maybe I shouldn't have come," I say.

"Why not? Why would you say that?" she asks quietly.

"I don't know."

"You did the right thing coming, Alina." She kisses my forehead and cups her hand under my chin. Her skin is dry and cool. She looks at Jazz for the briefest of seconds and almost smiles.

"Thank you, Petra," I say, standing a little taller. "But there is one dead. A new recruit. Abel."

"Abel? You mean Aaron."

"No, it wasn't Aaron. Aaron's fine, I think. It was Abel. He was Pod Resistance only."

"I don't know the name. Jazz?"

Jazz opens her eyes, looks up at the ceiling, and then back at Petra. "Never heard of him."

"Are you *sure* it wasn't Aaron?"

I nod. "Silas said you authorized him," I say, but with Petra's shrewd eyes on me, I'm not sure. Did Silas tell me that or did Abel tell me that Silas had received authorization from Petra? "I think Silas told me."

"You *think*?" Petra says.

"Silas definitely told me." If Silas didn't tell me that, if Petra has never heard of Abel, then who was he? Why would he lie to me to get into the Resistance and then die for the cause?

"Well, if this Abel is dead, we needn't worry, Petra," Jazz pipes up. Petra nods. I swallow and clench my jaw.

"So tell me, if they had you flagged, how did you pass security?" Petra asks.

"Uh . . . I . . ." I stutter, not knowing how to tell her about Bea and Quinn.

"Don't be ashamed. We've all found creative ways to survive," she says. In order to escape, many members of the Resistance, especially the girls, have had to offer up their own bodies to the stewards in exchange for safe passage through Border Control. Some recruits have betrayed friends to get across, and there are those, like Petra, who have murdered for freedom.

"I befriended a Premium," I begin. Petra nods.

"Did he hurt you?"

"It wasn't like that. We didn't—" I stop to arrange

my thoughts. "He was with an auxiliary, a girl, and they found a way to get me across. They followed me and—" I pause. "They saved my life again a few hours later when a drifter . . . Well, that doesn't matter, but they followed me and saved me. We were nervous about leaving the drifter behind so we brought her with us. She's a little old woman. She isn't a threat to anyone. I meant to give them the slip but we were chased and I couldn't."

Jazz has given up pretending to meditate and is watching me with large eyes. Petra breathes in and out deeply through her nose. She pulls her hair out of her face and secures it behind her head using a small band.

"Don't tell me." She covers her eyes with a hand.

"They're upstairs. Not the Premium, but a drifter and the girl. I'm sorry. I'm so sorry."

Jazz gasps and starts to wriggle. Petra steps back, perhaps to prevent herself from striking me. She takes her hand from her eyes.

"You've compromised our way of life to save a drifter?"

"No, I—"

"Where is the Premium?"

"He got captured, I think. Nowhere near here. Or buried alive. A tank came and fired at us. I managed to get to the Underground with Bea and Maude. I couldn't very well leave them. He didn't make it." Until now I've tried to believe that

Quinn's alive. But the chances of that are slim. And though he annoyed me so much I wanted to hurt him, my stomach tightens when I think of him writhing for breath. He was a Premium, but he wasn't the worst of them. He didn't deserve to die. I can't tell Petra this. To her, no Premium, especially one whose father works for Breathe, can have value. A tree in the stadium is more important to her than Quinn's life.

"So you've brought two civilians here. Do you even know who the drifter is? Do you know what she's done and what she's capable of doing?"

"Yes, Petra. Ex-Breathe. I thought you could use her."

"You thought? You *thought*? Do you remember the vows you took? The rules for protecting our project?"

"Yes, Petra, I just—"

"Your Premium must be alive. He must have led the zips here."

"He doesn't know where The Grove is. I think . . ." I take a deep breath. "I think *I* drew them here."

"You?" A thin vein in Petra's temple throbs.

"I stole a tank," I admit.

"You what?" Her eyes narrow.

"You what?" Jazz shouts, jumping up from the bed and standing next to Petra. "She stole a tank," Jazz repeats, tugging on Petra's coat. "Did you hear that?" Petra puts a finger to Jazz's lips.

"I thought we could use it. I didn't know that I—"

"You have started a war," Petra snarls.

"It's war now," Jazz repeats in a twitchy whisper. She pulls a curly piece of red hair into her mouth and sucks on it.

"Our goal is to be invisible. Did you forget that?" I shake my head. "Jazz, I need Roxanne and Levi," Petra says, and Jazz scuttles away. "You bring two unknowns and you steal from the Ministry. You also tell me that you recruited in the pod without authorization. Your stupidity is dazzling. I ought to expel you. We would be well within our rights to shoot you."

"I got the cuttings you wanted," I whisper.

"And we are being invaded as a result. It's a good thing Levi heard the zips in time for us to shut down or we would be dust already."

Jazz returns with Roxanne and Levi, and I'm glad for the distraction because nothing I could say would justify all my stupid mistakes. Petra's right: I didn't follow protocol and now people will die. People are already dead.

"Boss?" It's Roxanne. She wears an eye patch over one eye. She is vital to the Resistance because she is ruthless: both she and Levi are.

"We have uninvited guests," Petra tells them. "Tie them up and put them in a cell. The old woman is a drifter, so take precautions with her. And remove whatever tanks they're using. I'd like to be in control of their oxygen consumption from now on. Order Song to pump some air into the cell."

Song appears at Petra's elbow as though she's conjured him up with her words. "What level?" he asks.

"Moderate. No more than twenty percent. They'll get used to it."

"Don't make them prisoners. There's no need for the cell," I say. Maude is wily, but I'm thinking of Bea. "We can trust them. I'm sure of it."

"You're sure, are you? Well, I'm sorry if I don't value your judgment: it hasn't exactly been flawless lately, has it?" Petra places a hand on Jazz's head. "Go with Roxanne and Levi, my sweet. Take the prisoners' weapons and supplies. Don't feed them." Jazz skips toward the bunker door in her bare feet as though she's about to go to the park while Roxanne and Levi stomp behind her like bodyguards.

"Please. There's no need for this. Really, Petra, they aren't a threat," I beg. But it's futile. I know Petra well enough to know that the trees come first.

She moves away, leaving me alone at the back of the bunker. "Listen up!" she calls out, addressing the entire room. "We're out of lockdown for now. Go back up to your posts. But be ready to come underground again at a minute's notice."

"What will *I* do?" I ask, following Petra as she stalks from the room.

"You?" Petra's voice dips to a murmur and she rolls up the cuffs on her coat. "You'll spend the rest of the day in the shooting range practicing."

"Practicing for what?"

"You were brave enough to start a war, Alina Moon, now you damn well better be prepared to fight in it."

34
BEA

Dorian is showing us the sleeping quarters when I'm seized from behind. Before I can struggle free or protest, my mask is removed and I am yanked, gasping for breath, down several flights of stairs and thrown into a concrete room with no windows. Maude is thrown in after me, though she has it worse: she's blindfolded, gagged, and her hands and feet are bound with twine. The door slams and all the light disappears.

The air in the room is thin, and it's as much as I can do to crawl on my hands and knees toward Maude. I feel like vomiting from the dizziness. "Maude," I say softly. I am removing her blindfold when a dim light enters the room and a high voice bellows beyond the door.

"Leave the old woman as she is!" In the door is a grate,

which must be an opening for food, and in this grate is the shadow of a face.

"Let her breathe. At least let me take off the gag. She's an old lady." After a pause, the voice speaks again.

"Fine, but if she starts yowling, we'll come in there and shut her up." The grate slides shut. I wait for my eyes to adjust to the darkness. Then I untie the gag and Maude takes the deepest breath she can.

"Why didn't you leave me back in the underground station?" she says. Her voice is hard and angry, as though I did her an injustice by saving her.

"That's an awful thing to say, Maude. You won't die. I won't let you," I say, despite the fact that I haven't really the power to save Maude any more than she has the power to save me. "Do you think something awful happened to Alina, too?"

Maude punches the floor. "Alina betrayed us. TRAITOR!" she screams.

"Shhh . . . They'll hurt you," I tell her, taking her hands and wrapping them up in my own. Perhaps she's right about Alina, whose eyes were tinted with guilt when she slunk off.

There is no toilet, nor is there a bed or a chair or anything else to sit on. It seems to be nothing more than a large, airtight storage cupboard. I sit with my legs out straight, my back against the cold wall. Maude lets out a groan and rests her head on my shoulder.

"Do you think the boy made it?" she asks. "He was strong-looking. And not a bad boy. He might have made it, you know."

"I loved him," I tell her. She must know this already. "I don't know why I loved him. He was my best friend. I know he cared about me; he just didn't want me in that way. He hugged me all the time, you know. He hugged me so tightly I always hoped it meant something. Then he'd pull away and smile and say good-bye as casually as always. He broke my heart every day without meaning to."

"Some people are designed to do that," she says.

"Do what?"

"Some people are designed to break our hearts." On the floor next to me is what feels like a broken earring. I pick it up and turn it over in my hand.

"I miss him."

"You'll miss him forever, Bea."

"I want to go home. My parents will worry. They work so hard and they're always sick. When Mrs. Caffrey got pregnant, Quinn hated the thought of his parents sleeping together, but I wish mine would. They deserve to love each other. I hope that without me there they can afford to do that. I miss them so much," I say.

Maude turns onto her side and starts to hum. I feel myself beginning to doze. The room seems to tighten around us as my eyelids grow heavy.

I am shaken awake by Alina. "Come with me," she says, handing me an airtank before my eyes are even open. Maude is in the corner, rolled into a ball. She is snoring, still blindfolded and bound.

"What about Maude?" I pull the facemask over my nose and mouth and tighten the straps at the back. The air in the mask is dense with oxygen. I suck in a gloriously deep breath.

"She'll be here when you get back. It wasn't easy to convince them to let you out. Come on." The light in the corridor is painfully bright and I have to squint to see. Alina relocks the cell door. She stands in front of me sheepishly. "I promise I didn't do this to you," she says. "Are you hungry?" I shrug, too weary to respond. Alina leads me down the corridor, back up the stairs to the main level of the stadium, then up again. Dorian was showing us this corridor when we were grabbed. I glance over my shoulder. "We're just going to eat. Don't worry." Alina pats my arm. "Would you like to see something special first?" I shrug again. I don't think there's anything that would surprise or excite me anymore. Alina isn't discouraged: she takes my hand and leads me to a glass door. "We have to be really quiet," she says, and pushes the door open.

Inside the room are about thirty people without face-masks. Half of them are sitting crossed-legged and straight-backed on one side of the room, their eyes closed, their lips slightly parted. The other half have twisted their bodies into odd shapes: there's a girl standing on her head, her toes pointing into the air; there's a boy lying on his back with his legs straight and pulled up to his face so that he could kiss his own knees; there is someone sitting up with her legs wrapped around her neck; someone else is standing on one leg holding the opposite foot straight out to the side. Their flexibility seems impossible. "Do you hear that noise?" Alina whispers. There is a crackling sound in the room like static electricity. I nod. "That's their breathing."

"I don't need the mask?" I ask.

"*You* do and so do I. There's only about six percent oxygen in here."

"But how? What is this place?" I ask.

"A training room. Everyone practices twice a day for three hours at a time. You asked Dorian how he did it: well, here's your answer. Relaxation is the key to preserving oxygen. Petra read all about it and began the practice here at The Grove. Before The Switch, free-divers used to do it. It helped them relax and hold their breath under water. Everyone in this room is lowering their heart rates and maximizing lung potential."

I have a thousand questions, but Alina turns and leads me out of the room. We walk several feet down the corridor until we come to another glass door. Alina pushes it open and inside there are many more Resistance members. They are all wearing facemasks and the room is noisy and hot. Each person here is ferociously exercising and sweating on a digital machine. A few of them wave at us as we enter. Alina raises a hand and smiles. I've seen these machines in the pod; the Premiums use them to keep fit. There are people climbing and rowing and running and cycling. "I thought you said relaxation is key."

"You have to be fit. You have to be strong. A tough heart is another essential element," she says.

"But they need *more* oxygen to do this."

"Exactly. Not as much as you'd need. Everyone in here is consuming a different amount depending on his or her level, which is why they use the masks."

"Right," I say, as though this all makes perfect sense.

"Anyway, we better get to dinner. We're at the first sitting with Petra. We don't want to be late."

"I don't get how . . ." I begin. Alina turns to me as we walk.

"Most of the people here have conditioned their bodies to

subsist on whatever the atmosphere offers. They can explore the world without any supplemental oxygen. They don't run marathons without airtanks, but they can walk at a good pace and talk and, most importantly, survive."

"Does the Ministry know?"

"They know something. And that's why they want us eliminated. Can you imagine what would happen if we all just walked up to the pod and showed everyone how trapped they are?"

"You'd be shot before you got there," I say. Alina nods. "So anyone can breathe without tanks," I say.

"Not everyone: people who are old or sick still need airtanks. And for those of us who've lived in the pod, it's harder, too. You and I need tanks. For now, anyway. We've consumed such high levels of oxygen for so long that trying to breathe with less than our normal daily dose is painful. And it would kill us." We finally stop again outside a set of revolving glass doors. "Take off your mask. This room's airtight and we have some oxygen being pumped into it," she says. "If you feel lightheaded you can always put it back on."

About fifty people are sitting at a long table, and down the whole length of the table are platters of food. Alina pulls me closer and though I know the room has gone quiet and everyone is watching us, I can't help staring at the food: plates of berries—strawberries and raspberries and berries whose names I've forgotten, though I've seen them in films; platters of sliced vegetables and fruits of every conceivable color; steaming bowls of soup with green bits floating in them; thick pillows of crusted bread.

"How is it possible?" I ask, looking at Alina. I know Premiums can afford to buy some of these things from the biosphere, if they're very rich, but I've never seen anything like this. "You grew everything?"

"*She* didn't grow anything. She's not a gardener here. We choose people who know how to nurture as our gardeners, and I don't think Alina fits the bill." I recoil, expecting to be faced with a giant; I am surprised to see a slight, dark woman standing at the far end of the table. "She's one of our thieves. Though I think we may need to replace her. Would you like to volunteer?" she asks. I press my lips together at the smattering of snickers. This must be Petra. "Anyway, cheers!" The woman raises a glass in my direction and I nod.

Alina laughs nervously, then leads me to the table, where she introduces me to some of the Resistance. Dorian is there. He gives me an apologetic smile, and shifts down the bench to make room. "Welcome," he says. And then, "We heard she put you in the dungeon. Don't worry. She put me there at first, too. She'll let you out in a few days."

"Days?" a girl with tight spiraling hair says. "I was in there a goddamn month."

"You know, Leila, that might be because the first thing you did when you met Petra was scratch her pet," Dorian reminds her. Leila covers her mouth to stifle a giggle.

"Don't get me started on Jazz," Leila says, nodding at the little girl sitting with Petra at the head of the table. Leila piles her plate with berries and apple pieces and eats as she talks. "Yesterday, right, she sees me talking to Levi, and she comes right up to me and is all like, 'Relations between Resistance members is prohibited. Please remember that, Leila.' I almost wet myself laughing. Seriously. What age is she anyway? Five? I've been around longer than she's been out of diapers. She probably still breastfeeds."

"She's nine," Alina says. "And whose breast is she meant to be feeding from?"

"Nine? And she's talking to me like she's my goddamn mother. Man oh man, I could really smack that little brat sometimes," Leila says, popping a whole strawberry into her mouth.

"Keep it down," Dorian warns Leila. He turns to me. "She'll let you out soon. Be obedient. Show deference. To her and her pet." When I look back at the head of the table, Petra and the child are watching me. I try a smile. Jazz waves shyly and Petra takes a swig from her glass.

"She's testing you," Alina tells me in an almost inaudible whisper. "You look sad. She won't like that, because you'll be no use to her. Try to look angry. You're a disgruntled auxiliary and that's why you came with me. You're pissed off and ready to fight, okay? Try to look strong, Bea." I glance around the table and see what she means: everyone here is straight-backed and many of them have scars or bruises. This is no place for the weak; the weak stay in the pod, breathe deeply, take their vaccinations, and await rescue. Alina grabs a plate, bowl, and spoon from the center of the table and hands them to me. "Eat," she orders.

I begin with the soup, or at least I intend to begin with the soup and move on to the bounty of fruit. But the taste of the potato and what Dorian tells me is a vegetable called leek is so delicious, I fill my bowl with seconds of the soup and then thirds. My stomach is full to bursting before I've had a chance to sample anything else. Even so, I take a spoonful of blackberries and am chewing on them when Petra stands again. As Petra begins talking, I fill my plate with small pieces of food, which I surreptitiously tuck into my pockets for Maude. "We eat this meal together in the safety of our unlikely sanctuary," Petra is saying, "knowing it may be our last repast together. We give thanks to this place for its years of protection. We thank the earth. We thank the water. We give thanks to the plants and trees—the roots, leaves, fruits, and flowers. We give thanks to one another, to our comrades, for cultivating our gardens. We give thanks to the spirits of those who have died. We offer our devotion in the earth's name. We salute you." Everyone presses their palms together in front of their hearts and bows their heads. "So it is," she concludes.

"So it is," they chorus.

"Take her back to the lower level," Petra calls out. Alina stands and moves to the door. I follow. "Your name?" Petra asks. I try to speak, but my voice comes out as a sharp squeak. Several people mutter. Petra rubs her chin. Inside, my bones are rattling, but I stand up as tall as my tired body can manage.

"My name is Bea Whitcraft. I am an auxiliary. I want to help the cause," I announce. And I think this is true.

As Alina leads me back down to my cell, I pull out the pieces of stolen food. "What are you doing? What's that?" Alina gasps.

"Maude's hungry."

"If Petra caught you, she'd have had you whipped. Don't you understand?"

"She plans to let Maude die?" I ask.

"She could have killed *you*. She could have killed *me*."

"So let Maude go free now," I say. "Give her a chance at least. You could say she overpowered you and we could give her my airtank. What harm will she do?"

"And where would she go? How many days would the airtank last? She'd give us away."

"It sounds like we're all going to be caught anyway."

"I can't. I'd be breaking the rules. If there's one thing we have to do here, it's obey. It's the only way for the Resistance to succeed."

"Obey? That doesn't sound like you."

"I trust Petra. Look what she's built. She only managed it because she wouldn't allow people to violate her rules."

"Why can't you trust your feelings."

"The last time I trusted my feelings someone ended up dead." Alina's eyes harden and the skin around her mouth tightens, and I know there'll be no way to convince her. "Maybe Petra will find a use for her. Let's hope for that," Alina says. She opens the cell door, takes the tank from me, and gestures for me to go back inside to Maude, who is awake. Alina stands watching us a moment before shutting the door.

I can't keep the food down. I've lived on powders and chemicals for too long. No sooner has Alina closed the cell door than I vomit weakly, dribbling all over myself. "I'm sorry," I say. Maude strokes my face and uses the sleeve of her sweater to wipe my chin and swab my shirtfront. There were jugs and jugs of fresh water at the dinner table, but stupidly I didn't think to drink any.

"Could we get some water in here?" I call out. "And more air. I can't breathe." I move to the door and call again and again. No one answers, not even Alina.

"We'll be all right, darlin'," Maude says, and her stomach growls.

"I got you food," I remember, taking the small chunks of fruit out of my pocket and holding them to her. She paws the fruit suspiciously and then takes a piece of apple and gobbles it down, immediately reaching for another piece.

"Slowly," I say.

When she's finished, we sit back to back and try to preserve our energy. I feel weaker than I've ever felt. I call once or twice more and so does Maude.

But there is no one here to help us.

35
QUINN

We haven't exchanged any words in hours. There doesn't seem to be anything important enough to say. And it's dark by the time Silas leads me up a set of steps to a door where he raps a couple of times and waits until someone opens it. I just follow. I try to keep my eyes on my feet. I've sort of stopped seeing things.

We're at The Grove. It should feel unbelievable. It's an old soccer stadium. But how can I be excited about soccer?

My father. *Mine*. I can't get his face out of my head. In my mind he is turning into a devil. He'll have horns soon, a tail, and a smoking pitchfork. But he's still the father who took me to the park to play when I was a kid. The father who tickled the twins' feet at night when they should have been sleeping. He kisses my mother's belly before he goes off to work. He's that man, too.

Silas is whispering to someone, and minutes later a dark-skinned woman in a long coat is striding toward us, a whip in her hand, followed by a kid.

"Is it a family tradition? What is the meaning of this?" she says.

"I didn't have a choice."

"Follow protocol!" she shouts. "You've already taken it upon yourself to recruit members. It's a good job the Ministry killed this Abel character, whoever he was."

"What? No, I didn't authorize Abel. He told me that Alina—" She hits him square in the face with the handle of the whip. The woman is probably a foot shorter than Silas, with fists about half the size of his, but he doesn't retaliate. He stands there looking small and angry.

"I have never crossed you," Silas says. "Things have changed out there. It isn't what it was. We need new rules. And we need a plan. They've grown in numbers. They've gathered troops. A whole army is marching through the city as we speak. We have days to get ready at most. They'll obliterate us if they find us here. *Obliterate* us."

"You don't come with anything new. Roxanne and Levi were out today. Levi saw them. We have a planning committee set up to deal with this."

"No committee, Petra. It's too late for that. We should flee. Head for a northern division—Redwood or Poplar. Or we could go west to Sequoia," he says. So this is Petra. Alina spoke about her like she was some kind of demigoddess, but she's just a woman.

"No one is going to Sequoia. And don't presume to tell me how to run things." Petra raises her hand, though she doesn't actually strike Silas because the girl at her side makes a grab for the whip. Petra scowls, closes her eyes for a second, then turns to me. "So *you're* the Premium," she says, pulling me toward her by my tattooed earlobe. She pinches it and I yelp. I can't help it. "You're not as dead as Alina said you were," she says, and releases me.

"What do you mean? You know about him? Alina's here?" Silas asks. Petra crosses her arms but doesn't continue.

"Alina's here, Silas," the child says. Silas lets out a long sigh of relief. "She's in the shooting range. I can take you to her." Silas strokes her curly red hair and she smiles up at him.

"What about the others?" I ask. "Did they arrive too? Where are they? Can you take me to them?"

"We don't know who you mean, do we, Jazz?" Petra answers. The child shakes her head slowly.

"Quinn will be useful to us," Silas says, stepping in front of me slightly, which is really nice of him because Petra is swinging the whip again. "*Very* useful. He has connections."

"Useful? Yes. We may need a human shield when the

battle begins to rage," Petra says. "I hope he's bulletproof. Or foam-resistant."

"I'm sure I *can* help," I mutter.

"You have no idea what we even do here. Enough of this bullshit!" She clicks her fingers. "Levi, take the Premium somewhere he can't be any trouble." A guy grabs me and puts me in an armlock.

"Silas!" I shout. "Ask Alina about Bea. I need to find Bea!" Silas watches me being dragged away without giving any indication that he hears me. He doesn't know who Bea is, so maybe he doesn't care what happens to her.

But I care.

I really do.

36
ALINA

I brace my shoulders as I take aim, pointing the barrel of the gun at the space between her eyes. She stares back at me. My hand trembles. I'm taking aim at her head.

It was easy to get hold of these targets for practice. I was on the mission myself and it took less than an hour because every dilapidated clothes shop we came across had a bunch of dummies prostrate in their windows. But it's hard to shoot at this one. She has eyelashes and eyebrows, and even a bellybutton and nipples. She is too real. I aim at her chest instead and fire. Plastic pieces explode from her torso and she smashes against the floor. The noise echoes along the walls of the narrow room, which is insulated against sound.

I put down the rifle and go to her. She is fatally wounded. I touch her face. I do not want to practice shooting people anymore, even lifeless dummies. I don't know what's happened to me. Months ago I would have loved gearing up for a war. "I'm sorry," I whisper. She doesn't hear me. She is plastic. She is in pieces. She hasn't got a heart.

The door to the shooting range swings open and Jazz barges in. "What are you *doing*?" she asks. I jump up and brush myself off.

"Practicing," I say.

"Practicing what?" *I'm practicing grieving,* I think. I wipe my running nose with the back of my hand. "There's someone to see you," she tells me, holding the door open. I expect to see Petra; I expect I'm in trouble again. Then Silas slips into the room.

I stare at him, and at Jazz, who is beaming.

"Did she actually cut out your tongue?" Silas asks with a grin.

"I thought you'd been captured. I thought I was saying good-bye to everyone forever." I run to him and throw my arms around his neck. He's here and he's safe.

"I was lucky," he explains. "I thought I was finished for sure, but one of the stewards who arrested me was a Resistance member. I didn't even know him. He bundled us into the back of the truck, then called headquarters to say I'd attacked him and escaped. He gave me a couple of hacked pads and let me out by Inger's apartment. He took Mom and

Dad to a safe house. I have no idea where it is or how safe it is. It's in the pod; that's all I know for sure."

"But they're alive!" I exclaim.

"We have people deep in the Ministry," Jazz says.

"I suppose they wouldn't be safe if we all knew too much. I can't say how I'd react under torture. Maybe I'd give up my own mother," Silas says. I wonder how Abel reacted. He must have been tortured. And maybe he informed on us, because no sooner was he dead than I was being hunted. But I don't want to believe it of Abel. I want to believe he did the right thing. And that Silas would do the right thing, too. I want to believe that everyone would sacrifice themselves for the sake of others. For the Resistance.

"Petra claims she's never heard of Abel. Didn't you tell me that Abel was authorized?" I say, nodding. He frowns.

"Abel said Petra told *you* he was authorized. I assumed . . ." He looks up at the ceiling, then back at me. "And you thought Petra told *me*? Damn it!"

"That wasn't how it happened. I remember—"

"No!" he interrupts. "I heard nothing from The Grove. I thought you had."

Jazz gasps. "He was Ministry," she says.

"He wasn't Ministry. I'd know Ministry," Silas says. "I just don't understand."

"I'm telling Petra," Jazz says.

"The Ministry wouldn't kill one of their own. Why would they even *pretend* to?" I wonder aloud. "We planned to come here. If he was Ministry or Breathe or whatever, then why didn't he just let us lead him to The Grove?"

Silas rubs his nose and looks down at Jazz. "Don't say anything to Petra?" he pleads. He's right. We need time to figure this out ourselves.

"Why not? There's going to be a big huge mess because of Alina. She stole a tank," Jazz says.

"It's true," I say. I can't meet Silas's eyes.

"Don't flatter yourself," Silas says. "Our guy told me he overheard a senior Minister saying they've been planning a battle for a long time. He told me they noticed the number of tourists leaving the pod increasing and the number returning decreasing. They've been gathering evidence, training soldiers. I think you just changed their timing."

"There's no way!" Jazz declares with a scowl. "No one's been followed here. There's no way."

"You're probably right. They only know that most tourists go southwest, they don't know our exact location yet. They think we're gathered near the river by the old parliament buildings, but as soon as they realize their mistake, they'll double back. We have some time to get out, but not much." A light bulb overhead flickers.

"We're finished," I say. The stadium is the biggest

structure for miles and the Resistance chose it because it was relatively new and the least likely to cave in. Plus it's like hiding in plain sight. It isn't going to take a genius to target this place eventually.

"I think we should leave. I saw several hundred soldiers this afternoon. And I'm sure there'll be more," Silas says.

"I'll tell Petra!" Jazz says. Silas ignores her.

"In a few weeks this place will be a pile of rubble."

"No deserters. I'll tell!" Jazz screams, her hands on her hips.

"You should. Speak to Petra, Jazz." Silas rests an arm on her shoulder and she looks at him with a mixture of admiration and fear. "She listens to you. And I'm telling you, the army is on their way and they won't leave anyone alive. They mean to wipe us out. You're young, Jazz. You have your whole life to live. Tell Petra what's happening. Tell her you want to go. She'll listen to you. There are only a few of us who can't breathe yet. We could train quickly. I'm sure we could." He looks at me, but I have no idea how long it would take us to be ready. I doubt we could train as quickly as Silas is suggesting. It's taken most of the members of the Resistance years to conquer the atmosphere.

"And if not, we could carry tanks," I say.

"And why should I listen to *you*? You both came here with strangers. You don't know anything!" she yelps.

"Jazz," Silas soothes, stroking her shoulder.

"Petra is in charge and she makes the decisions. This is my home." And the only home she's ever known.

"Please talk to her. Even armed, our numbers make it impossible to win. Impossible," he says.

"I'm not leaving!" she screams, and hurtles out of the room. We stand watching as the door swings after her. The fluorescent light bulb continues to flicker.

"We're in trouble now," I tell him. "There's no way Petra will allow anyone to upset Jazz."

"I don't care. Jazz is the only one who'll ever convince Petra to leave the trees. Even she might not be able to."

"After all we've done here, do you really think we should run and let them destroy everything?" How can I abandon The Grove and all the trees? Maybe I agree with Jazz. Maybe we should stay and fight.

Silas reads my mind. "I can't allow us to stay and die. It would destroy Mom and Dad. I can't do that to them." This is something I hadn't considered, and I know how it feels, to be the one left behind.

"I understand." I pause, remembering something Jazz said. "What stranger did you bring here? I did the same thing."

"His name's Quinn. He claims to have saved your life. Did he?"

"Quinn's alive?"

"Petra's taken him," Silas says, looking away. "I don't know what she plans to do with him." He's keeping something from me, I can tell.

"Silas?" I ask.

He drops his head. "It's Inger," he says, and I realize why Silas looks so sad. I want to reach out a hand to comfort him, but I know it wouldn't be a comfort at all. "They took away his air and that was that. He's—" he tries. "I should've left the pod on my own. I should've left *him* alone. It's just that he was a tracker, and I wanted to make sure I found you, and . . ." He sinks to the floor and holds his head between his arms. I look at the fragments of dummy strewn across the floor, then crouch down next to Silas. I know this feeling, and I know it doesn't matter what I say. I won't be able to relieve his hurt. Or his guilt. I saw Silas and Inger together, and it was obvious how they felt. Inger is dead because Silas loved him. Abel is dead because I wanted him to love me. I feel connected to my cousin. And I wish I didn't.

The door bursts open and Petra marches in, closely followed by Jazz. She takes one look at the flickering light, reaches for a shotgun on the rack, and shoots it. Glass and plastic rain from the ceiling. I close my eyes, then shake shards of light bulb from my hair. Couldn't she have simply switched it off?

Silas and I stand up. His eyes are dry, but he is biting the insides of his cheeks.

"I am losing my patience!" Petra screams.

Silas puts a hand up to stop her. "We can rebuild somewhere else," he says.

"You won't defend The Grove?" she asks. For a moment Petra's face shows no sign of rage; she is simply brokenhearted.

"With what? Two hundred outcasts? We need tanks. Not just one. We need twenty. Most of all we need people."

"What about the trees?" she asks. Jazz takes Petra's hand and the two of them look down at the floor. A long moment passes before anyone speaks: we are thinking about the trees in the stadium standing tall and noble—beautiful and totally vulnerable. They will be the first to die because they are the biggest threat. Then Petra says, "I won't make prisoners of long-serving members. You may leave whenever you wish. But do not mention any of this to the others. I won't have mayhem here." Silas nods. "Well, *we* won't go, will we?" She looks down at Jazz, who smiles hesitantly.

"Bea and Quinn. You'll let them go, too?" I ask.

"Who? The Premium and the girl? No, of course not," Petra says, waving away the suggestion.

"They'll be fine here," Silas tells me.

"They won't. They've been pod dwellers their entire lives. And they saved my life. I can't leave them behind."

Petra, watching me, says, "So you'll stay. You'll stay and fight."

"That Premium I brought in is more valuable than you know. Maybe with his help we *could* be ready. Maybe he could buy us time," Silas says. He looks up at the ceiling for several moments, then nods resolutely. "Maybe he could buy us a couple of weeks and we recruit in the meantime," he says.

"I'm listening," Petra says.

When Silas has finished explaining that Quinn's father is probably the army's general and that Quinn has just watched him murder Inger, Petra is wild with rage; her neck goes red and she grinds one fist into the other hand. She intends to hurt Quinn regardless of how ashamed he feels. She intends to get revenge. Silas lets her rant. We watch as she boils up and simmers down again.

He insists there's a better way to use Quinn. And when he hears about Maude his plan solidifies; he has a way to use her, too.

Within an hour, Silas has come up with a scheme that could save everyone.

37
BEA

It must be morning, though I've no way of telling. All I know is that we've been in here for hours without water, light, food, or sufficient air. Maude couldn't keep down the fruit either, and the cell stinks. Her movements are getting slower. She won't even sit up anymore but lies dozing on the floor, rattled out of sleep every hour or so by a nightmare. I've tried to sleep myself, sitting up against the wall with Maude's head in my lap, stroking her matted hair and listening to her breathing.

I have no idea which side I'm on anymore. I know the Ministry keeps us down, keeps my parents working day and night, keeps us pumped full of oxygen so we've no way of surviving without Breathe, and in the pod I'll never be in a position to help my parents unless I marry a Premium, but at least there was the illusion of liberty. The Resistance claims to stand for freedom and justice, despite the fact that so far they haven't shown us any mercy—and I'm certainly not free. They fed me, but they don't care about Maude at all.

Alina would remind me of Maude's ugly past, her part in the destruction of the trees. What does that matter now? She's no harm to anyone and anyway, I can't marry the two images of Maude in my mind: the killer and the dwindling woman I now hold in my arms. I try singing little songs to her, songs my mother sang to me when I was a child. She seems less agitated when I sing.

"Baby's boat's a silver moon sailing in the sky,

Sailing o'er a sea of sleep while the stars float by.

Sail, baby, sail out upon that sea,

Only don't forget to sail back again to me."

The door is flung wide open. They're dragging Maude from the room, her head bumping on the floor like an old soccer ball, and without thinking, I leap at them. "Get off her! She's sick." To my surprise they do as I say and stand back. Petra enters the room, her hands clasped in front of her.

"I'd be quite happy to use her blood as war paint. But you care about her. And he cares about you. So you survive a little longer." I have no idea what she means and I'm too concerned about Maude to unravel riddles. "Leave the hag and bring the girl. I'll get the boy. We'll meet in The Symposium."

Now it's me being hauled from the room, and Maude is

awake and squinting at me in fright, her arms outstretched, pleading with me not to leave her.

"Please give her water. Don't let her die this way," I say as they strap a mask onto my face. Petra moves toward Maude and glares down at her.

"We'll water her," Petra tells me. "And wash her. She reeks."

Minutes later I'm alone in an oxygenated meeting room and they've taken away the airtank again so I can't leave. I've been planted in a chair at an old wooden circular table facing away from the door. I try to remember what Petra said when she came into the bunker. Something about me caring for Maude and that being important. Why shouldn't I care about Maude? Haven't they worked out we're not the villains?

The door rattles. I don't turn around to see who's coming in. I've decided I'm going to appear indifferent because it's obvious that it's my own foolish compassion for everyone I meet that's my enemy. I need Petra to think I don't care about anyone else and maybe that I don't even care about myself.

"I'm not one for sentimental reunions, so I'll be waiting outside." It's Petra. I hear the shuffling of feet and the door closes. The room is heavy with silence, and it seems to swell the longer I sit there. Still I don't look around because it feels like a trick. I stare at the broken clock on the wall instead. I have no idea how many minutes pass without my moving an inch or letting even a scintilla of sound pass my lips. And I would have stayed this way, I'm sure, if my stomach hadn't given me away. It gurgles loudly and that's when a voice fills the room.

"Hello?" he says, and I know, without turning around or hearing even a fraction of another syllable that it's him. I throw my chair back. Quinn is standing next to the door. He's blindfolded, his hands bound. He looks tired, but he's alive.

"Quinn!" I gasp and run to him. I imagined this scene in my mind—I replayed it over and over again. I thought I knew how I'd react. I thought I would run into his arms. But now, I come to a halt inches from where he's standing and carefully untie his blindfold so he can see me. When he does, he shakes his head and presses his lips together.

"Bea," he whispers, and steps closer. I feel his breath on me, and shift my weight into my heels, creating a little more space between us. His face is covered in bruises. I reach out, and he closes his eyes. He flinches when I touch the scab on his chin.

"You made it," I say. Neither of us speaks, really looking at each other for the first time.

"Alina's cousin found me," he says at last. He opens his mouth to say something more and stops himself. He shakes his head, then tries again. "I've got so much . . . so many things to tell you. I made the Leadership Program . . . it was fixed. And that's not the worst of it. When I tell you who I am, who I belong to, I wouldn't be surprised if you never . . . well, if you never wanted to see me again."

"You're alive," I say, allowing my weight to fall back into my toes and our noses to touch. And that's when it happens: he kisses me. I expect him to pull away, to keep the kiss platonic, but he doesn't; his lips stay locked to mine until I feel them part slightly and Quinn breathes into me. I reach my arms up, fold them behind his neck, and press my body into his. Finally he steps back and looks at me again.

"You have green eyes. I never noticed that," he says.

"Yes," I say. "They've always been green."

And he kisses me again.

38
ALINA

Petra leads us all into The Symposium and I get a good look at Quinn sitting at the other end of the table, Bea nestled against him. He no longer looks like someone I can make fun of. In fact, I wonder if it's really him.

"Sit down," Petra commands. Silas and I sit at the table opposite Bea and Quinn. Jazz is in the middle next to Petra, and Roxanne and Levi are opposite them. Quinn nods at me shyly before turning to Bea. She has been locked in a dark bunker for twelve hours, yet she looks more alive than ever.

"What's the status?" Petra asks Roxanne and Levi, who've been out scouting the area all morning. Roxanne clears her throat and rubs her uncovered eye with her thumb. When she stops, it's red and watering.

"We suspect a full attack very soon. There's been gunfire

and sporadic explosions no more than three miles from here, very close to the city center," she says. "They're basically destroying anything standing."

"Didn't I tell you?" Silas says.

Petra turns to Levi. "And what do you think?" she asks.

"They're on to us," Levi says. He folds his arms across his broad, bare, tattooed chest and gives Quinn a glare of pure hatred.

Petra waves her hand in Quinn's direction. "Silas seems to think that this Premium parasite may be related to a ranking officer. Were you able to find out anything?"

"General Jude Caffrey *is* in command of the entire army." Bea takes a sharp breath. Quinn shifts in his chair. After a moment, Bea puts her arm around Quinn.

"You understand my dilemma. We can't simply let him go," Petra says, looking at Silas and me now. I don't speak and neither does Silas. This isn't a question and we already know what's coming. In fact, this whole conversation is more for effect than anything else: we've already negotiated a plan; we know exactly what's going to have to happen for Bea and Quinn to be allowed to leave The Grove. Petra continues. "So this is the deal: the Premium and his girlfriend will be allowed to leave." Bea blushes. "You will get yourselves rescued by the army and tell them you found a way to escape. Then you'll lead dear old dad away from us to give us time to prepare. And I mean *far away.* We will discuss details. As soon as Roxanne and Levi see that the army has been misinformed of our whereabouts, the two idiots who brought everyone here will be free to stay or go, as well as the hag downstairs."

"Maude Blue?" Quinn asks, looking at Bea.

"I will get word to you in the pod that I'm satisfied, that I've released the old lady. Then you can both get on with your ignorant lives. If I'm not satisfied, I'll kill her—and eventually I'll kill you. Whether or not you eventually give us away is up to you. I presume you will. The apple doesn't fall far from the tree, after all," Petra says. She's underestimating Bea and maybe she's underestimating Quinn, too. They would both make excellent Resistance fighters if they were given the chance.

"You promise you won't let Maude die in the meantime?" Bea asks.

"We promise," Jazz says, speaking up.

Bea smiles, totally satisfied with this pint-size guarantee. "We'll do it," she says.

What she doesn't know is that it doesn't matter whether they drag the Ministry off the scent for a few days or not; Petra will see to it that Maude Blue lives on, at least until the old drifter helps us carry out the second part of our plan.

Jazz stands up and skips toward Bea and Quinn. She is

smiling and as she raises her hand to Bea's face I think she's going to stroke her, but instead, she digs her nails into Bea's skin and draws four scratches across it. Quinn jumps up to defend Bea, but he can't because his hands are still tied behind his back. Jazz turns to him and coolly socks him square in the mouth. There is a crack as Quinn falls back into his chair. Now it's my turn to stand up.

"We didn't discuss this. It wasn't in the agreement!" I yell. Petra squints and presses her lips together. Silas takes my elbow and pulls me back into my chair. "Bea doesn't deserve this," I hiss so only he can hear me.

"We don't want the Ministry to think they escaped us without a fight," Petra says. Jazz nods, gives Bea and Quinn a pitying look, and returns to Petra's side.

"Couldn't you have warned them?" Silas asks, in his even-tempered way.

"Quinn's face was scratched up anyway," I add.

"Authenticity!" Petra declares. "We do not want it to look staged, do we? Anyway, they should count themselves lucky. Levi offered to break a couple of arms."

"A couple of legs," Levi corrects, and Roxanne titters, though I have no idea why this is funny.

"So I'd say a punch and scratch from a nine-year-old was getting off lightly," Petra says.

"Hey, I'm almost ten. And just because I'm young doesn't

mean . . ." Jazz begins, but I don't listen to the rest of what she's saying because I am watching Bea. She casts me a look, which is at once alarmed and disenchanted. She must think that everything I said about the Resistance is a lie.

"Get them ready," Petra tells Roxanne and Levi, who march over to Bea and Quinn and start to shepherd them out of the room. It's only then that I realize it might be the last time I ever see either of them. I jump up and block the door. I have so much I want to say. I have to thank them for saving my life. And I want to apologize. They were happy until I came along and ruined everything.

"Move," Roxanne says.

"Alina, you're really getting on my nerves," Levi grunts.

"I want to say—" I wring my hands and try to find the right words.

"Thank you," Bea says. She smiles, leans forward, and kisses my cheek. I have no idea why she's being so nice. She has every right to take a swing at me. To hate me forever.

"Yes, thank you," Quinn repeats. He smiles too and nods. He doesn't try leaning in for a kiss. He doesn't even look like he wants to.

Levi pushes me out of the way and Roxanne nudges them forward. And then they are gone.

"Get back in here," Petra calls from the table.

I slink into the room and slide back onto the chair next to Silas.

"Maude Blue should be here," I say. We need her if we're going to plan a safe route through the city to get new recruits. She knows where all the drifters are. Plus, when I last saw her, she looked sick, and I owe it to Bea to keep Maude safe.

Petra nods. "Release her? Are you sure you can defend yourself against Maude without those two to protect you?" She smirks and Jazz stifles a laugh. When I glance at Silas, even he is biting away a smile.

I'm furious with all of them. Yes, they did save me from a frail old woman. When I had no one else, they rescued me. There's more to it than that, of course. They showed me I'd become cold and hard; I'd forgotten myself, and without even looking, they found me. *They* did that. My friends.

"I don't care. Go ahead and laugh," I say.

"Oh, I don't think it's funny," Petra explains. "I think it's pathetic. You're not like this."

"Like what?"

"Afraid."

"I'm not afraid," I say. Petra's eyes widen and she looks at Silas.

"Considering what we're about to do, where we're about to go," Silas says, "you should be."

PART IV

THE BATTLE

39
QUINN

We have full airtanks, and now the bruiser with the dodgy eye is bellowing instructions at us. I try to concentrate on the orders, though my mouth is still throbbing.

"Focus!" the bruiser barks.

"I am," I tell her, and spit a frothy mouthful of blood right at her feet. She pushes me, and I stumble backward into a pile of breathing apparatuses.

"Mess with me and you might need to borrow this," she says, pointing at her eye patch.

"He's listening," Bea assures her, and within minutes, the steel door slams at our backs and we are alone.

"You okay?" Bea asks. She touches my face with her gloved fingertips, already wet from the snow.

"'Course I am. You?" She nods. Bea's hair is tangled, her

clothes smeared in mud and dust, and her lovely green eyes have dark circles beneath them. She looks like she has fire in her, like she's finally alive.

"So which way should we go?" I ask. Bea pulls out a frayed map, examines it, and points to a dark alleyway between two tall buildings ahead.

"We have to get away from The Grove and remain unseen for at least five miles. Then we get picked up and say we've been walking north for a day," she says, folding the map and pushing it into the inside pocket of her jacket. When I don't speak she continues. "I have to do this, Quinn. I know you don't want to betray your dad, but I have to save Maude. And I think I hate the Ministry. Please do this with me."

I can't believe she imagines I would double-cross Alina or Silas. "Is that what you think of me?" I ask. Bea shrugs. She can't know how it feels to know that the person who taught you to tie your shoelaces is a killer. Her dad is one of the kindest people alive, and so is she. If my father is one of the cruelest people alive, then what am I? "Can I hold your hand?" I ask. It's all I can think to say.

Bea nods and reaches for me.

The farther south we go, the deeper the snow gets and the harder it is to navigate our way along the narrow roads.

Sometimes we're forced to cross a major junction or cut through a site of ruins or an old parking lot where we could easily be spotted, if not by the army then maybe by a crazy drifter.

My cracked ribs are throbbing and I have a pounding headache. I don't tell Bea. I want her to think she can count on me. I'm clinging to her with one hand, and in the other I'm carrying a knife in case we run into any trouble.

As the evening draws in and our legs start to seize up from the cold, we hear a noise. We both stand and listen, and when we're sure it's a tank, I wrangle with the valves on our tanks so that our air supplies plummet to dangerous levels; our story won't check out if we get picked up with a bounty of oxygen. We step right into its path. The tank shudders to a halt and the hatch snaps open like a mouth. Bea pulls off her scarf and begins waving it frantically. At the very least we want them to think we mean to surrender. A gun appears. Then a voice.

"Down on the ground with your hands behind your heads. Both of you. NOW!" Two days ago, I might have thought this whole drill was a bit over the top and shouted something snarky at the soldier with the gun. Now, I lie facedown in the snow and wait to be tied up.

Once the soldiers have us securely bound, they drag us to the tank and order us to climb in. When we've no longer got guns aimed at our heads, I begin the indignant Premium pantomime.

"When my father hears about this, you can be sure you'll be made to pay for the way you manhandled me." The soldiers look at each other. "Do you know how many tanks drove right by us without stopping? We've been walking for *days*."

"You Premium?" a soldier with a gun on his lap wants to know.

"What do I look like? Some sub?" The soldier cranes his neck toward me so he can get a gawk at my earlobe. "Would you like me to pull down my pants so you can do a thorough investigation?" I ask. He shrinks back and pushes another soldier forward.

"Who are you?" this soldier asks.

"My name is Quinn Caffrey, Jude Caffrey's son. He's pretty senior at Breathe." All sound is sucked from the tank as every soldier looks at me. All I've given them is my father's name, but in this tank, in this war, the name Jude Caffrey has power. And that means I have power, too. The soldiers start shuffling and whispering. "You've heard of him then? Listen, I've been held captive by the RATS. Right now, all I want is to get home. Can you take us back to the pod?"

"Get on the horn!" someone calls out. There's a frantic scuffle as two or three of the soldiers reach for the radio at once. Eventually they get hold of my father. It takes them several minutes to convey the fact that they've found his son and an auxiliary girl in the middle of the combat zone. At first it sounds as though they have to remind him he even *has* a son. I can't hear every word my father is saying, what with the crackling over the radio and the clamor of explosions on his end, but what I do notice is that his voice remains entirely unmoved, even after they've explained, in brief, what's happened to me. My father gives the soldiers in the tank orders to escort me back to the pod and that's it. *"Over and out."* Over and out? He doesn't ask to speak to me or tell them to check I'm okay. For all he knows my vital organs could be failing. Has he thought about that? He just orders them to take me home and it's 'over and out.'

40
ALINA

When Maude steps into the dining hall and pulls off her face-mask, I hardly recognize her. I sit there trying to remember where I've seen the face before. It's Dorian who escorts her in and at first I think that maybe she's an old relative of his or something. I'd never have believed a makeover could change someone so drastically. It's not even one of those surgical makeovers the Premiums are into where they get their noses turned up and their lips plumped. All they've done is given her a wash, cut her hair and nails, and dressed her in a fresh set of clothes. It's magic.

"That's her?" Silas asks. I described a horror. I warned him that he'd want to pull his sleeve across his nose to obscure the smell of old sweat and earwax. She sits opposite us and grins at the table piled with food. Her teeth are still stained and broken, but the scum buildup has been removed. She fills a plate to brimming with thick pieces of fruit and is about to stuff a large chunk of apple into her mouth when she changes her mind and takes a dainty bite of some bread instead.

Maude finally notices me. "Where's the other one?" she caws, filling her mug with cider and guzzling it. Her eyes dart up and down the table looking for Bea.

"Petra explained why you were released," Silas says without introducing himself. "There's a mission for you." Maude's eyes, cold and suspicious, rest on me.

"What'av you lot done with her? I ain't helping you do nothing till you tell me where you're keeping her." I want to tell her the truth, but I can't in case she refuses to help us. What does she owe the Resistance? We have to deceive her as we deceived Bea and Quinn.

"Bea will be released once we have a full army. We need to recruit the drifters. That's where you come in," Silas tells Maude. His tone is firm, like the voice that comes over the loudspeakers in the pod announcing the deadlines for receiving new vaccinations.

"That weren't part of the deal. She didn't say nothing about holding Bea."

"What *did* she say?" Silas asks.

"I weren't listening," Maude admits and coughs some of her dinner back up onto the plate.

"Drink more water," I tell her.

"And be ready to leave by sunset," Silas says. He collects an armful of pears from the table and strides out of the dining room.

"Where is Bea?" Maude asks again once Silas is safely out of earshot. "Please tell me. I thought we'd buried the hatchet, you and me."

"Bea is . . . Bea is . . ." I stutter.

"Careful," Dorian pipes up. He's been silent the whole meal. I hardly noticed him sitting there.

"Mind your business, you," Maude tells Dorian, lashing out at him with her fist. "Where *is* she, Alina?"

"You'll see her as soon as we get back from the mission," I lie. And wouldn't the truth hurt more? That Bea is gone and never coming back? I have to pretend not to know this myself.

At sunset the training stops. Swords and guns are put down and everyone comes to wish us well. Little mementos and good-luck charms are pushed into my hands and a few people start to murmur blessings. If Silas and I were denounced when we brought unknowns here, we seem to be making up for it now. We're being hailed as heroes all of a sudden, and we haven't even done anything yet, which makes me wonder: is this mission total lunacy? Silas was probably right the first time: if we want to stay alive, we should run. And we could.

As soon as we get out of here, we could head west and never come back.

Jazz snakes through the swelling crowd, sidles up to me, and presents me with a small white shell. Its ridges are smooth. "I'm sorry I smacked your friends," she says.

"Where did you get this?" I ask, holding the shell in my open hand.

"It was my mom's. Dad bought it for her on the day I was born. He was going to turn it into a pendant, but he never got around to it. I keep it in my pocket."

"I can't take it," I tell her. Shells are valuable. They import them into the pod from the coast and people pay a lot for them. You know someone has money if he's wearing shells or has them displayed in his house.

"It isn't for keeps. When you get back, you can give it to me again," she says. I thank her and put it in my breast pocket.

"Ready?" Dorian asks. Within the last hour he's somehow managed to convince Petra that he's vital to the mission as well. At least that's his story. It could be that she's sending him to spy on us.

"No!" Maude complains. She's been fitted with warm new boots and given a coat that belongs to Jazz. "I demand a phone call. I want me lawyer. I had a date arranged for tonight. At least let me call to apologize to the poor fella." This gets a snicker from a few people.

I throw my backpack over one shoulder, Maude's backpack over the other, loosen the valve on my airtank, and follow through the throng of people to the door. As I leave, I glance over my shoulder. Petra is standing back from the crowd, watching. There's something behind her rigidity that I've never seen in her before. I keep walking and when I look back at Petra for a second time I can name it: fear.

It's more like a blizzard now, the wind choking up our route. And the weather is not all there is to worry about. We have to listen for the rumble of the approaching army, too. With the storm so heavy, it would be easy to mistake zip blades for a whip of wind or marching feet for the distant crack of thunder.

Apart from Maude, who is barely able to shuffle forward through the snow, I'm the least experienced. I should feel safer tagging along with Dorian and Silas than I did when I led Bea and Maude to The Grove all on my own, but for some reason I'm much less confident now. Maybe it's because I know too much. Even with Silas to protect him, Inger perished. Maybe it's because I don't have to be brave anymore, now there are others to take my place up front. Or maybe I'm giving up.

We walk for what feels like hours, Maude at the front of the group, and when we make our first stop, it's only to check a map and eat half a pear each. Maude's face is stiff from the cold and even her eyelashes are rimed with frost. I try to hold her face in my gloved hands to warm it. She hisses when I come close. I don't have Bea's way, I suppose. Dorian sees this and removes the balaclava he's been wearing. He hands it to Maude without looking at her.

"Wear that," he says, and immediately she slips it over her head and hides her face from the storm. "We can't have her dying before we get there," he whispers when he's next to me again. "If anything happens to Old Maude, The Grove's done for."

41
BEA

We're invited into a meeting room, though in reality it's an interrogation chamber. Two burly stewards sit at a desk opposite us, staring. We're told we need to wait for their boss to arrive before we can begin. I'm not sure that's why we have to wait at all. I think they're using the time to intimidate us. I try not to look terrified, pretending I'm so exhausted I might fall asleep right here in this chair.

Our story is that the soldiers saved us from the driving snow, so if that's true I have no reason to be afraid; all we're doing here is helping the Ministry understand what happened. More than that, we're helping to fight terrorism and bring our captors to justice.

Quinn is trying a different tactic. He keeps tapping his foot and tutting. He turns around occasionally to look at the colossal ticking clock on the wall behind us, and once or twice he's demanded to see someone in power. "He's on his way," one of our babysitters says, adding, "sir," with a little too much emphasis. I don't know that the arrogant role Quinn's playing is doing us any favors as they seem to be increasingly annoyed and suspicious of us.

The door eventually creaks open and a hulking figure strides in wearing an expensive antique fur coat with a collar that covers his face. He brushes snow from his shoulders and, taking off the coat, throws it at our minders, who stood sharply as the door opened. At first I have the impression I've seen him before, and I start to run through a mental catalogue of all the places we might have met until I realize that I've never met this man anywhere. The reason I recognize him is because I've seen him on the screen—on the news and on political broadcasts, on posters and in displays at school. Towering over us is the Pod Minister.

He examines us over the bridge of his bulbous nose. One minute he is scrutinizing us, the next he turns to the two stewards and bellows, "I'm cold!" The steward holding the coat steps up to offer it to the Pod Minister, who cuffs the steward on the ear. "Not the coat! Get me a drink!" The stewards scurry out of the room and return quickly with a tray.

"Caffrey Junior," the Pod Minister says, reaching forward to shake Quinn's hand.

"Pod Minister," Quinn answers, standing.

"You've had quite a journey, I hear," the Pod Minister says, and plonks himself down in one of the chairs. He unplugs a heavy stopper from the bottle in front of him and pours a large glassful. He leans back in the chair and sips at the drink. The room fills with the sharp smell of whiskey. "Thirsty?" he asks. We both shake our heads. "I got a call this evening saying we found two missing persons. I couldn't believe it when I heard the full story. Even now I almost don't. It's curious because one of our tanks spotted a lone boy in a location very close to where Communications tracked the last signal from your pads." Quinn frowns as though he doesn't understand the connection. "And, do you know that no one has ever escaped the terrorists before? You've achieved quite a feat." The Pod Minister swirls the whiskey in the glass and inhales deeply before taking another vigorous mouthful. Quinn doesn't speak up even during this long pause.

"The thing is," the Pod Minister continues, "I had a report that you accompanied a suspect out of this place a few days ago. So . . . you helped a terrorist leave the pod and she turned on you. That's what you're saying?" Quinn nods. "Well, to start with, I'll have the stewards who permitted the girl's escape reprimanded. I presume they were open to some kind of bribe."

Quinn looks down, ashamed, but remains silent. I keep my

mouth shut and literally bite my tongue so I won't be tempted to say anything. No one wants to hear from me. "Tell me, son—exactly what *is* going on?" The Pod Minister runs a hand through his thinning hair and grins.

Quinn sighs and gives the Pod Minister a shameful look. "Her name was Alina. I . . . I . . . It's sort of embarrassing." The Pod Minister leans forward in his chair and the stewards, who are now standing by the back wall, start to look interested. "I liked her, you see. And, well, when she asked if she could come with us on our trip I, well, you know. When she tells me she wants to go too, I think that I'm in with a chance. You know?" The stewards begin to snicker as my whole body aches at the memory of Quinn's infatuation. Does he still feel that way about her? Is it possible to fancy a person one day and forget her the next? "So I gave her Bea's pass and bullied my way through Border Control."

"So this trip was all planned?"

"Yeah. 'Course. I mean, I didn't tell my parents about Alina because they'd have given me *the talk*. Every time I meet a new girl they remind me how dangerous it is to get naked. I mean, I'd be lucky, you know." The stewards are now bent over, trying to subdue their chortling.

"Why did *you* go?" the Pod Minister asks, turning on me all of a sudden, spraying my face with droplets of whiskey. Before I can speak, Quinn cuts in.

"Bea had never been outside the pod and I invited her to come with me before I met Alina. I couldn't exactly tell her to get lost." He pats my knee in the most irritating display of condescension. "I never told her Alina was coming, too."

"You're a sub," the Pod Minister declares, insultingly. He smiles and watches me carefully. In fact, this whole time his expression has been calm, pleasant even. But I know that underneath the smile is suspicion and rage, and I don't want to be on the receiving end of it. I am about to speak up when the door swings open and Quinn's father appears. He stands by the door looking at Quinn, not speaking, and steals a glance at the Pod Minister. Next to me, Quinn shudders.

"Ah, Jude, there you are, my man. Do come in," the Pod Minister says, scraping a chair across the floor and offering it to Mr. Caffrey.

"I had no idea you would be here," Mr. Caffrey tells the Pod Minister. "I could have handled this. You're much too busy."

"Come come, Jude. Nothing goes on that I don't hear about, you know that. And then I heard your poor son had been taken prisoner. I thought it my duty to come down here and make sure he was okay. For you. Ha!" Mr. Caffrey sits down in the chair being offered to him.

"Well, I'm embarrassed, Pod Minister. I promise you, he won't see daylight for a year," Mr. Caffrey says.

"What? Punish the boy? No, no, I don't think there'll be a need for that." The Pod Minister pushes an empty glass and the decanter of whiskey to Quinn's dad, who pours himself a generous measure.

"What the hell were you playing at?" Mr. Caffrey demands to know after he's downed about half the glass.

"Father, I . . . I . . ." Quinn stutters. He can't get the words out. He's more scared of his father than he is of the Pod Minister. A large vein in Mr. Caffrey's neck throbs and before Quinn can put up his hands to protect himself, Mr. Caffrey stands and smacks him hard across the face. Quinn lets out a small whimper and holds his face in his hands.

I know that to them I'm nothing, and that my word means even less than nothing. "May I speak?" I ask anyway, my voice barely a whisper. The Pod Minister stares at me, his smirk a challenge.

"Why, of course. Ha! Speak up, sub. Speak up. Tell us what you know."

"When we got out of the pod, she took us off in a strange direction. We hadn't planned on it. She said she wanted to explore some of the old houses. And we knew that was dangerous. We'd read all the guidebooks and we knew the structures were unsafe, but we went anyway. We shouldn't have. As soon as we went through the door, we were ambushed. Five or six of them came out of nowhere. We were to be used as hostages. They knew Quinn's dad was senior. We don't know how," I say. "I think they thought he was in the army though." The Pod Minister snaps a look at Mr. Caffrey.

"Don't ask me. Even my wife doesn't know," Mr. Caffrey assures him.

"We were blindfolded and bound and told to march," I continue. Quinn holds out his wrists to show them the chafing from where he really was bound. They both glance down at his wrists and then at the welt Jazz left on my face.

"Where did they take you?" Mr. Caffrey wants to know.

"We were going south. They didn't mention a place. But it was coastal for sure because they talked about boats."

"And eating seaweed," Quinn adds. This is an odd detail but the Pod Minister nods approvingly.

"Their hub is a boat?" Mr. Caffrey asks.

"I think so," I say.

"But how are they managing to grow—" Mr. Caffrey begins. The Pod Minister cuts him short.

"Classified!" he shouts.

Mr. Caffrey takes another gulp of whiskey, having almost let slip what no one in the Ministry wants revealed: there are trees out there.

"What I'm curious about is how these two *heroes* escaped the terrorists," the Pod Minister wonders, lingering over the word *heroes* and smiling again. "Sounds very dangerous."

Quinn's rehearsed this part, so I sit back and let him take over the story. "On the second night, while most of them were asleep, a group of drifters attacked. I couldn't see how many in the dark, but there was pandemonium and the punk who was meant to be watching us ran to help the others. We managed to crawl away and got as far as an underground station by the time the brawl ended. We heard them screaming and looking for us. Eventually they gave up."

The Pod Minister raises his eyebrows. "Wow! Isn't that something!" he exclaims. "It's almost hard to believe."

"My son isn't a liar, Pod Minister."

"Of course not, Jude. I didn't say that, did I? But I need to be sure." Another steward steps into the room, moves toward the Pod Minister, and whispers in his ear. "Well, bring her in, won't you," he says.

For the final time the door opens. Clicking footsteps echo in the corridor and then Quinn's mother enters the room. "Oh, Quinn, you're okay. You're okay!" she wails. She totters toward Quinn and throws her body across him, pressing her breasts into his face. Mr. Caffrey looks away. Mrs. Caffrey rarely hugs her children, and I have to be careful not to roll my eyes as I watch her performance.

"Hello, Mother," is all Quinn can manage. I want to reach out and take his hand.

"So, Quinn. If you had to swear to me that you're telling

the truth, would you?" the Pod Minister asks. Quinn nods emphatically as he tries to extricate himself from his mother's embrace. "Well, good. Good." Here the Pod Minister looks at Mrs. Caffrey and licks his lips. "And if I made you swear on the life of your unborn brother, would you still claim to be telling me the truth?" Quinn looks at the swell in his mother's body as Mrs. Caffrey stands up straight. I have never liked Mrs. Caffrey, but she is so tiny she looks like a pregnant teenager rather than a woman in her forties. I can't help shuddering at the thought of something awful happening to her or her baby.

"Cain. What a thing to ask!" she exclaims. She is half smiling, as though testing a joke. "Jude, tell him he's crossing the line. You're crossing the line, Cain." She looks at the whiskey in the Pod Minister's hand, and in her own husband's, and doesn't sense that the Pod Minister is completely serious.

His smile turns into a snarl. "If I find out you've been lying . . ." he growls. Mrs. Caffrey gasps and rubs her belly. "And as for you and your little girlfriend here. Well, that simply goes without saying. So tell me. Where does the Resistance live?" I try not to look anywhere but in his eyes. A long moment passes. No one breathes. I try to weigh the value of our lives and Quinn's unborn brother with the lives of everyone living in The Grove. "Can I have your guarantee that if we go south, we'll catch your terrorists?" the

Pod Minister asks. He is only looking at Quinn now. The entire burden of the decision is on him. If Quinn wanted to, he could betray Alina and Silas and everyone at The Grove. They did nothing to win his support. And what does he care about Maude? Everyone in the room is motionless as Quinn opens his mouth to speak.

"That's what I heard, Pod Minister. The terrorists are in the south," Quinn says. And so there's no going back. And there's no knowing what will happen when they figure out they've been duped.

The Pod Minister claps his hands as though Quinn has performed some extraordinary feat and turns back to Mr. and Mrs. Caffrey. "Ha!" he yells. He smacks his hands on the desk and I flinch. "HA! HA!" He drains the remaining whiskey from his glass, stands up, and grabs his grotesque fur.

"Get back out to the field, Jude," he commands as he exits the room. "And when you find them, radio in. I want to know the exact moment we raze their hideout to the ground! Ha! Good job, Caffrey Junior. Bloody good job. Ha!"

The Pod Minister disappears down the corridor, followed by his two lackeys, and Mr. and Mrs. Caffrey are standing together in a desperate embrace. I've never seen Quinn's parents hug in this way. I've never even seen them touch each other. Quinn is watching them. His body is visibly trembling now. I reach out and squeeze his leg gently, to comfort myself as well as him, and he takes my hand in his, but quickly lets go as his father turns back to us.

"You're telling the truth, son," he says. "Because if you aren't—" Here he stops. If we're lying, then what? Why doesn't he finish the sentence? Even Mr. Caffrey, the army's general, hasn't got a plan. "If you're lying, it's your life I'll see they take, not his," he says, putting his arm around his wife.

Mrs. Caffrey's eyes are transfixed on her husband. "Jude," she whispers. She won't look at Quinn. She won't defend him. All she can do is rub her belly and repeat her husband's name again and again. I want to scream at her. I want to shout, *Quinn was once your baby, too!*

"It's nice to see you both," Quinn says, and with that stands up and walks out of the room. I don't ask if I can follow him because the interrogation is clearly over and neither Mr. nor Mrs. Caffrey is taking any notice of me at all.

I chase after Quinn, calling his name as he sprints down the corridor and crashes through the exit. I can't keep up, he is running too fast, and when I finally push open the exit myself, someone catches me by the hand. My first instinct is to lash out.

"It's us, love." I look up and my mom and dad are beaming at me. "Oh, God, you're safe." They wrap their arms around me.

"I have to catch Quinn," I say. I try to struggle free.

"What's that, love?" Mom asks. Her eyes are red. She's obviously not eaten or slept in days. I don't think I've ever seen her looking so old. She looks like a grandmother. She must have thought she'd lost me. I lean into her shoulder and start to cry.

"I have to catch Quinn before he does something stupid," I sob.

42
ALINA

We've been walking for half the night, the blizzard worsening and our progress slower the farther we've trekked into the city. To keep ourselves from spiraling into lethargy we've sucked handfuls of snow and eaten pieces of frozen fruit. At first we'd worried about the army seeing our tracks and wasted precious time and energy trying to erase them, but it became clear that by morning any tracks we made would be covered beyond discovery. Our real problem is going to be finding our way back to The Grove in the storm.

"Location number one!" Maude finally shrieks over the drumming of the wind.

"You sure?" Silas hollers back. He pushes past me and stands next to Maude. We look up at the building, an immense structure made entirely from rusting metal posts and splintered glass.

"If that thing collapses, we'll be sliced open," Dorian says.

"You sure this is it?" Silas asks again.

"I'm not senile." Maude shuffles forward through the front doors and we follow, glad to be out of the wind. "Bruce?" she calls out. "You here, Bruce? It's old Maddie Blue come to have a talk with you. Bruce?" she sings into the intricately designed crystalline dome of the building. Only Maude's voice and the sound of our boots squeaking against the tiled floor echo in the atrium. "Bruce?" she shouts, her voice betraying some impatience.

"A shopping city?" Dorian whispers, gaping at the long-ago looted shop fronts. "It looks like a cathedral." He bends down to pick up a watch. "Would it be stealing if I kept this?" he asks. Without waiting for any of us to respond, he drops the watch into the pocket of his coat. The floor is strewn with shiny objects, and I'm tempted to take something myself. As I stoop to retrieve a silver hair clip from the tiles, a noise travels down from a floor above and we all scramble up the stairs to find its owner.

"Bruce! We wanna talk, that's all. We ain't gonna do nothing bad to you. It's your old pal Maddie. Let's get a look at ya!"

"Come any closer and I'll shoot!" a voice calls. We stop climbing the stairs and look up again to see a bearded man clothed in a rainbow of color leaning over the railing and pointing a rifle. He's filthy, the grime making his skin dark and grainy.

"You ain't got no bullets in that thing," Maude cackles, and keeps walking.

"Don't move, Blue. I swear I'll let this thing go."

"You needn't try and fool me, Bruce. Even if you had bullets, you ain't got your glasses on. You can't see a blasted thing."

"Last warning!" he bellows.

"Maude, maybe you should stop," I say. I try to grab her but she's already too far ahead.

"If you can see, tell me how many people I got with me," she says.

"That's it," he calls. He looks through the scope, aims the rifle in our direction, and as his finger is about to engage the trigger, he bolts from the railing and disappears. Maude howls with laughter.

"He's off to plug himself in." She's right: he wasn't wearing an airtank, so he must have been holding his breath, unless he's somehow figured out how to withstand the atmosphere.

On the top floor, Maude leads us directly into a shop with wooden boxes and silver tubes covering the shelves. Bruce is in there, sitting on a grubby velvet armchair, the sides leaking stuffing. The rifle on his lap is pointing in our direction.

His air is coming from a solar respirator much like the one Maude had. No sooner has he pressed the mask to his face than he removes it again, and with his other hand puts a brown, oblong object between his lips. He inhales deeply, holding the mask up to it and allowing oxygen to envelop it, so it stays alight. The tip smolders and then smoke is billowing from Bruce's nose and mouth. He looks like he's on fire.

"You're still on those things?" Maude says. "One lung takes in the air and the other one takes in the dirty smoke, does it? They'll kill you, you twerp. And what a waste of bloody oxygen."

Bruce takes another slurp of air followed by a puff of the fiery cigar. "If I'm dying, I'm gonna die smoking," he announces. "No air in the atmosphere. But there's plenty in this thing," he says, and kicks the solar respirator. "I ain't brainless. Got me ways," he says.

We don't know much about Bruce except that he's a drifter and that he has a bilious hatred of the Ministry ever since they abandoned him. He's also the reason all the drifters live apart. In his view, they're safer alone, not so prone to being exterminated in one fell swoop. He coughs and Maude, like an awful echo, coughs, too. "Well, look at you, Maddie Blue. You turned out all right." He pats his knee and winks. "Here, take the weight off those pegs."

"You should be so lucky," she says.

"Oh, too good for me, now you've teamed up with Breathe again are you, Blue?" he asks.

"Oh, do shut up, Bruce. These here are kids of the Resistance."

"Resistance? Planting a few weeds and sitting around chanting all day? Don't make me laugh."

Silas steps forward and shakes Bruce's hand. "Not anymore. They're after us and we're building an army. We need all the men and women we can find to fight. We want you to be the first. Come fight with us. Help us gather up the rest and come with us." I have to say I expected more of a sales pitch. Why would Bruce join us if there's nothing in it for him?

"The Resistance thinks we're scum," he says, still alternating between air and smoke.

"The Resistance has plenty of reasons to hate you. We also need you. Simple as that," Silas says.

Bruce smiles and nestles himself into the armchair. "I'd say you're desperate coming out in a storm like that."

"Eager," Dorian corrects. He's carrying the backpack of airtanks, which he finally drops. "We know you can fight. And you know how *they* fight."

"What's in it for me?" Bruce looks at Maude, raises his eyebrows, and smacks his lips together. The thought of it is too much. Silas ignores him.

"Dorian, show him," he says. Dorian unbuckles his airtank, takes off his facemask, and puts the whole apparatus on the floor. He stands watching Bruce, breathing without any difficulty whatsoever. He's only been wearing a mask because of the strenuous walking we've been doing and even then, his oxygen level has been very low.

"Well, I can do that. You saw me. No big deal," Bruce says. Dorian takes a piece of red apple from his pocket and offers it to Bruce. The old man takes the food in his filthy hand and marvels for a moment before stubbing out the smoldering cigar and shoving it into his mouth. "Fruit. Well, that's nice. You lot managed to grow something. Fine. What difference does that make to me?" Several minutes pass and Dorian continues to watch Bruce, as alert as he was when he first removed the mask. No one speaks except Bruce. "So what? He can hold his breath. Big deal."

After ten minutes Bruce finally stops berating Dorian and says, "You'll wanna put that mask on again, sonny. It's bad for the brain." He turns to Silas. "Is he holding his breath?"

"I'm breathing, and if I can, you can. We all can. Come fight with us and we'll train you to do it." Dorian leans down and retrieves a small airtank from his backpack. "You'll need this."

Bruce looks up at Maude. "Not even a kiss?" he asks. Maude steps forward and kisses his cheek.

"Happy now?" she says with a smile.

"I'm convinced! That's what love will do to you, I suppose," he says pinching Maude's behind as he stands up.

The storm rages as Maude and Bruce lead us to an old school where a whole family of drifters live: a mother, father, son, and daughter. Even with Bruce and Maude calling out as we enter the building, an arrow scarcely misses my head and strikes the wall behind me. The parents are old. The journey will be hard. The Grove has a doctor, though, and that's what convinces the children to unplug their parents from the solar boxes and get them ready for the journey.

Next we swoop in on a church where we hear the drifter before we see her—a high soprano voice sings out some aria to rows and rows of empty pews. She is tall with pin-straight hair. She doesn't notice us filing in and, thinking it would be impolite to interrupt her in the middle of a performance, we slide into the back pews. When she finishes, we all clap. The shock of seeing us standing and applauding causes the poor woman to lose her balance and almost knock herself unconscious on the marble altar.

All night long we slog and search, looking for our new army. Every hideout is different and every encounter dangerous. The drifters have only managed to survive by viciously attacking unsuspecting tourists or, at the very least, defending themselves from them. And they are so distrustful it isn't easy to convince them. Dorian has to perform for many of them and Maude and Bruce have to threaten others. Even so, some still refuse either because they are afraid of us or afraid of the storm. Many won't give up their solar respirators, or, in the saddest cases, are simply waiting for death and not willing to try to outsmart it.

As dawn begins to blush, we turn around and head back to The Grove, followed now by a mass of hawkish drifters. We've managed to round up almost twenty of them and get guarantees from fifty more that if we come back with air-tanks, they'll join us. And they'll recruit their friends. So this will be Roxanne and Levi's job: to arrange a team to collect the remaining drifters now that we have a complete map pin-pointing all their locations. And then we must train them, improve their breathing, and prepare them for battle.

"Is this going to be enough?" I ask Silas as we trudge back along the icy roads.

"I hope so," he says. "Because we've got nothing else."

43
QUINN

I sit there, silent, as my father explains to Lennon and Keane that I was kidnapped and almost killed by a band of bloodthirsty terrorists. I have no idea whether or not he believes the story he's telling, but the twins stare at him and then back at me with their mouths open, chewed up dinner on display. "Were you scared?" Lennon asks.

"Yes," I say. My father squints at me, daring me to contradict him, so I try to retell the story; I have to make everyone believe we really were held captive. "They stuffed rags in our mouths and tied our hands. If we spoke to each other they punched us here." I put my hands against my upper body, which still thrums. Lennon stares and Keane rubs his hands along his own ribcage. My mother puts down her fork and rolls her eyes as though I'm talking about some gory film I've seen and not my own life.

"No need for the details," she says.

"If I met a terrorist I'd use my spear to stab him in the eye. He wouldn't get away from me," Keane says.

"Yes he would. It's a plastic spear," Lennon reminds him.

They spend the rest of the meal devising ways to torture and kill the so-called terrorists. My father nods approvingly, encourages us all to be hungry for revenge.

I didn't want to come home. When I burst out of the Justice Building earlier on, I was thinking about hiding out somewhere else. But I couldn't exactly live on the streets. I'd have been picked up the second I shut my eyes. And I couldn't go to Bea. It would've been the first place they'd have looked. So I dragged myself home, if I could even call it a home now that I know my parents don't care whether I live or die.

When I came through the front door, my parents were standing in the hallway hanging up their coats. They could hardly look at me.

I slink into my bedroom after dinner, and my father follows me. He sits on the edge of my bed looking at the pile of dirty clothes in the middle of the room. "I can't say I'm not disappointed," he says.

"Sorry," I say, as though *I* have something to be sorry about. "I shouldn't have trusted Alina. I shouldn't have bundled her through Border Control. I know that."

"Yes, well, generally you need to start showing more discretion."

"What do you mean?"

"Your friendships are suspect. You're too old to be palling around with auxiliaries, so it's about time you and Bea cut ties. People will start to talk." My heart jumps and my hands begin to sweat.

"She's my best friend," I say.

"Not anymore. Keep away from her. Your mother and I have bigger plans for your life than an auxiliary wedding. Cain Knavery's daughter is a year older than you. Pretty girl. Sharp." I know Niamh Knavery. When he says she's sharp, he means she's cruel. And she's had a stack of boyfriends since the beginning of the school year. Even if Bea weren't in the picture, I wouldn't touch Niamh Knavery with rubber gloves on.

"I understand, sir," I say. If I'm going to help the Resistance, I have to play the game, and if that means nodding a bit and pretending to agree with what he says, I'll do it. I have to.

"By the way," he says, standing up, "I don't know what the terrorists told you about my job, but whatever you heard, keep it to yourself. Your mother is fragile and the twins are young."

"I don't understand," I say. I take on the face of the Quinn who lived here only days ago and my father eats it right up.

"Well, that's fine," he says. Without saying good night he turns and leaves the room, pulling the door tight on his way out.

I retrieve an airtank from under the bed. I need to start training to exist with lower oxygen levels. I have no intention of living in this pod, or this house, one minute longer than I have to.

44
BEA

We are back in the pod for two weeks before we have lunch together. It's important we avoid each other in public now that Quinn's dad has vetoed our friendship. We have to meet in secret, in the caretaker's closet with brooms and mops or in hidden corners of the tech room. Quinn comes to my place sometimes, but only at night and not too often. We both have the same free period today, so we're using it to meet in the canteen with the freshmen, most of whom we don't know. The canteen is a muddle of clanking plates and hungry voices.

"Cain Knavery was over again last night," Quinn says.

"What did he want?" I'm not sitting in the seat right next to him, which is where I want to be, but two seats away. We're facing the same direction and talking without looking at each other. Quinn is wearing a cap that hides his face.

"Blood. He's sick of scouring the coastline. He wanted to know if I could remember anything else that could help them pinpoint the location. He's not happy."

"So he's afraid?"

"He didn't seem afraid exactly. He was irritated. He got so wasted he almost broke my wrist urging me to tell him more. He spent the evening laughing at nothing. Ha! Ha! He gives me the creeps. Niamh and Ronan had to come with a driver to pick him up once he keeled over. Ronan basically had to carry him out of the house." Quinn raps his fingers against the table. I wish I could touch him.

"Imagine having a dad like that. I feel sorry for them."

"For Ronan, maybe; *he's* all right. But his sister? Ugh."

"So what did you tell Cain before he passed out?" I ask, as my art teacher, Ms. Kechroud, comes into the canteen. Quinn pulls his cap down a little farther.

"The same thing I always tell him: 'South, that's all I know, Pod Minister.'"

"We're running out of time."

"You don't have to tell me that. I don't know how much longer they'll keep searching before they figure out that we lied. I wish there was a way we could step up our training."

Whenever Quinn comes over to my place, Mom sits in the living room, happily convinced we're making out, while really we exercise and practice breathing with reduced air. Quinn stole a couple of tanks from the cellar in his house and so we've been gradually tightening the valves and learning how to live on less and less oxygen, just in case. We are also practicing meditation and the relaxation positions Alina gave me a glimpse of. We aren't much good. We need more time, and really, we need a teacher.

When Quinn can't come over, I practice alone. But despite all the hours I'm putting in, it's always hard to breathe on reduced air when most of the day I'm breathing in more than I need. Quinn thought about buying Premium Pure Air so we could use it all day, gradually tightening the valves as we got stronger, but we'd just be drawing attention to ourselves. People would notice me especially. They'd know Quinn bought the air, and we aren't supposed to be seeing each other anymore.

"Have you figured out a way to get across the border?" I ask.

"I'm working on it," he says. He stops eating and starts to massage his temples.

"What is it?" He looks at me quickly, opens his mouth to speak, then bites his bottom lip. "Tell me, Quinn. What is it?" Ms. Kechroud has her lunch and is looking for a place to sit. She scans the room without spotting me and luckily chooses a place by the door, away from us.

“We shouldn’t have met here,” Quinn says.

“Don’t change the subject.” I throw down my fork in frustration. Quinn puts his head in his hands. It’s the first time since our return to the pod that we’re bickering and there’s no need for it. “Quinn, please,” I say more gently.

“The Pod Minister is impatient. He talked a lot about you. I think he was threatening me. I think he knows we’re together. He might be having me followed. It’s not unthinkable.”

Before I get a chance to respond, a shadow appears over us and when we look up, Riley and Ferris are standing there. Ferris has had a new set of veneers fitted that are too big for his mouth.

“Guess who made team captain?” Ferris asks, picking at a large mole on his chin. He leans in close, and I have to cup my hand over my nose because the smell of his aftershave is so strong.

“The coach is blind. Can you believe he chose Ferris over me? When have you ever heard of a defender being captain? It’s ridiculous. We ought to have Coach replaced. I’m gonna tell people he watches us in the showers. Damn auxiliary,” Riley complains.

“Not now,” Quinn says.

“I thought you two weren’t friends anymore,” Ferris says to Quinn, looking at me.

“She borrowed something. I was getting it back,” Quinn says, patting a notebook on the table. Riley reaches for the notebook, but Quinn snatches it first and stuffs it into his backpack.

"So, Bea, when are you going to let me take you out?" Ferris has managed to pick a hair out of his mole and is examining it in his hand. "Maybe we could double date," Ferris says to Quinn. Suddenly Quinn's smile vanishes and he glares at Ferris.

"And I could come, too. When Niamh is done with candy-ass Quinn she'll no doubt wanna cop a feel of a real man," Riley says, running his hands down his own body. I have no idea what they're talking about. Under the table I stretch out my leg so my foot is touching Quinn's.

"Oh, God, it's Ms. Kechroud. I didn't show up for detention with her last night. Let's roll out of here," Ferris says. He grabs Riley by the shirt and hauls him away. "Bye, Bea!" he calls.

"Shit!" Quinn says when they're out of earshot. "They're the last people I wanted to see." I don't say anything. I wait for Quinn to explain what Riley was talking about. He doesn't. He takes his tray to the counter to clear it off. I wait a few seconds, then follow him.

Once we're out in the yard he leads me to a hidden nook where the water fountain is and finally turns to me. "When she was over last night, my father organized for Niamh Knavery and me to go out next week. I had to say yes."

I think of Niamh Knavery, her long spindly legs and mammoth breasts, her shiny hair and perfectly proportioned face. I hate the idea of Quinn and Niamh alone, maybe at dinner or seeing a movie in the dark, and I feel my hands curl into fists.

"But we're still together," I say. I want him to do whatever it takes to help the Resistance. Even so, I don't want to lose him.

"Bea, I want *you* and no one else. I promise." He leans on me, pushing me toward the wall, and kisses me hard on the mouth. Then he steps away and takes my hands.

"What are we going to do?" I ask.

"I think it's time you went into hiding. If they decide to make an example of me, there's at least a chance my father will intervene."

"Where will I go?"

"Meet me at the three-B tram station after school. I'm going to leave my pad in my locker and you should, too, in case they're using them to track us. Bring a bag of clothes. I have an address," he says.

"I don't want to endanger anyone, Quinn. It isn't right."

He takes my hand and kisses my palm. "I know you don't, but they're the only people we can trust. It isn't safe in the pod anymore."

45
ALINA

I'm in the shooting range every day training drifters. Some of the older ones, who brought their own guns with them, take one look at the dummy and hit the bull's-eye the first time. I send them on their way, down to Levi for cardiovascular training or to Petra for yoga and meditation practice. Those who've been defending themselves with knives and swords need a bit more help knowing how to aim the rifle and keep it steady when it goes off.

Once I'm done with drifters, the Resistance members come up to practice. Most of them need no training at all; they've become accomplished snipers and could hit a running man from five hundred feet. Jazz was sent up by Petra a few minutes ago to do drills. Surprisingly, as she fiddles with the gun, she doesn't even seem to know where the trigger is.

When I try to give her a few words of instruction, she pushes me out of the way and stamps her feet.

"Don't tell me how to shoot or I'll point this baby at you! Tell me *where*." The other Resistance members in the range look over at us. Dorian is up here, too. He sneers, aims his rifle in Jazz's direction, and pretends to shoot, stepping back to give the effect of the gun going off. I shake my head and bite away the smile.

"See that dummy there? I want you to plug her little finger." Jazz gulps and points the gun at the target. She shoots and staggers backward, almost falling over from the force of the blast.

"There's something wrong with the rifle," she says when she realizes that all she's managed to hit is an old vent in the wall.

"There's nothing wrong with that piece, Jazz. I just used it."

"I'm telling you, it's broken!"

Dorian coughs and sputters in the lane next to us, and I turn my back on him because if I look at his face I'll laugh out loud. Then I'll be in real trouble.

"Here, try this," I say, handing her a pistol. It's smaller and I hope that the force from it when she shoots won't send her flying. She aims for the dummy again and fires. She takes only one step back this time, steadies herself on me, and sucks her teeth.

"Target down," Jazz tells me, pointing to the dummy's knee, which she's managed to hit.

"I said her little finger," I remind her.

"You did not! You said hit her leg." She turns to Dorian. "Isn't that what she said?"

Dorian puts down his gun and steps over to us. "Jazz, have you been practicing?" Jazz nods vehemently, then puts her thumb into her mouth and starts to suck on it. Dorian continues. "The thing is, when Petra tells me to come up here and train, well, sometimes I go down and sit with the trees. Have you ever done that?" Jazz nods again. "And sometimes, when I look at those trees, I wonder what it would be like to climb up into one and just sit there. You know, just sit there all day."

"Can you keep a secret?" Jazz asks. Dorian turns his head to reveal a willing ear. "I do that all the time. I climb the trees and imagine all the things that the world used to have. And I imagine things *I* used to have. Like my parents." Here she stops and looks at me. "Petra said your parents died." My stomach does a somersault.

"They're missing, yes." Dorian rests one hand on my shoulder, the other on Jazz's.

"How about we go down to the trees now," he says. Jazz looks at the pistol she's still holding.

"I never practiced. When the army comes, I won't be able to fight."

"We could go to the trees for a while and come back here for an intensive course in gun fighting later," I say. Jazz cheers and dashes out of the room.

"She's so young," I say. Dorian shakes his head and takes the heavy rifle I've been holding and places it on the rack.

"We all are, Alina. We're all really young."

46
QUINN

I don't know what's come over me, but I've got a really bad feeling—like a sour pain in the pit of my stomach. At lunch today I couldn't bring myself to tell Bea how vile the Pod Minister was when he came around for dinner yesterday or how anxious my parents were to arrange a date with Niamh. Plus, last night I dreamed they came for Bea. They dragged her away by her feet, her head cracking against the ground, and there was nothing I could do about it. Even when they threw her out of the pod, I just stood at the viewing station watching her gasp for breath.

I meet Bea at the tram station and she is all ready with a packed bag. She agrees that we have to find a place for her to hide, and there are only two people who will be able to help us find somewhere safe: Alina's aunt and uncle.

When we step out of the winch, we turn right and start searching for the door to Alina's apartment. They all look the same, as most do in Zone Three, white with a letter and number above a peephole. "We're looking for J fifty-two," I whisper to Bea, who is squinting to read the characters above the doorframes.

"Here," she says, and presses her ear against the outer door. "Are you sure you got the right address?" I nod, join her at the door, and ring the bell. We wait for a minute and when no one answers, I ring again. We stand for another few minutes, but nothing happens. I ring again. And then again and again and again. "They must be at work. Or what if they were arrested? Now what?" Bea says. I have no idea, now what. Bea's not safe at my house, and I know I couldn't trust Riley or Ferris with her life. I slump onto the floor and Bea sinks down next to me. "Do you think Maude's okay?" she asks. I've hardly thought of Maude since we've been back, although that's exactly why we're back here at all: Maude was their guarantee that we wouldn't betray them.

"I'm sure she's fine. She's probably plugged into some solar respirator wielding a machete." I try to sound light. I put my arm around Bea's shoulder, kiss her cheek, then turn her face toward mine and kiss her on the lips. It never gets old, kissing Bea, and when we're kissing, I don't forget everything like I did with other girls. I don't space out. When I'm with

Bea I remember everything—my whole life feels like it's in that kiss—everything I've ever known is right there in her mouth. She rests her head on my shoulder and sighs.

"I hope they fed her. She isn't bad."

"Neither is Petra. Maude Blue'll be fine."

"Maybe I should go home. Mom and Dad were still at work when I left, and I don't have my pad anymore. I need to say good-bye. Let's try again in a couple of hours. Or tomorrow," she says. Usually I have terrible instincts and my gut tells me to do all kinds of things that get me into trouble, but this time the feeling is physical. There's no way Bea should go home.

"It isn't safe," I say.

"We don't know that for sure. Maybe we're being paranoid."

"You didn't hear Cain Knavery. He wants someone's head on a plate."

She doesn't believe me. "What's one more night?" she says. She presses the button to call the winch and within seconds the doors open and she steps inside. "You coming?"

"Wait!" A voice. I jump up from the ground and Bea steps out of the winch. I stand in front of Alina's outer door thinking it will slide open, but it remains shut tight. "Psst! Here!" the voice calls again. That's when we see two eyes peering at us from a crack in the door next to Alina's. "Who you looking for?"

"Alina's aunt and uncle," Bea mutters.

"The Moons. Can you tell us where they are?" I ask.

The door beeps and buzzes and when it opens fully, an old man appears.

"At a guess, I'd say you're on the run from the Ministry. Come on, get in here quick."

Old Man Watson, who could be a lunatic for all we know, agrees to keep Bea hidden until we can find a way for her to escape. I'm afraid to leave her, but we're running out of options, and with all the plants in his living room, he can be trusted not to hand us over to the Ministry at least.

"But what about you?" Old Watson asks. "The Pod Minister threatened you both."

"I have a plan. I'll be fine." Bea sees right through this lie.

"Stay here. Be safe," she pleads. The old man turns tactfully and shuffles to the other side of the room. Bea's right; in some ways, it makes no sense for me to go home. If they decide to arrest her, my arrest will follow. The Pod Minister wants answers and when it comes down to it, I have no idea whether or not my father will help me.

"It isn't enough to save ourselves. We have to find a way to tell people what's happening. We have to let people choose a new future." As I say this, I know it's true. I want to help other people. I want to make a difference and I can't do that in hiding. "If you find a way to escape, go to The Grove. I'll meet you there."

"No, Quinn," she says, tugging on the sleeves of her sweater and hiding her hands inside them.

"We'll meet at The Grove." I brush her hair out of her eyes and she smiles reluctantly. She looks so beautiful that for a second I just stare at her. I can't believe I've had this girl in front of me my whole life and didn't see her.

"I didn't want my parents to worry, so I told them what we told the Ministry. They haven't a clue about anything. Can you get word to them?" Bea asks.

"*I'll* do it," Watson says. "I'm not on any dead-or-alive list. Yet."

"How can we thank you?" I ask.

"Stay alive," he says.

When I get home, I know I'm right. My father is pacing the living room. He looks like he's about to have some kind of fit. Lennon and Keane are hiding behind the couch, peeking out at him. My mother is lying on the floor to relieve her back pain.

"Where the hell have you been? Don't you ever look at your pad?" my father bellows as I creep in and sit on the edge of the sideboard.

"I left it at school by mistake," I say.

My father squints. "Cain Knavery will be here in a few minutes. He might be bringing Niamh over."

"A fine girl," my mother says.

"What's happening? Why are you home so early?" I ask my father.

"Where is Bea Whitcraft?" He looks at me directly, like he's convinced he would spot a lie if I tried to tell one.

"How should I know? We don't hang out anymore."

"I got off the pad with Riley Weeze a couple of minutes ago. He says he saw you two at lunch." He shakes his head. "The stewards went to find her. She wasn't at home. Her parents say they don't know where she is. If you do, I want to know." He is speaking into the mirror, talking to my reflection as though he can't bear to look at the real me any longer.

"Why were the stewards trying to pick up Bea?" my mother asks. Can she really be that stupid? She was right there when the Pod Minister threatened Bea, me, and her unborn child.

My father whips around, grabs the collar of my shirt, and marches me into the hall. "The Ministry has searched the entire southern coastline, up and back—twice. I've tried to stall the Pod Minister, but he wants answers. Now tell me the truth."

I keep my expression blank. My father pushes me into the wall.

"I can't help you if you lie to me. You're practically asking me to hand you over. Don't try to protect her. It's happened before, you know. Auxiliaries have been trying to butter up Premiums for years just so they'll have someone on the inside. She isn't worth it, son. Save yourself. Save your family."

And this is exactly why he's been so desperate to see Niamh and me together; he wants the Pod Minister to have some grounds for keeping us alive.

"I don't know where the terrorists are. Bea was the one who heard them talking. She told me and I had no reason to distrust her. I did meet her today, and she told me she'd lied about hearing where they were taking us. She wanted to give our kidnappers a chance to escape. I'm sorry." My father pats me on the shoulder and steps back. He almost allows himself a smile, and this makes me sad; he is proud of me and it's because he thinks I've betrayed my best friend. Or maybe he doesn't see it that way; maybe he sees it as a sign of my loyalty—to him, to my family, and mostly to the Ministry.

"Where is she now?" he asks.

"She told me she was running away. She said she had people she could be safe with. She told me I should run too."

"RATS."

"I think so." I peer down at the floor, and at that moment there is a pounding at the front door and three silhouettes appear in the opaque glass.

"Let me do the talking," my father says, opening the door. "Welcome! Welcome! I put the whiskey on ice an hour ago. It should be nice and cold. And you've brought the youngsters!" Niamh and Ronan step into the hallway and smile politely.

"Niamh! What a beauty she is," my father says, taking Niamh's hand between his own and squeezing it.

"Ha! She didn't look like that an hour ago. And you should see her when she gets out of bed. A horror! Ha!" The Pod Minister barges right past my father and into the living room, where he pulls my mother up off the floor and kisses her right on the lips, his mouth opening slightly. My father lets go of Niamh's hand and follows him in.

"All right?" Ronan asks, offering me his hand in a perfunctory kind of way. When I shake it, I notice that his white shirt has a red paint stain down the length of one sleeve.

"You still doing the art, then?" I ask.

"Yeah," he says. "Why did you drop it? You were good."

"Me? No way," I tell him. "Ms. Kechroud said my pencil drawings looked like something a nine-year-old would draw."

Ronan shakes his head and runs his hand through his hair. "She's not a real teacher. You should come around some time and I'll show you my studio. If you like." He is about to say something else when Niamh nudges him aside.

"Quinn," she says. She looks at me from under her eyelashes. "I'm so excited for our date next week." She flicks her thick hair from her shoulders and pulls at the hem of her incredibly short dress. I've never met a person more in love with herself. Ronan rolls his eyes and strolls into the living room.

"Come on, you two," my mother says, tottering into the hallway and taking Niamh's hand. "Oh, what lovely shoes." The shoes are actually strappy sandals and the heels must be eight inches high. I have no idea how she's managing to keep her balance. She looks like she's about to go clubbing somewhere very hot and very seedy. How can my parents think this is better than Bea? This?

"Thank you, Mrs. Caffrey," Niamh simpers.

"Oh, call me Cynthia, please."

In the sitting room my father and the Pod Minister have already hit the bottle and are deep in conversation. When they see me, they stop talking. The Pod Minister beckons me closer with one of his ringed fingers. Ronan is sitting next to the twins on the couch looking utterly bored.

"Your father tells me you haven't been altogether truthful with us, Caffrey Junior." His breath stinks of booze; he must have been drunk when he arrived. He looks at Niamh and beams. "But we are all such friends, I think we can arrange something. Will you help us protect the pod?"

"Of course, Pod Minister," I say. My father looks relieved and refills his whiskey glass.

"I'll arrange it," the Pod Minister says.

I sit in the armchair opposite them. "Arrange what?" I ask.

"A sort of press conference. Tomorrow, while your father is . . . at work . . . we'll get you to do a little interview. There are murmurings of dissent within Zone Three and I don't like it."

"A press conference?" I say.

"Expose those dirty RATS for what they really are, so people will see what we're up against. Tell them what you know," the Pod Minister suggests. He raises his glass of whiskey and guzzles it down in one long slurp. He crunches on the ice.

"You're going to be famous, Quinn," Niamh says, running a cold finger down the back of my neck. I shiver and reach around to pull her hand away.

"Look at that," Mum says, seeing Niamh's hand in mine. "Now isn't that lovely." She smiles and so does the Pod Minister. Lennon and Keane grin, too. And then Niamh laughs, her head tipping backward theatrically. Ronan rolls his eyes again. The only person who still looks worried is my father.

"Quinn will be ready, Pod Minister. Don't worry about

that." My father moves toward my mother, and when he gets close enough to her, touches her tummy. He watches me the whole time, making sure I understand that my obedience protects our whole family. And I do intend to be obedient. I plan to tell my fellow citizens everything I know. I couldn't have asked for a better opportunity to tell the truth.

47
ALINA

The snow makes it difficult to climb, especially now that I'm reattached to an airtank, and if I didn't think this might be my last chance to sit in the trees, I'd shimmy back down again and tiptoe into a warm room. Jazz is almost at the top of the leafless oak next to me, nestled in against its cold trunk, humming to herself, and Dorian is almost at the top of his tree, too. When I get up to the same height as them I find a strong branch and brush away the layer of snow covering it so I can lie on my back along its length.

"You'll fall!" Dorian calls. I pretend I can't hear him. The blinds haven't yet been closed for the night. I stretch out, looking up at the black sky flecked with tiny winking stars. I can't remember the last time I saw the sky like this.

My breathing slows and I allow myself to be right here, in

the moment, savoring the peace. All the millions and millions of stars remind me, too, how small and fragile I am. And unimportant, really. If this branch were to creak and moan and break under my weight, and I were to plummet to the ground, the stars in the sky would continue to decorate the world. And even if every last tree disappears from our planet, the stars will still be up there. Flickering their good-nights.

No one speaks. We lie in our own trees for a long time, waiting for the sun.

48
BEA

"We took three trams to get here. Your dad was worried we'd be followed," Mom says, brushing my face with her hand. Her hair is white. I don't remember it turning this color.

I am sitting between her and Dad on the couch and Old Watson is in his bedroom listening to music, the volume politely blaring so he won't overhear any of our conversation.

"Why didn't you tell us before, love?" Dad asks.

"I planned to. I just didn't want to worry you as soon as I got back. You'd been through enough. Quinn and I were sure we'd figure something out," I say.

"Well, border stewards can always be bribed," he says, as though this is something he's accustomed to doing.

"You have no money." I smile so he knows I'm not accusing him.

"People need transplants and I only need one kidney. And one eye. Where there's a will, there's a way, Bea. I won't have my only child hunted," he says. Mom starts to fidget with the seam on her skirt. She knows it's no plan at all. It's true that people do sell their organs, but the process takes months, and only people under thirty-five are allowed to be donors.

"I really believed that you and Quinn were in love. But all you were doing every evening was homework and training. I thought—" She can't go on. This was her dream for me, that I would marry a Premium.

"He does love me. We did more than train." I blush, embarrassed. Mom smiles and so does Dad, but I don't know why since my marrying Quinn and living safely in the pod is out of the question. I'm about to remind them of this when Mom throws her arms around me.

"That fool. It only took him forever to notice you."

"I'll never be a Premium," I say.

"No, you won't," she says, and reaches over me to touch my father's face.

We hear something shattering in the next room and within a couple of seconds Old Watson hobbles in and begins rummaging though a stack of remote controls.

"Turn on the screen. Turn on the screen. The screen!" he demands. When he finds the remote, he presses a large red button and the screen comes to life.

I watch and wait, wondering what can be so important, when the Justice Minister appears. *"This is a Ministry announcement: Tomorrow morning we will be hosting a special live interview with Quinn Caffrey, who recently found himself kidnapped, tortured, and blackmailed by a dangerous terrorist cell."* The screen displays a photograph of a much younger-looking Quinn; he must have been about twelve when the photograph was taken.

"What's going on?" Mom stares at me as though I've organized this myself.

"Shh," I say, turning up the volume.

"The special event will be held at the Justice Building and spectators are welcome. Extra tram services are scheduled. We hope to see many of you there to support this victim and the Ministry's fight against terrorism. An antiterrorist march will follow the press conference. Good night," the Justice Minister says. The screen goes black before brightening again with an advertisement for a new brand of aerosol soap.

"Why would Quinn agree to do that? Well?" Mom is almost shouting, and Old Watson has to remind her to keep her voice down.

"He knows exactly what he's doing," Dad says calmly.

"And what *exactly* is that?" Mom wants to know.

"A message was sent to my pad from Lennon Caffrey's

code just before you showed up," Dad says, looking at Old Watson.

"And?" I ask. I hold my breath.

"I didn't understand it at all when I read it. I thought it'd been sent by mistake. But the message wasn't from Lennon at all. It was obviously Quinn who sent it. He wrote *Please come down to hear me speak tomorrow*. Or something like that."

Mom stands up and puts her hands on her hips. "So *what*?" she says. Dad looks at me, giving me a moment to work it out.

"So he's telling us to gather a crowd for tomorrow," I say as a thread of Quinn's plan starts to sink in.

"Exactly," Dad says. "Whatever he plans on saying, he's asking for some kind of backup, and what better than loads of auxiliaries?"

Old Watson steps forward and leans on my Mom for support. "I'll get out tonight and spread the word to as many people as I can. Door to door."

Mom nods. "We will, too."

"Help plan the crowd, but don't go down there tomorrow," I beg.

Dad stands up. "No more being pushed around, Bea. Now's the time. We have to do this. For you."

He's right. It might be our only chance. Quinn has practically asked my parents to get involved. And even if they didn't, the Ministry would soon get bored searching for me and target my parents.

"We should go now," Mom says. She thanks Old Watson and moves to the hallway, my father behind her.

"Be safe," I say, as Mom opens the door.

"We will," they say together.

"And we'll be back tomorrow after the interview," Dad tells me, and pats my arm. I kiss him lightly on the cheek and then my mom.

"Sleep well," Mom says, and turns away, her eyes tearing up. They step through the door and it closes with a beep.

Old Watson rummages in a cupboard and pulls out a walking stick.

"They never wanted to fight before," I say.

"They never had anything worth fighting for," Old Watson says. "Until now." And with that, he opens the door again, leaving me alone with nothing to do but imagine the fight.

49
ALINA

We are dozing when a piercing whistle slices the air. I sit up, throw my legs over the branch, and look down. "What's that?" I call out. I'm still half asleep, but Dorian and Jazz are already scampering down the trees.

"It's the zips," Dorian shouts. "They're back! Why didn't anyone close the blinds?"

And so it's started. If I'm really prepared to fight, today's the day to prove it. I take a deep breath and climb down the tree.

It's useless hiding in the bunkers. They've found us, and we'll be buried alive if we go underground. It's time to fight. There are people running in every direction, some of them already holding guns, others so taken by surprise they're still pulling on their boots.

I vomit. Without even waiting for me to wipe my mouth

clean, Jazz pulls on my arm and starts to tug me toward a staircase. "I never trained!" she squeals. "I never trained! Oh, help me, Alina."

"It's too late, Jazz," Dorian says. He glances left and right, then looks back at me and we stand staring at each other, neither of us certain what happens now.

At that moment Silas comes running from the lookout post, his eyes hell-stricken. He is pulling on a bulletproof vest and when he sees Jazz he grabs her. "Find Petra! We need everything and everyone. Rouse the sleepers, Jazz. And if you see Levi or Roxanne, tell them it's time to ignite that stolen tank. Go!" Jazz nods and dashes away, her small running figure a blur against the dawn. Silas turns to me and Dorian. "Get every remaining weapon we have in the shooting range. I'll gather everyone. This is it." Dorian runs away as Silas moves off in the opposite direction. I follow Silas.

"We're going to be okay, aren't we?" I ask.

Silas takes me by the shoulders. "Fight with gusto!" he says, and bounds off along the corridor, leaving me alone.

Dorian returns with a load of guns, drops them at my feet, and I begin distributing them as he goes to get more weapons. When Silas returns, he directs people into position.

At last Petra appears. She is carrying an Uzi and holding a megaphone. "No mercy!" she hollers.

So we take our positions and wait.

50
BEA

I can't eat breakfast, and even the hot drink Old Watson brews for me goes cold in the cup. I spend the morning pacing the apartment and switching channels on the screen, looking for coverage of the interview. Not that I need to; when the time comes, it's on every channel. "I should come down there with you," I say as Old Watson is patting his pockets and getting ready to leave.

"You should be rational," he replies, meaning I'm being emotional. But what he doesn't know is that I've never been very rational when it comes to Quinn. "If you disappear from the apartment, I won't know where you are and I'll have to form a search party to find you. So stay here," he says. I nod. Old Watson looks like he might be about to hug me, but thinking better of it, he nods brusquely and rushes away.

I turn to the screen as the voice-over comments on the impressive turnout and the exclusive interview about to come. I pick up the cold cup and finally take a few sips from it.

As the camera pans over a row of people sitting behind a desk on an elevated stage, Quinn appears. I put down the cup again and pull a chair close to the screen. He is dressed in a shirt and tie and sitting next to the Justice Minister—a round, red-faced old man who looks like he is about to fall asleep at any moment, despite the hoopla going on around him. Quinn is sitting quite still, his face looks gray, and his glare is fixed on some distant object beyond the crowd. He unfastens the top button of his shirt. Instinctively I unzip my cardigan a couple of inches.

"To those of you just joining us, welcome to Pod TV Channel 4," says the announcer. "The atmosphere here is electric and in a few minutes we should be hearing from the Pod Minister and Quinn Caffrey. After that, stay tuned for footage of the march."

Several pockets of spectators are holding anti-RATS placards aloft and cheering every time anyone on stage moves. I try to locate either my parents or Old Watson, but it's impossible; there must be a couple of thousand people down at the Justice Building, Premiums and auxiliaries all mixed in together. It isn't often this happens, and for a moment, I find myself smiling, until I'm startled back into the moment by a blast of high-tempo music.

I hold my breath as the Pod Minister parades onto the stage like he's a rock star, grinning and bowing as the cheers swell. He takes a purple handkerchief from his breast pocket and waves it in the air. "The Pod Minister is known for his candid interviews, but it's a rarity to see him appear at a public event like this. And the crowd is *loving* it," the announcer observes. As the music fades, the Pod Minister takes his place beside Quinn, ruffling Quinn's hair playfully as he sits down. He raises his hands and the crowd hushes. "Looks like it's about to begin," the announcer says, in case we're all such idiots we can't interpret anything that's happening for ourselves. Although maybe it's so we *don't* interpret anything for ourselves.

The Pod Minister taps a microphone hidden somewhere in his lapel and a noise like a drumbeat echoes over the airwaves. It makes me jump. The Pod Minister smiles. "These are trying times, my friends, trying times indeed," he proclaims. "Every day, our way of life, our very existence, comes under attack from the mindless barbarism of terrorists who seek to instill fear into our hearts. These people are fanatics whose beliefs we do not share and whose values are corrupt. They seek to destroy the pod and compromise our safety, hoping only to expose us once again to the horrors of life as it was during The Switch. And then there are those among us"—he gestures to the captivated crowd, the camera, and everyone at home, and the people sitting with him at the desk—"who wish to save this place and protect the life within it. Will we be tyrannized by the few? I know I won't. And I know you won't either. No. Together we will stand against our enemies and beat them down. Despite our differences, we will rise as *one* and proclaim our right to life. Our right, as humans, to breathe."

As he finishes his speech, he runs his hand through his hair and looks down at Quinn coldly, almost challengingly. I remember this look and I do not like it. Quinn lays his hands flat on the desk in front of him and stares at them. A few people in the crowd have thrown up their arms in celebration and are chanting the Pod Minister's name over and over. *"Knavery! Knavery! Knavery!"* He nods, and in that small gesture is the confidence of his supremacy.

"I gather you here today, my friends, to listen to a story of evil. This young man, a personal friend of mine, was stolen from us and tortured. He will tell us what he knows, and through his story you will see the face of our enemy." The Pod Minister sits down and turns to Quinn. "Would you please start by telling us a bit about yourself?" he says, pulling a small silver flask from his jacket and taking a drink.

My stomach lurches. Quinn looks so much smaller than I remember—the Justice Minister sitting on his one side, the Pod Minister on the other. He is trapped between them. What can he possibly do now? What can he say?

Quinn clears his throat and his microphone crackles to

life. "My name is Quinn Caffrey, and first of all I want to thank you for coming here today. Thank you for listening to me. I promise to tell the truth. I am a Premium, but I hope you will see that I represent you all." He puts a thumb to his mouth and chews on the nail momentarily. He has none of the Pod Minister's showmanship, but his tone is so sincere and humble there is an audible murmur of sympathy from the crowd. I feel so proud of him, and afraid for him, that I have an urge to jump up and race to the Justice Building despite Old Watson's warning. I want to be with him. I wrap my arms around my body and lean forward in the chair.

"We have no doubt you'll be truthful," the Pod Minister says, slapping Quinn on the back. "And what you want to tell us is that you were kidnapped by the RATS, is that right?"

"I was with them for several days and I saw how fervently they believe in their cause. It's actually scary how passionate they are."

"Yes! Ha!" the Pod Minister hoots.

Without being prompted, Quinn gets to his feet and straightens his tie. Behind him, a row of stewards are standing with their arms behind their backs, visors covering their eyes. They don't look real. But they look ready.

"During my time on the outside, I learned so much more about the war on terrorism than I ever could have learned here inside the pod. I was living in blissful ignorance while others were dying on my behalf. And what I have to say may be terrifying to many of you." His voice has found some volume and clarity. He is more the Quinn I know.

The Pod Minister squints as Quinn edges his way out from behind the desk and moves closer to the crowd. "I tell you all now, in sincerest truth, that you *cannot* trust Breathe or the Ministry." I cover my face with my hands and peer through the spaces between my fingers. The stewards do not move.

Cain Knavery takes another swig from his silver bottle and says, "Son—"

"We are prisoners here!" Quinn shouts. All of a sudden he sounds breathless. "They are overfeeding us oxygen. Outside many of us *could* breathe, if we knew how. I've seen it. The RATS want to save us."

"You see what they've done to him?" The Pod Minister stands up, pushes his way past the other officials, and moves to the center of the stage. When he gets to Quinn, he throws an arm around his shoulder. Quinn flinches. And so do I. "He's been delirious since we found him. I had hoped he would be able to address you, but . . . A terrible shame." The Justice Minister, his eyelids heavy, nods in agreement.

For a moment, no one moves, and then a voice from the crowd calls out. "*So you* aren't *overfeeding us oxygen?*" Then another calls, "*Yeah, what did he mean by that? We're paying for extra oxygen we don't even need?*"

"Overfeeding you oxygen? What do *you* think? Ha!" the Pod Minister asks. The crowd murmurs as Quinn manages to squirm his way out of the Pod Minister's hold and rushes to the very front of the stage.

The Pod Minister takes one step forward and stops. "Turn off his microphone," he yells to no one in particular.

"I have no reason to lie. And they are killing the trees. We'll never escape."

"They kill trees? What's he talking about?"

"We are trapped here. Forever!" Quinn continues.

The Pod Minister rubs his mouth with the back of his hand and glares at the crowd. "If you want to leave the pod, you are all free to go. No one is stopping you. Leave!" the Pod Minister shouts. "Open the doors! Let everyone out!"

The camera closes in on Quinn and he seems to look right into the lens. Right at me. "We can't leave, and he knows it. They have us addicted to their air."

"The interview is over. Quinn Caffrey is clearly mad," the Pod Minister says. He nods at the stewards who are lined up in front of the stage, and on cue, they begin to move, pushing the crowd back in an effort to force them to disperse.

"Don't be prisoners!" Quinn shouts.

"The microphone!" the Pod Minister calls out again. His face has turned pink and his lips are wet with saliva. "I said we are done here. It's time for the march."

"What are you afraid of?" Quinn yells. The Pod Minister smiles and comes right to the edge of the stage. I move away from the screen.

"I. Am afraid. Of *nothing*," he whispers. What looks like a bottle is hurled on stage and barely misses him. For several seconds nothing moves. The next sound I hear is Quinn's voice.

"Well, maybe you should be," he says.

"Turn off his MICROPHONE!" the Pod Minister yells again, pointing at Quinn as another object hurtles toward the stage, and then another. Soon the Pod Minister is forced to dodge the missiles coming from the crowd. He looks as though he intends to leap in among the people and personally take care of them, when he sees Quinn about to jump off the stage and make his escape. Suddenly the Pod Minister charges at Quinn and wrestles him to the ground.

Then many voices can be heard clamoring for attention: *"Let him go!" "We want the truth! Can we breathe outside?" "The PM's strangling him. Someone do something!" "He's just a boy! Help him!"* The stewards, a human wall at the front of the stage, hold out their batons.

"I'm coming!" I say aloud. But I can't take my eyes off the screen.

The Pod Minister pummels Quinn until several stewards bundle forward and pull Quinn to his feet. The Pod Minister brushes himself off and looks right into the camera.

"All *lies*," he wheezes. "Quinn Caffrey will be punished for public disorder, as will anyone else who is caught inciting violence."

But the crowd is enraged, and when the Pod Minister opens his mouth to address them again, his composure restored, they chant and hurl things onto the stage. *"Freedom! Freedom! Freedom!"*

That's when my parents appear. "Get out of there! What are you doing?" I yell. The stewards are trying to subdue the protesters who are still throwing things, and my parents manage to rush past them and clamber up onto the stage along with several others.

As soon as my father is close to the Pod Minister, he launches himself forward, punching the Pod Minister square in the jaw and knocking him to the ground. The crowd, for a brief instant, gasps collectively, and then everyone is hollering, shaking their fists, and catcalling. What my father has done feels like a victory, especially to auxiliaries who've spent their lives complying.

But the Pod Minister will not be beaten this easily. Lying prostrate, a trickle of blood running from his nose, he raises a finger and within seconds more stewards emerge from the recesses of the stage, spread themselves among the crowd, and begin to flail their batons. A steward strikes a young woman on the side of the head and she crumples to the ground like a rag. People begin to scatter, but even more stay exactly where they are, my parents included.

No one has figured out how to turn off his microphone, and Quinn is yelling again. "Fight for the right to air! There is life outside the pod. And there are *trees*. We could live out there! We—" He stops, his attention distracted. The Pod Minister is back on his feet. And he has a gun pointed at the crowd. Though not at the crowd, exactly. He is smiling. My stomach flips and I lunge at the screen.

"NO!" I scream. A shot breaks the momentary silence and then my mother is on the ground in a flowering pool of blood. My father looks at her aghast and turns to the Pod Minister when another crack swallows all hope and my father too is on the ground bleeding.

Quinn flails, but the stewards keep a tight hold on him and eventually drag him off the stage and out of sight.

And now no one can stop the crowd. The people are advancing on the Pod Minister and the thrashing stewards are unable to do anything to stop them.

I can no longer see my parents. I drop to my knees, as every noise in the world disappears and in my ears instead is a shrill scream, which, only after several seconds, do I realize is my own.

51
ALINA

The soldiers are advancing on The Grove from all directions. And behind them, around twenty armored tanks are grinding their way through the debris of the city. My instinct is to run, not fight. "What are you waiting for?" Silas shouts, his gun firing off a round of bullets.

I peer through the scope and pick off my first soldier. My first murder. My stomach turns and if I had anything in it, I'm sure I would be sick again. Silas is next to me, relentlessly firing his gun, and as he fires, he roars—guttural, primal. Maude is here too, along with about twenty drifters with sniper skills, and Dorian is on Silas's other side. On any other day I am sure we would make a formidable team. Today, we are too few.

Occasionally soldiers drop as our sniper wounds them and a few troops in the rear fall out of line in an attempt to dodge the bullets, but most are sprinting in our direction. Suddenly their tanks fire, splitting open whole sections of the stadium, and the soldiers run right through the openings.

I continue shooting as our stolen tank emerges and fires at the running soldiers. But the Ministry has twenty tanks, and we have only one, and within minutes, ours is forced to retreat as more vehicles bombard The Grove. I scream and fire off another round.

A zip flies overhead and at once The Grove is filled with choking foam, dust, and debris. We duck our heads. "Shout when you're ready to make a run for it," Silas says. Many of the drifters are already dashing for the lower levels.

"How many have we got sniping?" I shout.

"One hundred and fifty, give or take. I've positioned them at every side." That may be true, but if the other teams are as scared as this one, that number has just halved as our troops disband to save themselves.

"Let's go!" I shout.

"Follow me!" Silas yells. I reach for Maude, but Bruce already has her safely by the hand.

As we move down the back stairs we are forced to step across bodies to escape. Some are only injured, some clearly dead. The foot soldiers must have already entered the building. If we stop to help we may never make it out alive, so we keep moving.

We run as best we can along a wide corridor when another bomb hits. Through the shattered glass paneling we see a sight that makes each one of us stop running and gasp aloud: the forest we've spent our lives cultivating is shriveling up before our eyes. Black foam swells along the columns of trees and eats its way from branch to branch.

A small figure hurtles toward us. "Petra won't come out!" It's Jazz. She's hysterical. "Make her come out!"

"Where is she?" I shout.

"She says she won't let the trees die alone." Jazz tears away and gestures for us to follow. We scramble back down to the lower level where the roaring battle is muffled by the sound of the shivering, dying trees.

"Come out. Come out, please!" Jazz screams, her voice like sharpened metal. Petra is sitting on a low branch of an oak. Her hair is loose and her feet are bare. She was the one who made us prepare for war, who insisted we fight, and now here she is meditating her way to defeat.

"What in hell's name you doin' up there, you fruitcake?" Maude screams, shaking a fist at Petra.

"Get down here. Cut the crap, Petra!" I shout. I've nothing to lose and someone needs to bring her to her senses.

"What have they ever done?" she asks. She strokes a branch and rests her head against it. "All I ever wanted was to protect them. I failed. I won't desert them."

"You didn't fail. Get down and fight for them. Fight for yourself. The foam will eat through that tree in a couple of minutes and you'll be gobbled up along with it."

"It's too late. You all know it's too late. The zips are coming back. Another bomb and we'll all be dead."

She's right. It was crazy to think we could win. "We're leaving. Come with us," I say.

"Take Jazz," she says, and with that begins to climb the tree, moving closer to the foam. Two zips roar overhead.

"I'm going!" Silas shouts. When I grab Jazz's elbow and start to drag her away, she sticks her feet into the soil and becomes immovable.

"Help me get Petra down," she pleads. Her dirty face is lined with tears.

"We have to go. We are going to try to get down the river. We're heading for Sequoia. Petra wants to die here, Jazz. Let her," I say. There's no point in lying to the child. She deserves the truth. But Jazz won't hear the truth, or doesn't like it. She pulls herself from my grip and starts to climb Petra's tree. "JAZZ!" I scream. She doesn't turn back. She scurries up the trunk like a little insect and is gone.

Silas is behind me. "She's made her choice," he shouts. "We have to go!"

"But she's a child," I say to no one in particular.

We dash across the smoldering field to the west end of

the stadium where we raid the airtank stockpile, grabbing as many as we can carry. Dorian will be fine—and though Silas and I have spent the last two weeks in intense training, we will need it along the road. Maude and Bruce certainly will. No one seems to have made it to this side of the building yet and the potent gunfire in the northeast section of the building sounds horrific.

Dorian puts down his weapon and begins to unbolt the heavy door while Silas and I fit ourselves with airtanks and then ensure that Maude and Bruce have theirs, too.

"Get your hands up," a steely voice demands. When we turn, a broad figure in full army regalia is standing less than five feet from us, pointing a rifle in our direction. Behind him, ten soldiers stand with their guns aimed at us, too. I'm sure this is it, and I try to think of something calming so that when I die my last thought won't be a violent one.

"I know you," Silas snarls. "You murdered my friend." He steps forward but Dorian and Bruce manage to restrain him.

"Shall we shoot him, General?" one of the soldiers asks.

Maude snorts and spits at the soldier's feet. "Shoot me, why don't you, you little runt," she says.

"General?" the soldier presses, waving his gun between Silas and Maude.

"Little runt," Maude repeats.

"No. We need a few of them alive, so we can make examples of them."

"Didn't they make an example of your son?" Silas spits.

The general lowers his weapon and steps forward. Could this be Quinn's father? It must be. Silas continues. "I'm surprised they didn't publicly execute him, once they realized he lied to everyone. How many days did you waste down on the beaches? I hope you had fun making sandcastles."

"What do you know about my son?" the general demands, taking Silas by the shirtfront and pushing him into the wall.

"Your son saw you murder Inger. His name was Inger. Did you know that? Did you care?" Silas's eyes are full of fury. "Your son knows you're a murderer. That's what I know about your son. So, tell me, what do *you* know about him?"

I step forward. "Quinn knows what you did, and he's ashamed of you. He knows what you are and he knows what we are. He chose us."

The general turns abruptly and scrutinizes me. "You must be the infamous siren. You aren't half as pretty as I imagined," he says.

"General?" The soldier looks behind us at the corridor, which is filling with black foam. Regardless of which side we're on, if we don't all get out of here, we'll be eaten alive by it. Bruce and Dorian work on unbolting the door again and no one stops them. Maude tries to pick up her gun but a soldier spots her and steps on the barrel.

The general's radio sputters to life. Keeping Silas pinned with one hand, he pulls it from his jacket pocket and shakes it roughly.

"General Caffrey, General Caffrey. This is Sergeant Delaney from the pod," a scratchy voice calls out. "Speak," the general commands, talking into the radio's mouthpiece. "*We need the army back at the pod immediately, General. There's civil war breaking out here. I repeat, it's civil war. We need backup.*" The general looks at the remaining soldiers and points to the door. They move forward and help Dorian and Bruce get it open.

"Are the bombs in place?" the general asks one of the soldiers.

"Yes, sir."

"Good. Out that way. Quickly. Get one of the zips down here this minute. We've done our job. By dusk this place will be a ruin."

Suddenly an explosion rocks the stadium and the general topples to the floor with Silas as the rest of us do our best to stay standing. I am yanked by the arm and bundled through the exit together with the soldiers as plaster, bricks, and shards of glass rain down on us. Looking over my shoulder, I see Silas and the general scramble to their feet and follow. Another loud bang unsettles the walls and we back away from the stadium as thick black clouds devour the sun. The soldiers are no longer aiming their guns at us but instead at the stadium, as though it is a giant creature about to attack. A final explosion shoots debris skyward and we have no choice but to run because the stadium is collapsing, every outer wall giving up its fight. We turn and watch as the walls fall away and all that remains standing are the oaks, birches, willows, beeches, and other trees, covered by syrupy, spiraling black foam. Several of the soldiers look aghast at the shrinking, dying trees and then at the general, who is now on his feet. He merely lifts his chin in defiance.

"Sir?" one of the soldiers says. The general just shrugs. Several soldiers decide not to hold their positions and turn away while the four or five who remain aim their guns at us once again.

"To the tanks!" the general orders, and then these soldiers, too, are lumbering away.

"What now?" Silas asks, glaring at the general. Silas is pointing his handgun directly at the general's head. The general doesn't flinch or call anyone back to defend him. "I should finish you," Silas says.

"You should run, son," the general says, and without even looking at Silas, walks off through the snow and is gone.

52
BEA

"How much did you see?" Old Watson wants to know as he falls through the front doors, but the look on my face is enough to tell him I saw everything. And the look on his face tells me I wasn't wrong about what I thought I saw. "There'll be time to grieve later," he says, picking up my bag and stuffing it with the few things I've left lying around the apartment.

Old Watson goes into his bedroom and comes out with an armful of clothes. He walks toward me and covers my head in a coarse beret. "Now is the time to escape." I don't move from my spot by the balcony doors. I've been watching the anarchy through the glass. Windows have been smashed. The tram has been hijacked. There are riots in most of the streets. Everyone has gone mad and yet my body feels like it's been filled to the brim with liquid calm.

"We have to get a move on," Old Watson says. He turns off the screen, which is nothing but static.

"Let's go."

"I have nowhere to go," I tell him. Less than an hour ago, I became an orphan. It's a word I always thought of as romantic. Only girls in bonnets and boys in short, threadbare trousers can be orphans. How can this word have anything to do with me?

"You have to get out of the pod. It's chaos out there, your perfect chance. I know a way."

"What about Quinn?" I say.

"Quinn can look after himself." Still, I don't move. I examine the shape of my hands. Dad always said I had the same hands as my mother. He said I have slender hands that should play an instrument. I never played though; we couldn't afford it. "Bea, it won't be long before they start pumping halothane gas into the pod instead of oxygen. It'll knock everyone out. They did it before—years ago. Then it won't be safe to escape. Even if you have an oxygen tank, you'll be spotted. You don't have a lot of time." Old Watson forces me up and pulls me out of the apartment.

The streets are pandemonium. Swarms of auxiliaries are heading toward Zone One, moving past us in frenzied droves carrying makeshift weapons, and those who aren't marching that way are trying to stop those who are. There are mothers and fathers trying to hold back their children and children trying to restrain their parents.

"This way," Old Watson says, cutting through the crowd and dragging me down a dark alley. I follow him, but my knees buckle and I am on the ground. Maybe they've already swapped the air supply for gas because I can't breathe, not even a modest breath. Not only that, but my heart is slowing and one arm is beginning to twitch.

"I'm having a heart attack," I gasp. Old Watson is on his knees trying to get me up.

"No you aren't. I know it feels like that. But you're okay. Your heart is breaking," he says. He tries to lift me from the ground. "Get up, Bea. Your parents would want you to live." And he continues to talk, but I have no idea what he's saying because the pain in my chest is so strong it has cut off my senses. I cannot hear a thing, but I can see the light at the end of the alley and people dashing past. They are running. Everyone in Zone Three is running.

53
QUINN

Apart from a single dim light bulb hanging from a wire in the ceiling, it's dark. From somewhere deep inside the building, I can hear water gurgling. The stone floor has brown stains all over it, and there are manacles on the walls. In the corner there's a bucket in case I need the toilet and on the floor in the middle of the cell there's a thin, soiled mattress. There's only one thing they do in this room.

But they didn't chain me up. They just threw me in here and locked the door. There's no escape route anyway, unless I find a way to eat through stone. I've spent the last hour lying on the stinking mattress imagining the kinds of things they'll do to me in here. I imagine the Pod Minister's face, his wet mouth, as he personally rips out each one of my fingernails or teeth with a pair of old pliers. Death won't be enough for him. I shudder and begin to pace the cell.

I am scared to die, but death will be better than having to see Bea and tell her that her parents are dead and that I'm responsible for it.

The door buzzes to life and one of the stewards who arrested me appears. "You don't look like you're praying," he says, and chuckles, as though keeping me locked up were the most pleasant thing in the world. He strolls around the cell, his hands in the pockets of his pants.

"I'm not," I tell him.

"Well, that's probably best. I don't think angels visit this place much anyway." He stands under the light bulb and flicks it with his finger so that it begins to swing gently, carrying the light from one side of the cell to the other and back again. "So who are you working for?" he asks. "You a RAT?"

"I'm not working for anyone."

"We hear your girlfriend is a major player. I guess they'll let you buy your way out—her life or yours. Do you know where she is?"

"You've got to be joking."

He cackles. "It was worth a try."

"So when does the torture begin?" I ask.

"He'll be here to deal with you before long."

"Who? Who will be here?" So this guy isn't the interrogator. Of course he isn't: he hasn't laid a finger on me.

Any minute now the Pod Minister will storm into the room. He will put his hands around my throat and finish what he started. "Who am I waiting for?" I call out as the cell door bangs shut. "Who will be here soon?"

54
BEA

I feel myself being lifted off the ground and carried along the alleyway. "You're okay," I hear. It sounds like Old Watson, and it could be him, but it must be my imagination because he wouldn't have the strength to lift me.

I open my eyes and there's a man's face looking down at me. He smiles and says, "She's awake."

"Watson, she's awake," a different voice repeats. A woman. I struggle to free myself from the man's arms and manage to stand up.

"How are you?" Old Watson asks from behind me. I have no answer. It seems an absurd question.

"Where are we going?" I say.

"Like I said, I'm getting you out of here. Can you walk?" Old Watson asks.

"I'll try," I say. I hold on to him as I wobble forward.

"We'll be quicker if you carry her, Gid," the woman says.

"Is that okay?" the man asks. I shake my head no, and force myself to walk more quickly.

We move down alleyway after alleyway, changing direction when we come upon a mob. Everyone seems to be going in the opposite direction to us, and as we advance, we come across fewer and fewer people. At last the man and woman leading us stop, and I find myself right up against the unbreakable glassy shell of the pod, next to a garbage chute. Usually this is where we come if we have to throw away items too large for our home chutes, and usually it is monitored by stewards. Today it is deserted. "We're here," Watson says. He leans against the pod. He is sweating and breathing uneasily.

"Did they reduce the air?" I ask.

"I'm old, that's all," Old Watson says.

The man and woman smile gently and the woman rubs Old Watson on the back. "You should go with her. You should get out now while you can," she says.

"There is still work to do here. You can't do it alone," Old Watson tells her. Then he turns to me.

"This is Harriet. And this is her husband, Gideon." The couple smile. "When you get to The Grove, tell Silas you've seen them, that they're alive."

"You're his parents," I say, and they nod. I try to smile

because *someone's* parents are alive and that's better than nothing. But they are not *my* parents, and for a brief second I wish these people were dead and my parents alive in their place.

"Here," Harriet says, handing me an extra-large airtank. "Use it sparingly and you'll have four days, maybe more. I've it set to eighteen percent. You'll have to tighten it as you go. Move slowly."

"And take this. Go west," Gideon says, handing me an antique compass. "You can't use a pad. They'll track you." He hands me an antique map, too, and points to a dark spot. "That's The Grove. You'll remember most of the way, I'm sure."

"Ready?" Harriet says. She unlatches the door to the garbage chute and looks down into it. From somewhere deep inside the pod there is the sound of an explosion and an alarm begins to whir.

"That'll be the gas," Gideon says. He is carrying an airtank and slips the facemask over his mouth and nose. Harriet and Old Watson do the same as Gideon helps me into my mask. He slides a belt around my waist and attaches the tank to it.

"Watch out for glass at the bottom," Old Watson says, leading me by the hand to the escape route. I still feel weak. It's as much as I can do to climb up onto the lip of the chute.

I don't want to flee. I want to bury my parents. I want to find Quinn. I left him once before and it was the worst thing I ever did. I glance at Harriet and Gideon, and then at Old Watson, who nods sternly. "Go on," he snaps. I am about to protest, but I know that what I want is less important than what I have to do, and what I have to do is survive. For Quinn. For my parents. So I shove my body away from the edge of the chute and I am gone, devoured by the chute and sliding right out of the pod, just like any other broken thing.

55
QUINN

The door buzzes and a tall figure bursts into the room. I cower against the wall, and when I look up, I see my father, his uniform dusty and torn in places. "They sent me to deal with you. *Me!*" he shouts. "Do you realize what you've done?"

"Do you know what *you've* done?" I shout right back. "Do you know what you've spent half your life doing?" He takes off his cap, folds it, and pushes it into the pocket of his coat. When he speaks, he is surprisingly quiet.

"I've been protecting your way of life. Do you think it's easy to keep the Premiums in power? It isn't. And you have the audacity to judge me? You enjoy all the pleasures of my work and now you question the way in which those pleasures have been secured. Every fine piece of clothing you've worn in your life and every gourmet meal, all the air you breathe has been possible because of what I do."

"I don't want that. I want—" I pause.

"What? What is it you could possibly want that I haven't given you?"

"I want to be free," I say. My father squints as though I'm speaking a language he barely understands. He stares down at the floor and sighs.

"The Pod Minister has been killed. You'll be tried for that and executed." I nod. It's no worse than I thought. "Can you breathe without supplemental air?" he asks. I shake my head.

"I'm getting there," I tell him. He raises his eyebrows. He probably never thought I had it in me to be good at anything.

"So you trained," he says, and I nod. It feels like we are having "A Moment," the first one of our lives. Eventually he says, "You can never come back here, you know. Follow me."

"What are you going to do to him, General?" the steward who first questioned me asks, scurrying after us as we proceed down an unlit, tapering tunnel. My father turns and glares at him.

"We are treating him as we would treat any other terrorist. Now get back to your damn post!" he barks. The steward shuffles to his place by the cell door and watches as my father drags me along. We stop at the end, when we cannot go any farther. We are in front of a door marked with a black and yellow sign: CAUTION—AIRTANKS REQUIRED. "Good luck out there," my father says.

"Out there?"

"When I push you outside you'll have to scream and shout. Knock hard. Beg to be let back in. I know you can act." He half smiles and I realize he is only pretending to punish me; really, he is saving me. I clench my teeth to stop myself from crying. I know it would only annoy him. "I've left a few air-tanks outside for you. They're full," he whispers.

"Say good-bye to Mother and Lennon and Keane. And my new brother."

"Drama, even at the end," he says, unlocking the door and opening it. With a heavy sucking sound, white light fills the tunnel. And then he says, "In another world I think we would have been friends, son." I nod and hold out my hand for him to shake it. He sniffs and pats my shoulder. Then he pushes me outside.

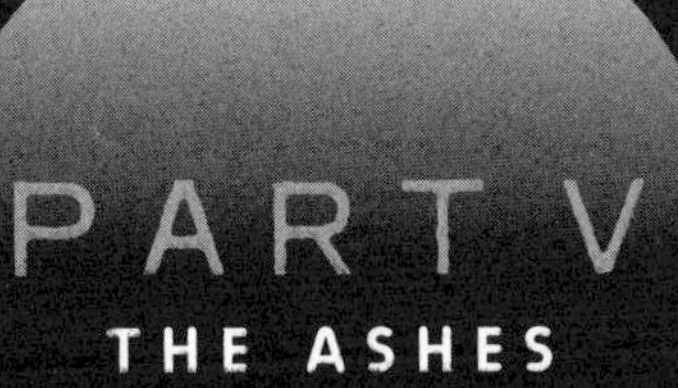

PART V
THE ASHES

56
ALINA

The water is forcing the rickety boat to smash against the dock with such force it's possible the old thing will turn into a wreck before we've even hauled up the anchor. The sails flap and huff. No one is speaking. We all look back one more time to take a mental picture of the land we are leaving behind. Buildings glimmer in the distance like small crystals, light glinting against their windows. I have an urge to go back. Now that we are here next to the winding gray river, I want to go home.

Maude and Bruce are sitting on the dock, their feet dangling above the freezing water. A couple of members made it along with us and they are standing in a quivering huddle waiting for instructions, as though Dorian, Silas, and I are their new leaders. I want to reassure them, but there isn't much I can say. We are sailing into the unknown, where we will all be at the mercy of strangers.

It is still snowing, and in a few hours the land will be covered again. The smog in the east is no longer threading its way into the sky. The Grove died a long time ago.

Dorian has a hand on my shoulder. "Maybe we should have surrendered," he says.

"Let's go," Silas says, glancing at him. "Our tanks won't last forever." He's right. We should go. We are taking the boat as far along the river as we can and from there walking to Sequoia. Dorian claims to know its location. And Silas has a map.

"We've lost everything," Dorian says, looking up at me, his eyes still bloodshot from the foam. I nod. We've lost everything. And what have we gained?

"We're alive," I tell him.

Just about.

57
BEA

The Grove is gone and in its place is a pile of black rubble and thick blankets of foam, suds, and withered trees. The debris is still smoking. It took me a couple of days to get here, using the underground stations as markers. I slept a lot, finding shelter among icy ruins. I wasn't scared. What did I have to be scared of? I walked for two days and didn't see another living soul.

And now I am at The Grove, the place I came to find refuge, and I am completely alone, with little hope of finding anyone alive.

I allow myself to cry. I have no idea where to go.

• • •

The sun rises and the black wreckage remains unchanged. I find a place to sit, where I open my flask and drink. Then I hear a voice.

"Bea."

It is so quiet, I close my eyes, afraid.

"Bea."

I turn and drop the flask.

And then he is holding me and crying into my shoulder and pulling at our masks so he can kiss me.

"Quinn," I whisper. He holds my face in his hands.

"Your parents—"

"I know," I say, and Quinn holds me again, wrapping me up in his thick coat to protect me from the snow. He rocks me back and forth.

"I'm sorry," he says.

Later we walk the perimeter of The Grove together, trying not to notice the bodies. And then a face, set deep into the rubble, blinks at me. I look away, sure my mind is playing some gruesome trick, but a moan follows and the black tree crushing the body shifts slightly. "Someone's alive!" Quinn shouts, and jumps into the debris. When he emerges, a small, soiled figure is holding his hand and stumbling toward me.

"They're heading west. Sequoia," she whispers. It's Jazz.

She's alive. She's covered from head to toe in dirt, but she's alive. And so are we.

"Then that's where we're going, too," I say.

Quinn looks at me and nods. "Yes," he says.

ACKNOWLEDGMENTS

It takes a whole heap of people to get a book ready. Rarely can a writer work in isolation.

Sincerest thanks are due to Julia Churchill and Sarah Davies, my glorious agents, and the whole team at Greenwillow, with a special mention to Martha Mihalick, who spent countless hours working on the manuscript to get it just right.

Many thanks to Lisa Wu and Felicity Williams, who helped me create a world that works, scientifically.

Thank you to my friends and family, and especially my husband.